Operatı

REVERT

One MI6 agents fight against terrorism suddenly turns him into an enemy of the state.

** Brian Fulton **

(OPERATION REVERT)

Copyright © 2018 by Brian Fulton

ISBN 978-1-912713-05-9

Printed in England

Table of Contents

Dedication 4

Chapter 1 – Jason Wright 5

Chapter 2 - Ian Stewart 35

Chapter 3 - Michael Mordha 49

Chapter 4 - Compromised 60

Chapter 5 - The two faces of Trevor 77

Chapter 6- A Painful Goodbye 85

Chapter 7 - A killer plan 99

Chapter 8 - Reassessing the situation 108

Chapter 9 – Vengeance is mine 115

Chapter 10 - The uninvited 135

Chapter 11 - Loose ends 141

Chapter 12 - The new king of nothing 154

Chapter 13 - Last man standing 164

Chapter 14 - History repeats itself 179

Dedication

I would like to thank my family and friends who have given me the encouragement to take this big step in my life. A HUGE thank you goes out to my wife Louise who has been my biggest supporter and advisor in completing of this novel. I also need to thank my children Ethan and Christian for all the hugs and kisses that kept me upbeat throughout the making of this story. I would also like to apologise to my parents for the number of C-bombs and other profanities that are heavily used throughout this book.

LOVE YOU ALL

Chapter 1 – Jason Wright

Where do I start? I suppose everyone needs a name to begin an introduction. Well, mine is Jason; I am thirty-two years old. I am five foot eleven inches tall, muscular build, fifteen stone on a good day, hazel eyes and short dark brown spiky hair. I was born in Northern Ireland and moved to Canada when I was only a few months old. This was because my father was under threat from the RVA (Republican Volunteer Army). They are one of a few Republican terrorist organizations that infest my homeland like vermin. I've built up a great hatred towards the RVA from a young age; this grew as I gained more of an understanding of who they were and what motivated them to kill.

Currently

I am sitting in a secluded part of Black Mountain overlooking the flickering lights of Belfast City with my best friend Mark. On a beautiful moon lit night in July. The moon was shimmering down its dull blue light over everything it touched creating a hazy atmosphere. The street lights seem to dance and glisten in the distance which made the sprawling and troubled city almost look alive. It was surreal. All you can hear up here is the faint hum of traffic which almost puts me to sleep. The local wildlife seems to be in slumber, ignoring our presence as we wait for surveillance information to be passed back to us in a live operation taking place below us in a Republican housing estate.

Sometimes I wonder how I got to where I am today and to be honest it hurts my head just thinking about it. I guess I always thought about Northern Ireland while I was residing in Canada and had made plans to move in with my grandparents after graduating high school. However, in 1996 to my delight, my family decided it would be in all our interests if we moved back home together due to aging grandparents and losing touch with loved ones. I was seventeen at the time and was soon to understand why my parents were so reluctant to make a move back home to a place they supposedly loved. I remember the excitement of making the transatlantic journey. The feeling of contentment, knowing it's not just a visit. We were about to re-establish ourselves back where we belong. Most of our family including both sets of grandparents lived in and around a picturesque part of the country called Cookstown located in County Tyrone. We had to move into our grandparent's house which was situated just on the outskirts of the town. We would have to stay there until my parents could save up for a deposit for a place of their own. It took them just over a year before they found a house we all liked in a growing housing estate in Portadown.

My story starts to take hold in 2002 after attending University in Londonderry or Derry as some people call it. I just obtained a degree in IT and was itching to find my dream job that would make me loads of money to buy a fancy car and a big ass house to park it in. Unfortunately, it was not going so well on the job front as I had to take a few jobs on temporary contracts and worked in some pretty shitty places. Gears and Son's sausage roll factory, being the worst of the lot. Never had I seen so many unhygienic people working together under one roof. They were coughing and spluttering over the freshly baked goods as they quickly trundled past them on the processing line. I even saw a few scratching in their ear and nose holes while wearing their latex gloves and what disturbed me, even more, was the fact they were still handling and packing the food with those same gloves. How I felt for the unsuspecting public, who were purchasing these products and all the contaminants that came with it. It put me off them for life. I will never forget the one positive thing the factory did for me. It forced me to rethink my life. I promised myself bigger and better things! And from that very point in my life, that's just what happened!

I never talked about my work or personal affairs with my family or friends as I liked to keep that side of my life private. There was no hidden agenda; I have always been like that. It was never an issue to other people as I made friends easily enough without giving too much away about myself. During my daily car journey to work, I started to take more and more notice of the army check points I encountered periodically on the roads. I had always admired how tough looking the soldiers were and how they always looked prepared for a fight! The way each one assessed a part of the surrounding area, looking for that small element that didn't sit right. Always alert and ever ready.

The massively armoured Land Rovers looked menacing. The exterior was painted dull grey which to me made it appear like a small tank. How that chassis took the weight of it was beyond me. The thick green glass of the bullet proof windows in the land rover looked intimidating to some, but I always thought they looked cool. The soldiers would usually block the road to allow a single lane of controlled traffic to go through and occasionally stopped and searched cars for weapons or wanted people.

They usually had a printed manifest outlining military intelligence that would help them highlight the cars they needed to focus on. I kept wondering what action the soldiers might have seen, how many terrorists they may have taken out if any? I used to think about the Army so much I applied to join it a few months later as I wanted to be a part of that team.

When I was in the recruiting office in east Belfast, I was watching a lot of the younger men checking out the Army holiday posters. These training trips are fully paid on behalf of her Majesty. I had to laugh to myself as I found it funny that for some of these boys that could have been the deal clincher for signing up. I had my own reasons for joining, and it wasn't for the free fucking ski trips let me tell you. The office looked minimalistic and the furniture uncomfortable. I sat down waiting for the recruitment officer to come over to me, but he was dealing with a potential recruit; the applicant looked like a fucking worm to me, kitchen staff at best. Stop slagging people off Jason, your better than that, I thought to myself. I kept looking over at the coffee machine, wondering if I would have time to have one before he calls me.

I stand up anyway and walk over to the clapped-out looking machine and search my pockets for change. Hmm, it looks like I don't have to pay as the money hole was blocked, fantastic; I will have another before I leave. Just as I am about to sit my ass back into the chair, the recruitment officer calls me over. "Jason Wright!" He shouted out as he stood up and leaned over his desk from his cubical, watching me approach with a grimaced look on his face like he has better things to do than talk to me.

As I walk over and sit down, I noticed we did it simultaneously.
Well, I am faced with a ginger cropped haired recruiting officer called Chris Pearson, as his name is engraved in brass on a little id bar across his left chest. I love building profiles on people and try to take everything in as he is talking to me. I start with the basics; he is clean shaven and well-spoken. Most likely attended college. A bit rebellious as he has a tattoo peeking just above his collar. His right hand has bruised knuckles from punching an object or some poor sods face, due to the coloration of the bruises, it must have happened at least three days ago.

Eye brows looked plucked, and nails looked too over done to be heterosexual. He is sloppy with his ironing as I observed double creases in his jacket and shirt. This would suggest his lack of ambition within the military, he is probably no higher than a corporal, not that I could spot any identifying ranks on his uniform, but rest assured a higher-ranking officer would never let such a small thing go unnoticed. The whiter patch of skin behind his watch tells me he has obviously not been in Northern Ireland the last couple of weeks and was posted or on holidays in a hotter climate. As I snap out of it and actually take in what the man had to say, he informed me that my degree would allow me to be trained as a Captain, to which I was over the moon with. Happy days!

I fill out the forms he has given me as he photocopies my passport and drivers licence. I thank Sargent Pearson for his time and make my way past the coffee machine again to take one for the road, for my train journey home. It's not long before I received a letter inviting me down to Ballymena for an informal lunch with a Colonel Lyndhurst. The days dragged by thinking about the meeting, but it wasn't really until the night before I was to go up to Ballymena when reality hit me.

This was the point in my life that things were possibly going to change for the better; the tide was turning so to speak.

When I was on the train to Ballymena, I couldn't help thinking why a lunch instead of a formal interview? I could not put my finger on it, but it seemed odd to me. I was looking around the train carriage and thought the train looked empty for this time of day. As the snacks trolley finally makes an appearance, I purchase two chocolate bars and a diet cola. The trip took no time as I was transfixed by watching the countryside fly past me in the huge picturesque windows of the train. At Ballymena station, the train slows to a crawl and then finally stops. I quickly gather my belongings and rubbish and depart the train with excited adrenaline running through my veins. The weather was overcast and a bit cold which was the norm for Northern Ireland. As I am walking towards the taxi ramp to pay for a lift to the base, I was hoping the rain would stay away as I hate having to keep fixing my hair.

I climb into the back of a waiting taxi and buckle myself in, I was building up in my head what sort of questions he was going to ask me and the possible model answers I could give back as I am sure he will be consistently probing my character for my suitability of the position on offer. I arrive at the gates of the Ballymena base and get out of the taxi. I am now walking towards the security barriers, and I feel like the whole place is watching me; which I don't know why but makes me a little nervous. I stand a little taller holding myself with confidence as I approach two steely eyed soldiers guarding the main entrance. I hand them my letter which was read in its entirety. They then check the visitors' roster for the day and confirm the information I gave them. I am searched and put through a metal detector before being given instructions on how to make my way to the mess hall. Walking through the base felt good as I had a sensation that I was surrounded by like-minded people with the same morals as I had. Coming into the mess hall, I couldn't help but notice Colonel Lyndhurst himself was the only person in the big empty room.

He was sitting at a table at the back and didn't look at me while I approached him; he appeared to be reading the papers he had in front of him, flicking through them quickly back and forth in his hands. I couldn't even tell you if he was reading them or organizing them. "Sit down Jason," He said without breaking his concentration on the papers he was currently looking at. "I understand you come from Portadown, did you have a pleasant journey?" he said. I replied, "Yes sir."

He then asked me what I fancied to eat for lunch even though it was only 10am in the morning. He recommended the grilled chicken and immediately proceeded to shout over to the kitchen our order without conferring it with me. Someone in the back of the kitchen shouted back "Yes, Colonel!" The conversation we had over the next hour had nothing to do with the army which confused me greatly.

After eating our early lunch, he looked at me and said: "You passed!" I was taken back as it didn't seem like an interview at all; it was all a little unbelievable, to be honest. The Colonel took me for a tour around the base and asked me what type of work I was interested in? I replied I would like to go into the intelligence corps as I wanted to fight terrorism in Northern Ireland. "Yes, that would suit you I think. You fit the profile of the kind of candidates we are looking for at the moment. I will make the arrangements", the Colonel replied. With that, he escorted me to the front gates and sent me off with a firm handshake. I am now standing in front of the base, wondering where the time had gone. I was feeling euphoric as I now felt I was important. With a huge grin on my face, I pull out my phone and use the number the taxi man gave me to book him for a lift back to the train station. On my train journey, back home to Portadown I was going through the conversation I'd had with the Colonel in my head, analysing what was said, trying to work out what made him say "You passed?" I could only think that this was too easy and that they had an ulterior motive for the decision.

I was honest about who I was and wondered if they had Intel on me already, did they pass me for that reason? I could just hear my friends telling me to wind my neck in. Still, I couldn't help myself connecting the dots, slowly building a picture of what they might want from me. The strange things that have happened to me over the years made a little more sense when I put them in perspective. When I was in my early twenties, I believed I was under surveillance by the security forces. There were plausible reasons behind why I would think this. I don't believe it was because I was a bad person, not evil but there were points in my life if I had to do over again, I would have taken a different path. I believe that certain people could be a focus for authority's due to the friends they hang around with. Was I guilty by association?

My circle of friends consisted of a wide range of people who come from every sort of background possible as I based my friends on who they were and not where they come from. This gave me an incredible insight into the many different sections of the community in Northern Ireland.

I met my 1st group of Roman Catholic friends at college through a few wood work classes we shared. We hung out together doing what mates do, going out clubbing, attended house parties and from time to time coming home drunk, with my friends singing pro-RVA songs, which I didn't take part in. They were good lads; I knew they would have my back if I got into any trouble which was the case on a few occasions. They stood up for me even though I didn't support their cause and was a Protestant. Their families were very friendly towards me, often having long chats, taking a real interest in what I was doing and how I was keeping. I remember this one time before we went out clubbing. I bought this tube of fake tan and swore this was my secret for pulling all the ladies. So, all the lads wanted to try it. We were all fighting for a spot in front of the hallway mirror, rubbing this fake tan on our faces and arms. It was a rare sight to say the least, when Brandon's mother came walking in and asked us what we were doing, with a big grin on her face. It's moments like this why I keep in touch with them, even today.

These were the friends I met with periodically.

I then have the 2nd group of mates that are made up of Loyalists Protestants and Roman Catholics. We would often poke fun at ourselves and each other with derogatory remarks about the other's religion, never taking offense. I met these fellas through work and friends of friends. We all had nick names which reflected a part of our personality. Some of the nicknames were suited like "Stains" who got the name from always spilling food and drinks down his shirt on a night out. "Mongol" was another name of a mate who always behaved like he had severe learning disabilities. He was fearless and always talked with a stupid put on accent which made us laugh, and others cringe. He also loved to walk around a nightclub trying to chat up as many ladies as possible using his radical theory based on the law of averages. Which to his credit actually worked as he would at least pull one or two during the night! We then have "Rock Star" who had the long hair and every visual characteristic that would associate him to that of an 80s rock god. Pulling ladies came easily to him as he stood out from the crowd. He is best known for not sharing his takeaways after a drunken night out. Then we have "H-Block" who is Roman Catholic; the name was given to him because of our stereo typical view of the RVA movement. He was once asked on a weekend trip over to England how he wanted his breakfast, to which I then blurted out "Shoved under the door!" referring to the way prisoners are served their meals.

We used to also make fun of him by connecting him with dirty protests; this was over silly things like, hurry up and bring H-Block a drink before he shits all over the walls. He liked the nick name too and gave as good as he got. Last but certainly not least we have "Browner". Aptly named because of the reckless way he drove his expensive sports car. If you got a lift off him, you would shit your pants during the car ride or come very close to it!

These were the friends I had the most fun with.

I then have a 3rd group of friends that were more sensible but still great fun to hang around with. It was also a mix of Roman Catholic and Protestants. This group usually liked to go out to more Roman Catholic areas such as Newry or Warrenpoint. We never joked about religion in this group, and everyone respected each other's beliefs. We had fanatic pulling competitions when we went clubbing seeing how many women we could pull in the night and the ranking of each one.

I have to laugh at this one time when we didn't pull any, and we were almost sobbing on the way home convinced we were ugly. We all loved the gym, and every one of us was vainer than the other.

This is the group of friends I hung around the most with.

I then have the 4th group of friends who through different social outings became very prominent in my life. These friends were people of influence. Their reputation earned through fear and respect. Their missions were highly successful and deadly. People would call them freedom fighters, family or even friends like I did but others would call them gangsters or even terrorists. These friends were broken down into two Loyalists associations which were the Ulster Commandos and the Loyalist Freedom Fighters.

These were the friends I learned the most from.

I can remember the first time I met my link to the Ulster Commandos. It was when I was a cashier at a petrol station which was nearby to where I lived in Portadown. This was one of the not so crappy jobs I did part time in my youth while at college. It paid for my new car and gave me a bit of extra money for clothes and of course the weekends on the lash. While working a Friday evening, I noticed the manager Tom faffing around with a wad of money which he counted two or three times before sticking it in a brown envelope.

"Jason," Tom called. "There is a man coming to collect the shop's oil money at 9 pm, make sure he gets this envelope." "No problem, does he have a name?" I replied. Tom shouted back, "His name is Ryan".

Tom was on his way out to support the men in his lodge at a protest taking place in a field near the M1. I belonged to the same fraternity but a different lodge and would be camping at the rally later that night after my shift. As Tom walked out of the shop, he said he would be back in time to lock up. I waved him off and helped myself to a few of the pick-an-mix beside the cash register. I was anxious to how the protest was going as it was bringing Northern Ireland to a standstill, so I turned on the radio to listen out for any news on it. Practically dead on 9 pm, a man walks up to the counter waiting to be served. I go back around the cash desk to see this huge fella in a very stylish and expensive looking black leather coat. He had a big smile on his face and looked friendly enough. "How are you mate? You got the oil money for us?" he said. I told him

12

I did and asked him his name to which he replied "Ryan." I then went into the back office to pick up the brown envelope for him. When I came out, Ryan had helped himself to a handful of the pick-and-mix.

He was shaking the sweets about in his hand while investigating the cigarette rack at the back of the counter. I handed the oil money over, and Ryan quickly stuck it in his inside pocket and left. I didn't think any more about it as it wasn't my money or any of my business and went back to listening to the news on the radio. As the weeks turned into months and the months turned into years, I found myself being on friendly terms with our so-called oil suppliers. I understood from day one it was protection money to fund the Loyalists group who operated in our area. They used to come in all the time selling counterfeit Euros and the latest pirated DVDs and dance CDs. I would buy a lot of stuff from them, and I would also give them a discount on their purchases. Swiping some items past the till scanner and letting others go straight into their shopping bag. I thought I was the big man by ripping off the shop as the owners were millionaires and had stores all over the country. So, I didn't feel bad about robbing the rich to help the working class.

It was New Years, and the boys were around again. I was invited by Ryan as a guest to his night club which was inside a football stadium on the outskirts of Lurgan. It was a Friday night, and I got a taxi there for around 8 pm. The party was huge and in full swing by the time I arrived! The music was rave, and I loved it! The lasers and strobe lights were almost going in sequence to the base of the music which was mesmerizing. The food was amazing, and the booze was in abundance. One of the guys came out of nowhere and dropped a couple of small pills in my hand.

I didn't do drugs, so I just stuck them in my pocket and thanked the guy for them. I was still in awe at the high-tech disco in a football club of all places; you can tell big money was spent on it. As I was being introduced to everyone, I felt like a king. Everyone was really nice and friendly. I was particularly enjoying being surrounded by the girls who kept asking me to talk as they liked my strange Northern Irish / Canadian accent. I was kissing one girl to the left of me, then the other on my right. The party was unbelievably good. I kept being dragged all over the place being introduced from one person to the other. Around 1 am a fella comes in and starts shouting that a well-known RVA man has been spotted twice driving past the front of the football ground. Half of the lads and two of the women walked out to investigate. I wasn't ready for what came next. Under one of the tables at the club, Ryan began to pull out a huge duffle bag and proceeded to dump it on top of the table. By the strain on his face while he was lifting it there was something weighty inside it. He continued to unzip the heavy bag which was jam packed with things that slowly began to protrude as he wrestled the zipper open.

It was like slow motion as everyone was pulling out rifles, locking and loading and running towards the exit doors with enough weapons to start a small war. The qualities of the armaments were second to none as they looked new or had been looked after well. I was shocked at all the different types of guns they had as I only ever seen weapons like these in the movies. All the men and a few of the women made their way past me and over to the weapons. Some already had guns on them. Ryan looked at me in a way almost to say, your move mate. I didn't hesitate; I went over to the bag and gripped a small machine gun from it. Ryan nodded and smiled. "Welcome brother." He said before storming out the side door with an AK-47. Most of us made their way outside and placed themselves strategically along the road, carefully positioning their weapons, waiting for their chance to riddle the unsuspecting RVA twat. My actions were automatic, I didn't think about what I was doing, I just did it. While we were waiting for this drive past to happen again, I was still in awe of the fire power they had. I wanted to hold the bigger guns, even maybe fire them into the air. We waited 30 minutes to see if we could spot the car again but knew he probably wouldn't risk another drive by. A few men stood guard outside as the rest of us headed back into the club. That famous volunteer would never realize how close he came to death that night.

We carried on partying and took turns doing watch throughout the night. I didn't get home until 5 am, and till this day; I still don't know how I got home. I just remember stinking of smoke, having more cash in my pocket than I went out with and a hangover from hell.

My parents were very worried and didn't sleep till I was home. Only for my sister telling me, I would have never known. I felt bad, but they had to let me live my life. I started to meet with the boys every so often at night clubs and on different outings in Belfast. I used to get excited when I got a text from them. I was one of the lads, a defender of Ulster. They continued to greet me with respect and made a big fuss over me which felt good. I remember one time they took a chair off this really big guy at our local pub in Lurgan where we often met at and gave it to me to sit on, as some kind of grand gesture. It was surreal, the guy gave his chair up without question; he just gave up without even making eye contact with the man. It was like he understood if he put up any kind of resistance it would end up looking like a challenge to their authority with all outcomes ending in the same way, the certainty of being beaten to death.

The pub we always hung out at was small; with most of the décor looking like it was last in fashion during the seventies. The low-level lighting in the pub gave the place a shadowy look and feel to it with windows that were small, and mirror tinted to only allow people to see out and not in. It stank of stale smoke, but you got used to it after a while.

There were all sorts of CCTV in and outside the place with the video being scrutinized every day by people looking for faces that didn't fit, developing profiles of patrons and keeping a data list of every car registration plate that entered their car park. The pub had doors that needed you to be buzzed in twice to gain entry to the pub. One door opened and the other stayed locked till it, in turn, was shut and locked before allowing the second door to be released. I found out later it was designed to prevent any one trying to run in and spray the joint with bullets. I never had to pay for anything as they always picked up the tab in the clubs and bars we often went to. They even gave me a grand to spend in Ibiza after Ryan inquired how much I was taking with me. "£500 wouldn't keep you, son," Ryan said while counting out the notes and then sticking it in my front pocket of my leather coat. It was the first holiday I took without my parents. All the positives I felt did not extinguish the shadowy presence I felt in their company which was always that of fear. I considered them my friends but I always, and I mean always chose my words carefully around them. As time passed I was officially sworn into one of the groups. I was then branded with a nick name "The Canadian" as my accent was strong and I didn't quite merge with the local dialect yet. They started me with low-level foot soldier jobs such as spraying graffiti in Republican areas, collecting protection money and selling counterfeit Euros. I even spent some evenings cutting down any road signs around the country that had any Gaelic dialect on it as that sort of stuff didn't belong in Ulster.

I was also to attend function's and rallies to provide support if Republicans ever tried to attack the events. I recognize that some of the stuff I was doing was wrong but I couldn't exactly say no, could I?

The internal feuding and rifts always made me nervous as you didn't want anything heading back your way as it was always shoot first ask questions later. The knowledge I gained whilst in their company was to put in a word, fascinating! I picked up new tips on how to dispose of evidence; for instance, you would be amazed at what chlorine does to destroy forensic evidence. To the way you would carry out surveillance operations, always working in four men teams, using the latest technology. We had bunkers everywhere and made sure we didn't have all our munitions all in one place to make sure any losses through police or military finds were minimal. When we had to transports stuff, we made sure to give the police a false taste of how we smuggle money and weapons just to take their focus off how we really moved our stuff about which was using more of a public transport method.

We also had a great way to launder our money, we would ask our people to hand in a bundle of cash worth up to ten thousand pounds to the police and say they found it in a field. The police would hold it for a short-allotted time and if no one could prove they lost the money it would be handed back to the person who found it. That's how we bought our fancy cars outright with clean cash. We also had friends in high places which were a huge help in our fight against the RVA. There was Intel handed to us that was so intricate that you could make accurate predictions with it as to when and where to hit, who to kill, where they frequented, patterns in movement. Without mentioning names, we had a high-ranking Republicans mobile phone movement traced over two weeks on a digital map with different colour lines representing the different days of the week 1 and week 2. It even had a time scale on it. Unfortunately for him, it made our job all too easy. It made me almost pity the security forces as to what they were up against as they had their hands tied with red tape but ours were not!

We also had our pick of weapons as they were smuggled in on fishing vessels from Morocco and other countries that did not care who they sold arms to as long as we had the world accepted currency, US Dollars, we could buy pretty much anything we wanted. One of the sneaky ways we used to get past the coastguard with our contraband was to have several submerged plastic tubes which kind of looked like torpedoes. They were attached underwater at the stern of the boat and travelled about five meters below the waterline behind us. They were also painted dark navy so they couldn't be seen from the surface of the water. So even when we were boarded they didn't find anything.

I was always surprised how much stuff we could fit into them. I was enjoying all these jobs that paid me extremely well and thought about making it a career. It was all fun and games for a while until my friends tested my loyalty to the group. I had to kill two RVA men called Gabe and Peter McClean. I can remember the moment I was asked like it was yesterday. I was having a few pints with Ryan as we normally did in Belfast when Ryan just came out with it. "Jason, I need a wee favour off you." "Anything!" I replied. "Good lad, knew you wouldn't let me down. I need you to kill two fellas for me." Ryan said. I laughed at first but Ryan wasn't amused and just blankly stared at me while taking long drags out of his cigarette. I suddenly felt the hairs on my arms and neck start to rise as a cold chill went through me. I nodded and said, "no worries." Ryan then stubbed out his cigarette and downed the remainder of his pint.

He then got up on his feet and put his hand on my shoulder and leaned over near my ear and said: "I'll fill you in with the details later tonight." He then patted my shoulder twice before walking coolly out of the pub. When I got over the shock of the unexpected request, which in reality I knew was eventually coming. I took myself outside of the pub for some fresh air. I was already semi mentally prepared for this test.

I thought I was a hard man, but it didn't stop my guts turning and I understood all too well the consequences of turning down such a job offer. What helped me through it was later that night being told who they were and the evil deeds they had done. They have been on the news numerous times for terrorist related offences, but they never stay behind bars for long. When they appeal the charges, they always seem to magically be dropped due to lack of evidence or introduce serious doubt to the charge. It made what I had to do next much, much easier. They didn't give me a gun; I had a cut throat blade and a tiny stun gun. They gave me information on how to immobilise the brothers and use the blade to slice a major artery which in this case was the inside upper leg. It was to look like a mugging that went horribly wrong.

I got a taxi from Belfast to go home that night after being prepped at another pub which belonged to our group. I had literally one day to prepare. I didn't sleep much that night as I was racked with nerves. I got a bus into Lurgan and made my way over to a safe house where I got into gear that would disguise me as a Republican local. This was the easiest part of the mission. The club I was going to had no dress code and all the local scumbags were seen to frequent the place. I remember from my Intel that my targets would be there most Friday nights.

I was dropped off near the centre of Lurgan and began walking towards the rebel strong hold, making sure I avoid the police cameras as previously planned. It becomes all too apparent as to why the lads did not give me a gun. The six bouncers at the main entrance searched each person methodically. You could tell who the RVA were as they just sailed past security without so much as a glance. My turn to be searched comes quickly but they find nothing. I have my weapons stuck in my hollowed-out rubber soles of my shoes.

While I was using the toilets in the club, I get my killing tools out and assemble them in a cubical. I placed them in my jean pockets, so I could access them easily now. I was amazed how relatively easy it was to sneak in so I felt things were going my way. Nevertheless, I took out a little package I hid in my under crackers and unwrapped it. I wet my little finger in my mouth and rubbed the fluffy white powder in and around my gums in a circular motion and then a little on the tongue. Just a few hits of coke to keep my senses sharp. The boys recommended it to me for jobs like this. I tried coke for the first time the week before to experience the effects. WOW! I can see the attraction as it keeps you really focused for a few hours at a time. I get out of the cubical and make my way over to the sink and mirror to wash my hands and fix my hair when I see my reflection. I nearly laugh aloud as I couldn't believe I was wearing this shitty top.

Don't get me wrong it was a nice navy polo shirt, but the sports team on it was everything I hated. I get the cologne guy to let me have a few sprays of his best stuff before leaving the gents toilet. As I grab a pint and scan the place over, I start to relax and enjoy the mission I was on. The music and atmosphere complemented the setting I was now in. I see a beautiful lass staring at me across the bar, and I stare back making sure she knew I noticed her. She had piercing blue eyes with long brown wavy hair and a body that would make a super model cry. I play it cool and turn away from her to make it look like I wasn't eager but unfortunately when I turned back she was gone.

My heart sank a little as she was perfect in every way, well almost every way I smirk to myself. I do however catch a glimpse of my targets and move closer to them as I need to have them continually in my sight. I need them to notice me and understand in their minds that I am not a threat to them. So, I start dancing with a few ladies near them to get their attention. All goes well, and they seem relaxed in my presence, so task one was done. Task two is to find a girl to walk with me behind my targets as the best place to hide is in plain sight. I feel a bit shit about this part of the task as I will only be using her to complete my mission. Plus, I have to knock her out.

As I was chatting up the ladies, I noticed this woman at the bar who was being a complete prick to the bartender. She gave him such a hard time and was so demeaning towards him I decided to use her as my walking partner. I made my excuses and left the girls I was with and make my way over to her. As she was walking to the dance floor, I bump into her knocking her drink out of her hand. "You fucking dickhead!" she shouts at me. "I am really sorry, how about I buy you two of the same as an apology?" I answered back to her trying to be as charming as possible.

"Fine, let's go!" she said in a strained voice while rolling her eyes. At the bar, I started to compliment the way she looks telling her that she was stunning and no one in the club was her equal. I was continually feeding her inflated ego. Which wasn't impressing her. As I was paying for the drinks, I made sure she saw the wad of notes I had in my clip to give the appearance I was a wealthy man. Too easy, I thought to myself as she was then all over me like a rash. Love or money as the saying goes. Task two complete. As I try to keep her at bay, I am continually watching the RVA pricks. Keep getting pissed boys I thought to myself, this after all, is your last night on earth.

The music stops, and the flood lights suddenly burst on illuminating every corner of the club in a brilliant white light which signalled the club was about to close. The bouncers were as always starting to kick out everyone like they do every weekend. I was in front of my targets going out the door, so I pulled my girl close to me for a lingering kiss against a wall outside until the boys had passed me. As the lads started their long stagger home, they took their regular route along Brownlow Terrace which is a semi secluded street which was perfect for what I was about to do. My Intel was impeccable. I also had no trouble convincing my girl to come back to mine and used her to keep the distraction off me in case the boys glanced behind them. I was gaining on them. I quickly got my blade and stun gun ready.

You know what? They never looked back once! ZAP! My girl was down. It was like a slow-motion ballet. Then ZAP! ZAP! In the neck of the two lads who dropped like a ton of shit. All three were out cold. The effect of the stun gun is short lived, so I had to work fast before they had the chance to come round. I quickly confirmed their identities before taking their wallets, watches, and rings. Their stuff was to be kept for later in case we needed to send a message to the RVA that we did it. I made the cuts where I needed to and then add a few more to make it look like a struggle. Some of the cuts I made spurted blood wildly in all directions. My face, arms and Fenian polo shirt were covered in blood.

I couldn't help thinking these dirty fucks may have all sorts of diseases and couldn't wait to get all these clothes off and shower. Now I have to erase my presence from the kills. I smeared their blood in every crevasse of the blade, but I used one of their hands to do it. This took away any prints that I may have put on it. I then took the other brothers hand to place the blade close to him. This was to make it look like they fought the attacker and got cherry picked of their possessions by the local hoods. As I get up to leave the area, I zapped my date again, so I could get at least a five-minute head start before she starts to make any noises.

As for the RVA cunts I left behind, well, I know they will keep their mouth shut. I was officially now a foot soldier in the Loyalist army. My reputation grew and was no longer walking on egg shells within the group as I passed my initiation with flying colours. This then brings me back to the strange occurrences that were frequently happening to me. I can remember this one time at College I was doing a graphic design course and was given a brief to design my own night club. The brief to me was piss easy; I was an expert with graphic design software and was convinced I was going to achieve a high grade. All we had to do was gather research; put together a few ideas for the interior and exterior of the building before making a final proof of a night club using 3D graphic software. I had the bright idea to drive to Belfast one night and get my friend Jamie to take some pictures out the window of my car as we drove past the clubs. The car I had at the time was brand new with eighteen-inch alloys, a white paint job, super-size spoiler on the boot and tinted black windows. It looked bad assed! I knew we would be doing this in style, maybe even picking up a few ladies along the way.

I wanted to take the pictures of the clubs from my car, so I didn't look like a dick with a camera with people jumping in front of my shots as I didn't have the temperament for idiots. Jamie took the pictures for me out the window of the car as I pulled up next to each of the clubs. We got some nice pictures of a few night clubs and a few phone numbers if memory serves me correctly before calling it a night and heading home. I was at my grandparents' house the next day when my father rang and spoke to my mum in an irate manner. "Jason! Laura!" my mother shouted, "We have to go home right now!" We said our goodbyes in a rushed manner and proceeded to the car where our mother was ignoring our questions to why we were heading home in a hurry. My mind was wandering about all sorts, but I was completely confident it had nothing to do with me. The sky was a beautiful pink dusk colour as we pull into our cul-de-sac, you could see all the neighbours out on the road, then the police Land Rovers, Police cars that were marked and unmarked along with the police constables and soldiers surrounding our house.

I didn't feel nervous as I didn't have anything at the house that would get me into trouble, but I did, however, change my mind as we pulled into our driveway, this was maybe something to do with me. My dad had his arms folded across his chest standing very solid. He was the only figure in the middle of all this I could instantly recognise right away. He was in a heated exchange of words to what looked like a detective. I say this as the man he was engaging in a shouting match with was not wearing any paraphernalia to connect him to the police or army. My mother's lips were trembling and her eyes wide. She was not taking this well and looked like she was going to break down in tears. The atmosphere was tense, and I was now convinced they were here for me. The detective and the rest of the officials stared at our car as a few police men and some of the soldiers approached us slowly, starting to take positions around our vehicle. We all stayed in the car as we were almost waiting for permission to get out. I see the detective, and my father walks quickly towards us. They opened my door right away and said to be calm as he held my arms and directed them to the roof of the car. They then began to search me. As they emptied my pockets and placed the contents on the roof, the detective was talking to me, but all I could hear was him mumbling at me as things began to slow down.

I was trying to take everything in that was happening around me. I'd look over my shoulder and see my father looking at me; his eyes were lit with rage. If there wasn't this circus going on, I think he would have caused me damage without even hearing my side of the story, that's if I knew what the story was to begin with. I was excited and nervous about the attention I was getting and was confident that my reputation was growing even bigger thanks to my nosy neighbours who will no doubt be spreading the word on the current antics. I even bet one or two of them will even exacerbate what happened, here's hoping I laughed to myself. "JASON! Stop fucking sitting there like you're some hard man, you little bastard!" Dad said through gritted teeth. I was sitting in the living room on the couch; I can't even remember walking through the front door? "If I find you were up to anything I will break your neck before throwing you out of this house." my father said with his face inches from mine; I couldn't stop staring at his huge canine teeth as his voice began to raise and his spittle hit my face. I know he loves me, he just shows his concern for me in a different way. My father ranted on about how he had spent the last few hours trying to stop these men from tearing our house apart looking for a gun!

Only by chance did my father know the man who oversaw this team, otherwise our house would have been totally wrecked looking for a non-existent gun.

The detective interrupted and explained to me that they had a search warrant and said: "We know you were in Belfast last night, we know this because we have your car on CCTV and traced the number plate." he said. That was fast I was thinking to myself. The detective continued; "We saw a bright flash of light coming out of your car and which could have been a muzzle flash. The report made to the Police, was from a bouncer that you'd tried to shoot him." the Detective continued.

I explained my circumstances and handed over my camera film to be developed and looked over by CID to verify my story. Everyone was staring at me whilst I was speaking. After what had seemed like no time, the circus that was my house, dispersed leaving me with a still irate dad and upset mum.

I was invited to the Portadown police station to pick up my camera and printed photos a few days later. Each of the photos was professionally printed out on A4 glossy paper which led me to believe they were examining every little thing in the photos. The Police men laughed about it and how such a little thing ended up being blown out of all proportion. That was Northern Ireland for you, innocent things like that could potentially end in a bad way. My dad still gave me a rollicking over my antics with the camera and what I did. Looking on the bright side of things, I did get two rolls of film developed for free, result! I then kept thinking about how excessive that response was by the security forces and why they would react that way with me?

On a very sunny day a few weeks later, I was on my way to the town centre to buy a new amp and stereo system for my car. I got into my car that was always parked in front of my parents' house. While in a seated position I lean out of the car and check underneath it before starting the ignition. I was told by my associates that this was the done thing to do to keep safe from bombs, as they all did it. I unexpectedly noticed an aerial; it was about three inches long sticking out my front passenger side wishbone. I felt my heart race and thought this was it; death has finally caught up with me. I nearly took the door off trying to run out of the car and into the house, thinking each step away from the car was a blessing from God.

No blast could be heard as I fall on my face in the hall way. "DAD! There is a bomb under my car!" I shouted. My dad came rushing down the stairs and went out immediately to investigate the underside of my car. I shouted over to him while walking back outside it was under the passenger's seat. My father went to the passenger side of my car and got on his side to get a better look at it.

"What the fuck?" said my father while staring at the inanimate object protruding out the hole. We both scrutinized the aerial and wondered how it got there? We looked at it for a while before my father lost patience and ordered me into the house. He then got into the car and kept the door open while he drove it.

Keeping the door open while driving a vehicle limits the blast pressure of a bomb. Nothing happened. He then pulled my car over, and we both looked at it again. As soon as we clapped eyes on the aerial it started to retract back into the little hole. My father then grabbed me by the arm and brought me across the road and up the street away from our house. "You know what that is?" my father asked me. "No?" I said. My dad went on, "that's a fucking bug in your car, the security forces have been listening and tracking your movements! What THE FUCK have you been doing? Have you put your family in danger, HAVE YOU?!"

My father kept shouting at me, and it was at that moment I started to acknowledge the error of my ways. I was dragging my family into something that had nothing to do with them; because of my bad life choices, I was putting my family at risk. If the spooks in the army were taking an interest in me, you can almost guarantee the RVA movement would be as well. They don't exactly care or take into account innocent bystanders when they want to take out a target. A bomb discriminates against no one. Within no time, I got rid of the car and bought a new one. I didn't want to tamper with the device and wanted it as far away from me as possible.

With these series of events I started to stay away from the Loyalist groups and as the years faded by so did the memory of my name amongst the ranks. I was a civilian again. I concluded that the interview at the army barracks was a sham; they must have used my national insurance number against me to sabotage my interviews for any jobs I went for until I finally went and sought the army out for work. I could keep calm under pressure, my hand would be steady even in the most distressing of situations, and I can tell you I have been in a few. I also had a nose for avoiding trouble as I always calculate my actions and probable outcomes to a high degree of accuracy. This turns out to be a set of skills the government would like me to develop further. The security forces saw the potential in me as an undercover MI6 agent that would work on operations in Northern Ireland and the Republic. I was never asked about my past endeavours or to divulge information on the people I used to knock about with. I wouldn't anyway; I'm not a fucking rat, I'm a patriot, loyal to my Queen and country. On a lighter note, while working for the government, I started to hear all sorts of rumours about MI5 and MI6 being part of the Illuminati organisation. A lot of my staff thinks it is entirely possible as the agency is engulfed in dodgy emblems such as the All-Seeing Eye. Even the art work on the wall has a weird look, almost all of it conveying some sort of hidden message.

I like to keep an open mind about it. The facts will always present themselves, so I was confident one day I could get to the bottom of it. To be honest, it keeps me curious about the organisation I am now working for, but I am more interested in my own country and solving their problems. Six months into my new job I am sent by my employers to a small B&B in a village near Whitehorse. There is around twenty of us being trained for different areas in the security service. We are not allowed into the base or the "Sweatbox" as it has been lovingly named by recruits until we have passed certain checks. There is a time clearance that we must stick to, so once we are in the base, we stay there for four weeks. I never make any attempt to be friendly with my peers as they are the ones who stand in my way of the leadership role I am after. I wanted to stand head and shoulders above the rest of them, and that wasn't going to happen if I started to let my guard down.

Training was beyond intense and very unpleasant at times, but there was no way around it, it had to be done. Even the days when my energy was sapped from me with endless workouts and anti-interrogation techniques that would deprive you of sleep for days at a time. I stuck at it. I made myself angry during these exercises and used it to my advantage as it made me even more determined to finish what I started. After successfully passing my training I was given my first assignment in Poland. It was the longest two years of my life. Most of the friends I use to have, now gone. All the while lying to my family and what few friends I had left, that I was in England working as a police officer. But now I am a success as I finished top of my field and now guaranteed leadership roles within the secret service. I was told at my low-key graduation by my mentor that I needed to be a ghost. I needed to blend into my surroundings and become that invisible man that takes everything in and lets nothing out, and that's just what I did.

Over the next three years, I was living in and out of different countries doing assignments I would never have dreamt of. Learning about things I wish I was never exposed to. You know when people say ignorance is bliss, it's true. There are images I can never get rid of, those awful thoughts of helpless victim's crunch around my head like glass. All those memories of faces frozen in death, their innocent lives snuffed out by cold blooded political killers, it changes you indefinitely. The laws have more clemency and tolerance towards terrorists and killers than the victims could ever hope for. My hands are ever bound by witless white-collar law makers, which makes my job hugely complicated in every way and slows my progress in bringing long overdue justice to the victims. I sometimes would look at the stars on a clear night and just burst into tears for no reason as I am over my head and well out of my comfort zone. I am turning into a wreck, but I keep it well hidden from everyone as it would show weakness.

I need to play it cool, or it could end badly for me. The agency has no empathy, no understanding or mercy for the weak. I am slowly finding out that the agency has an agenda which is clearly not in the UK's interests. Their agenda is hidden as we fight their war and everything else is considered collateral damage. I need to make my way back to Northern Ireland. I have done everything they have asked of me. Investigation after investigation, I consistently find myself locking horns with senior agents over the way I handle my cases. I continue to bring criminals in and connect them with hard evidence, undisputed evidence which is then, in turn, transforms into light sentences and acquittals as most of these psychotic terrorist killers are agents. My blood boils at the clemency they are shown!

It makes me remember a quote in the bible "Woe to those who call evil good and good evil; who put darkness for light, and light for darkness."(Isaiah 5:20) The quote from Isaiah fits what I am feeling right now. The sense of evil people walking this earth and allowed in politics. I don't want any part of it! To me it's easy. If the laws don't bring justice to the victims, I WILL! I changed completely, almost overnight. As I have a lot to answer for in the eyes of God. I will be paying for my atonement by doing good from now on. Regardless of what my puppet master's orders are. Evil is evil, put whatever spin you want on it. I will be a champion for good, this I swear. And for over seven years I did just that. I brought justice to the innocent and leak information beneficial to my vigilante brothers. The criminals now more than ever sense a presence they never felt before, it was called justice. Rumours and whispers of rogue agents that operate above the law spread throughout the underworld. Putting fear and uncertainty back with the criminals who were once untouchable are now themselves vulnerable. I did all this under the very nose of my handler's. As long as I did what I was told, and it didn't go against my new found moral code, I had free reign for my side line projects. I was doing so well at the agency that I was given my very own team to lead, on an operation called REVERT.

Back to the present:

On a beautiful moon lit night in July; I am sitting in a secluded part of Black Mountain overlooking the flickering lights of Belfast with my best friend Mark. We are talking about our weekend and other crazy shit, just passing the time.
I am listening to Mark while drifting in and out of focus trying to follow the distant lights of the cars going up and down the M1 and around the little twisty roads of the housing estates. I was excited; I have been after this terrorist child killing bastard for years. Mr. Mordha is 38 years old with a new age hippie look to him. He now has a man bun in his hair, which is a big change from the shitty dreads he had. I guarantee that fucker never sees a bar soap but once a month.

This piece of shit has over twenty souls that I am aware of to his name with three of them being children. He goes by many aliases, Martin, Sean, with Gérard being his latest name change. The agency always uses the Christian names when building a portfolio which reveals the marks true identity, which in this case is Michael Mordha. This cunt gets funded by deluded American plastic paddies who think it's alright to donate to support groups for the RVA who in turn fund RVA bombs and guns that kill innocents on both sides in Northern Ireland.

They believe in the deluded Irish cause that masks the genocidal killings of men women and children who they think shouldn't be living in their country, even though those British families have lived there for hundreds of years. Then the same American plastic paddies have the audacity to cry about terrorism when it visits their country. Words escape me when faced with the sheer hypocrisy of the whole thing. The American wannabe Irish Republicans biasedness towards Ulster Protestants is beyond sickening! Could you imagine trying to explain to God when you die why you felt it was right to support the killing and maiming of a section of the community in another country because you feel they should live somewhere else because you don't agree with their culture or religion? Thank God, most Americans are not like that, just a minority of idiots that can't think for themselves.

The mess that is the RVA is cleaned up partly by temps from MI5, and MI6 from time to time. "Temps" is a code word we use for paramilitary killers. We pick them up from different groups and give them large sums of money to take out targets we think are a threat to the country. This is how the government keep their hands clean. You hear about a gangland killing on the news; we see orders that have been issued and carried out. Due to the nature of the job, it's better not to form a friendship with any of the temps as they don't normally last too long in the land of the living as they often get killed through greed. The more jobs they do for us, the more cash they get but the risks are always the same. When they do get taken out, it is kind of a good thing for us as it ties up a loose end. When it comes to my own team, regardless of temps. I will study everyone in detail as secret service portfolio profiles mean nothing to me as I build my own views with each one of them. One of the temps I am using tonight is called Ian.

He has been with us for a few years and has been most useful so far, but has a bit of a temper. He is a Loyalist, which means he is loyal to Queen and country and usually from the Protestant community. Ian's tattoos were an interesting study into his persona. Firstly, all Ian's arms were inked using a bamboo tattooist which is the most painful way to be inked. This indicates he has a high pain threshold and therefore wouldn't shy away from a dangerous situation.

Secondly, he had two web tattoos, one on each elbow which can be interpreted in Northern Ireland as a sign of carrying out a successful kill. Not going to delve any deeper into that as he is now working for us. Nonetheless, if police connect him to any murders outside of his office hours, he will be facing prison. He also has a skull and dagger in the middle of his chest which has his old regiment named underneath it. It turns out that he was a former soldier who was once based in Yorkshire. For the most part, he had a very impressive record, but there have been notes added which appear to show Ian having a few discrepancies with regards to missing weapons and ammunition.

He was suspected but never formally charged with the crime due to lack of evidence. It would be an educated guess that said weapons are most likely now in the hands of Loyalist terror groups. Thirdly Ian is trained in mixed martial arts and believes himself to be a bit of a bad ass, and from what I have seen already with my own eyes, he is. Fourthly, I understand why he joined the Loyalist paramilitaries. Most likely due to a vicious attack, he had at the hands of Republicans. Everyone has a story; you just need to know where to look to find it. Ian's profile lets me know he was the temp we needed for this job tonight. Let's hope he doesn't fuck up.

The talkie was crackling beside me, "Hello, are you there?" a voice said. "Yes, Ian! What's the update?" I asked. "The rat has entered the cage!" I paused for a moment..., "Dry run?" I Inquired. "Yes, clean run," Ian replied. Bringing the radio closer to my lips, "Shake the cage!" I ordered. "Received!" replied Ian. I inform Mark that it was "Showtime!" While getting up onto my feet from my scenic perch, I lifted my AR-15 up and throw the strap over my shoulder. Mark also picked up his rifle, but he carried it differently from me, almost as you would cradle a baby which is endearing in a strange way. As we both made our way back to the car, Mark asked: "When can I get stuck into these scumbags?" I laughed and said, "You're very keen mate, be careful what you wish for mate as you might just get it" I replied. I was thinking about Ian when he mentioned that, and how I hoped he had followed protocol. He can be a bit of a loose cannon at times, to put it mildly.

Meanwhile

The street started to fill with people, among them armed RVA men frantically looking for the perpetrator or perpetrators of the gun fire. Which was our man

Ian who had to riddle Michaels house to start an internal feud as we had intel there was a possible power struggle happening amongst the higher ranks.

A few men entered Michael's house to investigate the damage done and to see if their hero was still in the land of the living. Michael eventually came out to cheers and roars of delight, from his neighbours in the estate. The men held his arms up and laughed at the incompetence of their would-be assassins and started to talk and speculate who had tried to take out Michael. No doubt their mobiles were going crazy to inform their political wing of their latest news and how to maximise the media coverage for this event. As I drive to the rendezvous point, I ponder about what Michael will make of tonight's events.

Little does Michael realise that what just happened was a strategic hit that will confidently create a feud between Republican paramilitaries which will hopefully thin out the ranks, if you catch my meaning? The RVA will eventually find the evidence we planted. No doubt they have a few samples of those left-over cartridges Ian left on purpose. Normally the cartridges of a sanctioned hit get caught in our improvised blowback scoop to leave no shells at the scene. We also file the bullet ends in different directions to create different metal scoring so forensics can't use them for evidence.

Before we riddled Michael's house, we tracked him for several months. The Intel gathered was very useful and all thanks to a very small tracker we planted on his van while Michael was getting his MOT. We now have his movements recorded and the people he was meeting named. After a lull in information, we really needed this avalanche of new data to get on top of this terrorist group.
Mark and I arrived at the meet and went over our next steps. Ian came strolling in with a big smile on his face. "Well, another rat scuttled," Ian said. "Yes, very good work but it will be all for nothing if our mole doesn't plant the evidence we need to start this feud," I replied.

"What evidence?" Mark inquired. "The tip-off our mole needs to make to the senior RVA man after he finds the planted rounds used in today's hit. The rounds will be placed in a rival Republican safe house. The shells used at Michaels hide out will match the ones planted at the safe house. The ammo is specific to one automatic weapon which in turn needs to be modified to fire the new bullets. Therefore, we will also plant the rifle Ian used in the same safe house. Someone will come across them, and it will eventually get back to Michael. If retaliation doesn't come soon, we need to initiate a further hit, maybe taking out a few low level RVA men," I stated. This is how the agency cleans the unwanted problems that still infest Northern Ireland. We try to get them to do the dirty work for us. I pull Ian to the side and inform him that I needed to meet with him this afternoon about a new operation I wanted him on board with. Ian nods and then waits with the others for me to dismiss them.

Now comes the hard part, waiting. I already knew the low-level RVA scumbags we needed to take out if we wanted to speed up events and how to go about it. Time at the moment wasn't our friend as I had to report back on the progress we were making with the feud. The agency needs Michael to be killed by one of their own for him not to become a martyr for the movement. There is no reason for us waiting about at the rendezvous point as this attack will take time to fester, so I dismissed the men and made my way home. The sky was clear, and the stars were bright. I am in and out of muddled thoughts when it sinks in about the number of hours I have put in again! My doctor is going to bollock me again if I can't keep my blood sugars in check as all I eat is shit while doing this job, I thought to myself.

Down the M1 past Lisburn, past Lurgan to pull off at the Portadown junction. I always do alternative routes home as a precaution as I am as much as a target as the ones I mark. I passed a car dealership to my left that has the most beautiful set of wheels sitting proudly on top of a car stand. I drive past it with envious eyes and the thoughts of someday climbing the ladder high enough in the agency to easily purchase one outright. I'm starving and know I won't be bothered to make anything to eat when I get home as it's too much of an effort. Fast food comes to mind, but none are open at this hour, so I pull into a petrol station and get a dozen doughnuts to eat. I am standing in line in the little shop at the petrol station, staring at myself on the CCTV screen. It was so blurry and in grey scale, how could anything recorded on it be used as evidence in court I wondered.

A blonde girl is behind the counter; she looks like she is new here. "Hello," I said in a tired voice. "Hi there, you look like you need your bed," she replied. "I do indeed," I said giving her a big smile while taking my doughnuts. At home, there was nothing on TV I wanted to watch, so I stuck the news on to see if we made this morning's headlines? Sure, enough under breaking news, we have a news station reporting a warped sympathetic version of events that portray the RVA as victims. The news station is trying to connect it to Loyalist paramilitaries not keeping the ceasefire. If only the public knew the truth. If only the people of Northern Ireland knew what sort of shady deals were being made behind closed doors on their behalf. It would shame the devil.

The news station added further insult to injury to have that twat Michael interviewed at the scene saying the RVA was showing restraint after being attacked a number of times by the British Loyalists. Michael, the hypocrite, says this while only last week killing two young men that were in the right place at the wrong time when an improvised explosion went off killing them both. Not much news coverage on that!

But I knew the evidence was key, and it never stuck to Michael. The way I look at it is, you don't get to lead a large rebel terrorist army without getting your hands dirty. Can't be done! Michael loved planting bombs; he got off on it. The huge following, he has in the Republican community was unreal, making him out a hero for killing indiscriminately. The RVA believe no one is innocent and any collateral damage as they call it is quickly dismissed with their broken record of how both sides have lost loved ones. There is no empathy, no reasoning, just killing for a dead cause. There will never be a united Ireland as the Commonwealth would then have an Island beside them that is friends with all the UK's enemies. Enemies that would want to see England blown off the map. The Agency will make sure that doesn't happen.

Anyway, their wannabe army doesn't see the clean-up operation happening right under their nose. I turn the TV off and head upstairs. I check in on my son Daniel who is three. I just lean against the door frame staring at him. The moon is shining through his window, dimly lighting his room. I was thinking to myself how beautiful and innocent he was just sleeping there. I went over quietly to him and gave him a kiss on his forehead. I pull his blanket up and tuck him in and closed the door over, just leaving a crack open in case he shouts for me. I get into the shower and scrub myself down looking at all the scars I have accumulated over the years.

The bullet wound through my right shoulder was the one that made me realise that the action wasn't always one way and that I needed to be more careful. I always wear a heavy tactical bullet proof vest now because of it. I do have other scars from my childhood, like my chisel mark on my face from shop class and part of my elbow that I ground off during a onehanded bike ride due to a half cast on my arm, but so what, doesn't everyone? I make my way to the spare room as my wife Olivia hates me waking her up; it has almost become a regular row we seem to have most weeks. I am sprawling out over the bed, and my eyes get heavy fast with my breathing ever slower, calmness takes over my body and I drift off to sleep. "BEEP, BEEP, BEEP!" My trip for the silent alarm goes off, and my heart jumps out of my chest. I lock and load my gun which is under my pillow, then jump out of my bed and head over to my monitor which is turned off. I quickly press the power button and impatiently wait for the images to appear on my screen to see what the hell's going on. I check the cameras and see two drunken twats in my driveway taking a piss over my car. I glanced over at my digital clock, 3:35 am, fucking never get a night's sleep! I quickly go down stairs and creak the front door open then head quickly and silently towards them. They were that wasted that I used one guy's head to knock the other out.

Now I am standing in my boxers over two unconscious men in my driveway. Shit, Olivia is not going to like this. I quickly go through their pockets to find their id and levied them both the cash contents of their wallets for pissing on my car. As I go through their wallets, it becomes apparent that the fine doesn't work out great for me as the pair of them only had twenty quid between them.

I do however find their id and information about where they live. I see one of them works for a welding agency in an industrial estate not too far from here and the other drives a taxi. I keep the IDs to run through more thoroughly later to make sure they are not caught up with any of the paramilitaries. I am enraged that these two pricks have not only woken me up and pissed all over my car, all they have for my troubles is twenty quid! "Mother fuckers!" I get on my mobile and order Ian to come over to my place as quickly as possible. I go back into the house and get dressed and make a brew as I wait for Ian to show up. Twenty minutes later I can see Ian rolling up in his Jag through my dining room window as he parks outside my house. I lock the house up and walk over to meet him. The night is cold, and the street I live on is quiet as people are in a deep slumber at this time of night. Ian makes very little chit chat with me which indicates the poor man is tired as he is never one to keep his gob shut.

I like the way he has asked me no questions about these two pricks and just gets on with the task at hand. We drag each of them over to Ian's car and throw them roughly into the boot. I don't give a fuck right now if any of my neighbours saw what happened, they know better than to cause problems for me. Wait that sounds bad. I wouldn't do anything to them but play the fool and insist I have no idea what they are talking about. I must keep reminding myself that I need to repent my sinful ways and be a changed man. Fighting for the innocent against all that is evil in the world today.

I ask Ian to drive to a super market near the centre of the town but on roads that avoid ANPR cameras. The government has these damn cameras everywhere that record all car number plates that pass them which are date and time stamped. They are then stored on a database for several years. The government can type in a registration plate and accurately track the car's movements in real time. Very useful for us and a great burden for the unsuspecting. We leave my area and get onto the back roads which are very narrow and full of dips and curves that will be shaking the crap out of our lodgers in the boot of the car. It takes a little longer than normal to reach our destination and pull up alongside the road. We jump out and make our way to the boot of the car expecting to hear muffled cries for help. We look at each other as it's eerily silent like we no longer have breathing guests in the trunk of the car.

I whip open the boot and to see the two of them still out cold but to my relief still breathing. We grab the men and drag them out of the car. Ian's guy has crapped himself as unconscious drunks do and the guy I have weighs a ton but nevertheless, we strip them down to their pants in an effort to punish these two pricks for taking liberties. We pull on our clavas and fire man lift their unconscious bodies a short distance towards the trolley station in the middle of the car park of a well-known supermarket.

I use my old hand cuffs to attach them to separate trolleys and spray the cuffs with my small bottle of oxygen bleach which kills all traces of our DNA and finger prints. I then stand back and admire my work when suddenly, I feel awash with guilt. I am not a heartless man; I leave them a pound each in their trolleys so when they wake they can use it to release themselves from the rack. They'd better wake soon as it's only a few hours till opening time and this is a busy wee supermarket. As for the cuffs attaching them to their trolleys, well that's a gift from me.

On the way home, Ian and I laugh about their predicament and how we could have made it worse. I feel so tired now; my eyes want to close and just sleep in the car. The soft eighties music in the car makes my eyes finally shut and go into a semi doze, the music makes me remember happier times in my life when things were simple and uncomplicated. The car comes to an abrupt stop which snaps me against the seatbelt and instantly awakens me. "Your stop boss!" Ian said. I give him a dirty look and pull myself slowly out of the car. I tell Ian I will see him later at HQ which is a lie as I have no intentions of going up to Bangor today. As I lock the house door behind me and make my way upstairs into my bed. Around 6:30am I can hear my little monster getting up.

I then get prepared for what is inevitably going to happen next. My door slowly creeps open, and a little face peeks around. My boy makes eye contact with me, and a big smile covers both of our faces as my son comes running and jumps onto my bed and gives me a big cuddle. He is getting so strong; I can feel my neck crack at times when he does it. I have so many plans for him. I think about my son often, wondering what he will be like when he is older? What type of career does he want? Will he hang out with me when I am an old man and shoot the breeze?

I love him to bits as he is the one thing that is consistent in my life. He is unbiased and wants nothing from me other than to be his daddy. I wish I could say the same for my wife that all she wants from me is to be a good husband and provider, but I felt like we have drifted so far apart that we are only together for the sake of our son.

Those words haven't been spoken between us yet, but it's just a matter of time. "Daaaad," Daniel said in a semi quiet voice, "I want chocolate." "No chocolate, its morning time" I replied. I grabbed his hand, and we both went down stairs to the kitchen. I have now crossed over from being "sleepily tired" to "tired awake" as my second wind kicks in and feel more alert in myself. "Well little man, do you want cereal or toast?" I ask.

"Chocolate," Daniel replied. I pour him a bowl of cereal and give it to him. When will I learn not to negotiate with a three-year-old? My son eats his breakfast as we both watch the cartoon channel in the living room together. We are eating our breakfast when the mail flap suddenly snaps as letters are posted through the door and as usual Dutch our dog goes mental outside barking at the postman. The little man runs from the living room to retrieve the mail, and I quickly follow as Daniel likes to open our letters by ripping them apart.

God love him.

Chapter 2 - Ian Stewart

Ian was sitting in a stolen car in a well-known Republican estate in Belfast. He has his window rolled down a crack to let the cool night air in and let the gentle twirling smoke of his cigarette out.

I hate this waiting game Ian thought to himself. I feel pumped and ready to do this assignment, but that bastard has yet to show up, and it's boring the shite out of me. I was only parked a few houses up from where Michael was now living. The man liked to move around a lot and was very hard to follow which makes this intel we have on his new digs, very significant for the agencies plans to start an internal feud. His house looked very out of place compared to the rest of his neighbours.

His home looked like a fort with all the security cameras, sensor lights, dogs and a five-foot iron fence with a security gate to finish it off. Michaels Republican palace probably had bulletproof windows, not that it would matter with these new state of the art ballistics I had locked and loaded. The Republican estate the house is situated in was notorious for churning out new brain washed recruits, ready to shoot someone in the back for their pathetic RVA movement. The estate never seemed to sleep. If you watched carefully, you could see the odd face appear from the second-floor windows, ever keeping watch, ready to alert the estate for battle.

The estate was quite similar to others I had seen before. It had the crudely painted curb stones in green, white and orange plus they had the Tri colour flags on most of the lamp posts. It was an eerie sight as the place looked a little deserted and too quiet for my liking. I was watching the flags limply blowing in the wind when I get fixated on bouncing headlights coming down the road. It looks like a van, which seems to be slowing down behind me which makes me nervous. I play it cool as I sink low into my seat and watch the van trundled past me and stop a few houses away from Michaels place. As I strain my eyes to get a better look I can see an outline of a person getting out of the van on the passenger side. The van does a three-point turn and honks as it speeds off down the road past me. The man waves goodbye to the driver, and then I see him! Yes, yes that's Michael! I wait for a few minutes and let him get settled as I want to make sure he is in his living room when I riddle the house with bullets. I pick up the talkie beside me to talk to Jason, my overrated MI6 boss. "Hello, are you there?" I said. "Yes, Ian! What's the update?" Jason replied. I excitedly proceeded to inform him that Michael was finally home. "The rat has entered the cage!" I wait for a reply, "Dry run?" Jason asks. Meaning did I have a plan of attack with a safe escape route. "Yes, clean run," I replied.

"Shake the cage!" Jason said firmly. "Received!" I replied as I threw the talkie onto the passenger seat. Ian took his woolly hat off his head and slowly unrolled the rim and stretched it out before him. He then took a long draw from his cigarette and burned two holes into it for his eyes to see through. He then put the woolly hat back on and stretched it slowly over his face to make a balaclava. Stubbing out his cigarette on the dashboard of his stolen sports saloon. He proceeded to cock his automatic rifle and gave it a once over before getting out of the car, calm and cool like he has done this a thousand times before.

He proceeded to walk up to the house while taking short glances all around him as if he was expecting trouble. Quickly and without hesitation, he unloaded his clip into Michaels hideout. The bullets began creating massive craters in the pebble dashed wall and cutting through the bricks and windows like they weren't even there. The drapes in the living room caught fire due to the heat of the bullets pummelling through it. Ian made sure he got rounds into every room of the house. The large calibre weapon was spitting hot smoking shells all over the street, and the deafening echo of the automatic gun fire was rattling the windows of the nearby houses. The gun fire stopped, and the last empty cartridges could be heard clinking onto the ground. Ian then made a hasty retreat to the car where he threw his smoking rifle into the passenger seat before speeding off into the night.

I make my way back to the rendezvous point after ditching and burning the car; I had used. After our short briefing, Jason asked me to meet him later that afternoon for an assignment he wanted to use me for. I'm fine with that, so long as the money is good as I don't have a day job to go to. I am making my way home after popping in to see my on-off girlfriend Emma when my phone rings. It was Jason again! What the fuck does he want now? "Hello?" I said answering my mobile. "Ian, I need you down at my place in 20 mins!" Jason ordered and disconnected the call. Going to be a long night Ian thought to himself as he pulls on his trousers, before making his way to Portadown. I let Jason know I'm outside his place, I can barely muster any enthusiasm for anything else. Next thing that happens leaves me questioning Jason's mental sanity. Needless to say, two poor fuckers have got on the wrong side of him and we ended up causing them some upset and grief. I leave Jason at home after the night's shenanigans, I don't understand that guy sometimes as he often says I'm the loose cannon, hypocritical prick! I drive myself home and manage to get some sleep before dragging myself into work at HQ for 11:30am. It's a bit of a dump inside with areas of peeling paint and poor plastering patches dotted about the place. They would need to knock it down and build a better headquarters that would represent the police force in a better light. The compound that surrounds it, however, is first class! I would hate to be the terrorist that fired on this station as the defences would be devastating on the poor sods.

The building perimeters have advanced automated weapons that pin point the sound/flash source of firing weapons and then, in turn, hit them with controlled bursts of heavy calibre projectiles. Death is guaranteed instantaneous. These security measures are never on until the building has been actually hit by munitions. The walls also host a variety of manned and other automated high calibre weapons that would shred an armoured truck and of course anyone hiding in it. Plus, to make it all legal the barracks is swarming with CCTV inside and out, which is streamed and stored in data clouds, held on SD drives in London and Belfast. The armour and reinforced concrete wall make this a safe place but the only stickler is the mortars as they can fly over the high walls, but the automated systems would make sure that whoever fired the mortar would never do it again. On a lighter note, it has lovely helicopter bays and the most spectacular sea view a military headquarters could ever hope for. I wish I had a full-time job here, Ian sighed. Ian knew all too well, in their eyes he was nothing more than an expendable killer for hire.

As Ian walks into the MI6 operations room in the basement of the building, he quickly scans across all the agents' busy working at their stations. He stands strong and puts on his game face, trying not to show the disappointment of truly not belonging to the agency. Trying to make his presence known, he shouted aloud "Where is Jason?" All the people in the office stopped for a moment and looked up at Ian without saying a word, until one by one, they went back to work. That could have gone better, I thought to myself. Maybe I was coming across rude, but that's just my nature. I realise I have a bit of a reputation for losing my cool and wrecking things in the office. Probably the reason why everyone tries to give me a wide berth.

Fuck them! I walk a little slower to try to rile up these pencil pushing pricks even more. They think they are above me, even though it's me that pulls the trigger, me that puts my fucking neck on the line, me who has the fucking minerals to do what they can't! Fucking English pricks! Northern Ireland is more loyal to the crown than any of these wannabe MI6 cunts! My anger is building again, and I am desperate to smash something or even someone, but I don't. The eyes, they never lie. You can see it in my face not to approach me as I'm wound tight and ready to explode! I walk into meeting room one and sit down at the conference desk. I let out a deep breath and try to take in what they are talking about as they have already started wittering on about today's brief. It's of no importance to me as my only ever input is saying yes, I will be there or no I won't. I don't even need to be here as I am but a tool for a job, but they make me come in any way. I love the fact I get to take out Republican terrorists legally or any terrorists for that matter which threatens our wee country.

People might call me a terrorist, but I fight against those that wish to destroy my heritage and hurt my people. I do what the government has failed to do time and again, protect its citizens from murdering bastards. The government used to say they would never deal with terrorists, ha ha ha, what a joke! You ever hear the saying "that you would be robbing Peter to pay Paul?" That's the best way I can describe the mess that is called "The ceasefire". I do the jobs for British intelligence as it firstly, it pays well and secondly, it allows me to send information back to my comrades to take the fight directly to these RVA scumbags. That's the only way I can sleep at night otherwise I would be nowhere near these fucking white-collar hoods. Do I feel I am working above the law? I could say yes, but that would make an assumption on my part that we have a tangible working law to begin with, which we don't! If we take into consideration what terror, bombs, guns and murder get you, well that would equate to a right to stand for a seat in our government! How's that for fucking crazy?

They hand me a paper folder that is stamped with "Operation REVERT - Eyes Only." I put the folder in front of me without opening it. Trevor is again talking away, and as usual, he is oblivious to the people around the table using their phones and laptops, not really paying any attention to the old man. The agents all know it's a white wash game the British government is playing and have lost all respect for the roles in which they play in Ulster, or they just don't give a damn about any of it. Ian moves the folder closer to him on the table and opens it up. This must be the mission Jason wanted to talk to me about.

It seems that Trevor is poking his nose into this "Operation REVERT" again looking at this brief as it has been amended by him according to the notes twice already. Don't get me wrong, what little I know of Trevor is that he is good at data gathering, and his plans for assignments are always impeccable which is why he always gets involved with the big job roles, but it looks like he has watered down the plans by cutting the size of staff down and reducing funding and management. This name "Operation REVERT" that the agency gave the project; it gives me a little hope for the future. Operation REVERT means to return to a previous state, practice, or topic. I start to get a good feeling building up inside me, not unlike an excited sensation as I start to put the pieces together and realise that this cease-fire with the terrorists was part of a master plan to kill off the RVA and their supporters. The old divide and conquer strategy. The hard-core RVA movement has already split with their political wing or near enough for reasons best known to them.

I know the money and arms coming in the country for these terrorists have dramatically dwindled to nothing over the years, and the threat they pose is nothing significant as they now rely on homemade weapons which have been literally death traps for a few of them. I say this in regard to the failed homemade mortar round that exploded in the hands of an RVA man a few months ago. Rumours were that it was a very messy clean up. What essentially the government are doing according to this document, is slowly making it very distasteful to support the RVA movement as fewer and fewer Republicans jump for joy at their terrorist acts. There are good people on both sides of the community, all they need is a chance to escape the bigotry of the hard-lined dinosaurs in their own area and realise we are all God's children. That we all need to respect one and other like the great man Martin Luther King said not so long ago with his "I have a dream" speech.

The more I read, the more I thought, you sneaky, sneaky bastards. Well done! Well, I am the rough tool they need to bring a means to an end in this conflict. I didn't kid myself; I always knew my role in the agency. The promise of a short life, great pay and with no recognition of any of my heroic deeds. I am expendable, ten to a penny. It is the only reason I am allowed to be here at this table. I have made my peace with God and am ready to die fighting for this country, how many in this room can say that? Whether I go to heaven, well that's an entirely different matter altogether. That's for the big man upstairs to decide. I am now reading my role in this master plan. Well, it's a bit different to what I am used to. To be honest, the last job they gave me to pepper the house of that scumbag Michael was a breeze, so I was hoping for something similar. They want me to pose as a taxi driver in Warrenpoint? Sounds easy enough but why? I read on and it becomes apparent it won't be as easy as I first thought. I would be a mobile interrogation centre on wheels which is a new one to me. There is a section outlining the specs of the taxi I will be driving. The taxi itself is protected with Dynamic Armour which is fucking amazing for this day and age. This is the same advanced armour used on military vehicles which protect it against kinetic energy penetrators and other high explosive projectiles. I feel safer already; I laugh to myself.

There are Taser pins that push through the back seats of the cab with a hidden push point to activate it which would render the passenger or passengers immobile. You can control the amps and volts of the current which could turn a little shock into one that was lethal. It becomes more apparent through each paragraph I read that this taxi is for exploiting potential whistle blowers from within the RVA community. As I keep reading about the specs of the taxi, I become more impressed by the tech they have crammed into it.

The front of the windshield acts as a monitor to show data on various parts of the glass which will be invisible to anyone looking into the cab as all windows are electrically atomised to blur and deflect light. The hidden cameras situated around the outside and inside of the vehicle will be used in conjunction with facial recognition software to ID potential targets. "Ian, IAN!" Trevor shouts. I look up to everyone staring at me. "Well?" Trevor asks. "Well? Well, what the fuck do you want?!" I replied. "Can I see you in my office!", Trevor commanded in a sharp tone of voice. As I get up, I place the folder under my arm like a newspaper ready for a read on the shitter. I casually walk into Trevor's office and closed the door behind me. "I take it you like your new assignment?" Trevor inquires. "Yeah, it's alright," I replied. "I would like you to go through the assignment with Jason to see if there are any changes that we need to make to the mission to reduce detection. It will be largely an intelligence gathering operation before and we'll need you to clean up what needs to be cleaned up". Trevor continued. My blood boils, as I struggle to put the words together to give back a response to Trevor's request. "Once again, my years of experience are overlooked by you! You bureaucratic fuckwit!

Why do I need... you know what, if you can't trust me to do a fucking simple recon job you can go fuck yourself as I have more experience and prowess over the years in the military than that wannabe cock Jason!" "Did you even look at the file I gave you? It's not just a recon mission." Trevor replied angrily. "Right... I will have another look at it again." I told Trevor. "That's a bit of tough shit now you fucking moron," Trevor said angrily. "I have had enough of your fucking autistic mood swings to last a life time, and in this unit, your antics are becoming more of a liability every day for this agency. Any fucking wonder Jason keeps you on a short leash with your fucking tantrums ever ready to shit all over our operations that have been methodically planned for months on end. You're a fucking liability and are suspended until further notice." Trevor shouted at me while I was walking out of his office.

I will read the file again later and give Trevor a few days to cool down. Why do I keep putting myself in these situations? I can't even have a civil conversation with these spooks without being defensive or difficult. I do however know why I am always abrupt and quick tempered, but I have always chosen to ignore or maybe even deny it. It could have something to do with my blue and red tablets I take, which is a common side effect of HGH (Human Growth Hormone). I need it to stay in shape as I am approaching 45 years old and can't produce the testosterone I need to build the essential muscles I use for the type of work I do.

I need a coffee! I can just imagine everyone's fucking delight that I am suspended. Fuck them; they need me more than I need them, pricks.

They can come and find me when they are ready to go with this new operation. Who could replace me? No one, that's WHO! I head to the canteen and grab a black coffee to go. I try to make a point to be nicer and practice on the people passing by me in the hallway as I make my way out of the building. "Hello, nice day, isn't it?" I ask a colleague in passing. "Hey, there missy!" I shouted giving this beautiful woman a wink and a smile. This is easy; I could be nice all day if I wanted to. I make my way out of the building and head towards my car when I hear footsteps running up behind me. I turn around quickly to see Lynne approaching me. "Ian wait! I need your file back. Trevor has sent me down to get it off you!" she shouts. I take out the pages discreetly and hand her the folder as I get into my car. "See you later Lynne!" I tell her while I close the door. Lynne walks off towards the entrance to the building. I know I have seconds to get out of here before she realises there is nothing in the folder. I quickly drive to the security gates, and the barriers lift to allow me to pass. I can see Lynne opening the folder. Shit! She is running over here. I roll out of the gates very quickly and speed down towards the coastal road. I can't go home for the minute as that will be the agency's first port of call; I hope they tidy the place up after them. I head down to a quiet little fishing village I know called Portavogie.

It takes about 25 minutes to get there, but what a view it is along that coastal road. On a good day, you would swear you're in the tropics when the waters turn a clear aqua green against a brilliant blue sky. I love it up here. Someday I am going to buy my own place up here by the sea. As I slowly drive into the centre of the small village, I pull into a petrol station. It's nearly 2 pm when I start to fill the car up; my stomach starts to grumble. I walk into the shop to pay for the fuel when I feel compelled to check out the sweets. I'm not going to eat sugar as that makes you fat so I settle for a diet cola. I suddenly realise on the way back out to my car that there is a beautiful wee chip shop by the docks that do the best scampi. I decide to grab a bite to eat and pull my car along the docks to read this assignment in peace. As a rule of thumb, I always park with my back to a big wall so I can observe anyone approaching and have my car ready for a quick getaway. I can see all the usual big boats tied up and that tame seal the fishermen always feed in the port. The wee seal has been hanging around the docks here for years. I could watch him all day, but I need to focus my attention back onto the brief as I want to know more about my role in this operation. When I read further about the taxi, it mentions it has an automated facial recognition system which is streamed to HQ to analyse and build profiles on the people in that area. It monitors faces? I scratch my head; how do they have the tech to do this. I read on. The windscreen highlights possible people with links to the RVA movement along with painting the known people of interest in red as credible threats.

The agency has located two RVA units around Warrenpoint and has discovered a huge catchment of weapons that all need to be destroyed. Due to the weapons being stockpiled within close proximity to the active RVA units, it would be a forgone conclusion that they intend on using them very soon. Intel warns, that if the internal feud doesn't take place soon and with the desired effects, plan B was to go into immediate effect. We kill all the problems at the source. Ian's eyes start to widen as he contemplates what he just read. Ian continues reading about how they intend on carrying this operation out. The RVA marks will be dispatched during a 110-minute window. They also want the main players to be killed in such a way as not to make them martyrs, so it must be made to look like they left the country. Their bodies are to be kept and disposed of in international waters using concrete coffins. That's how they took out a problematic bomber called Nigel Haroon last May. There was a lot of

Republican uproar about it when his case was thrown out of court due to lack of evidence that would suggest he was assassinated by British intelligence. MI5 knew Nigel would be back into the Republican ranks within weeks, so they waited till they got evidence confirming this before a kill order was issued. I feel myself grin as I am looking forward to this part of the job. Just like old times, I thought to myself, here's hoping for option B to be chosen. FUCK! One problem, I forgot I was suspended. I need to get Jason to fix this for me, after all, he owes me for that Portadown job we did together, among other things.

I put the papers above my visor and finish off my scampi supper, "Yum!" I think to myself as I scrape my chips around the bottom of the box trying to gather up as much salt as I possibly can before wolfing them down. I then select my favourite FM dance music channel and turn the tunes up as I decide how I would get back into the game. I can't fucking think straight with all the shit that has happened to me today, so I do what was asked of me in the first place and make my way down to Portadown to speak with Jason. I get out of the car and pull out two freshly cloned plates I made last week and stick them on my Jag as I don't want to be stopped by the police or picked up on the ANPR cameras on my way to Portadown. Jay is not going to like me coming unannounced or that I have caused a shit storm down at HQ but he will have to get over it. I have to remember to keep my cool and accept Jason is my commanding officer even though he is nearly ten years younger than me with less experience and nowhere near my size and strength. Ian suddenly stops his mental ramblings about how great he is and laughs to himself, man I feel old! Ian starts to reminisce. It feels like only yesterday when I was sixteen and living in an estate off the Shankill road. I remember life was very different back then. Children were brought up with manners, and their parents knew where they were at all times. I was taught always to be respectful to others.

Sometimes it didn't matter how nice you were or courteous to somebody, as there are always going to be some people out there that will hate you for one reason or another. How can you love your neighbours when they themselves were unwilling to love you back? That's when I became bitter towards all Roman Catholics as they were in one way or another connected with the RVA movement. I suppose that's hypocritical of me to say as the same could be said for all Protestants. so that statement I will take it back. The fact that some of these terrorists believe if they confess their murderous killings to a priest, the priest actually has the power to absolve their sin? So, it begs the question why did Jesus need to die on the cross for us when a priest can forgive your sins?

Jesus went to the cross willingly, and his sacrifice was to atone for all our sins as his blood alone was the only thing that could save humanity from Hell. Since when did man think he could forgive himself for his own transgressions? I just don't get the way they think.

My mother, could never explain to me in a way that I would understand why the RVA hated us when we worshipped the same God but in a very different way? Protestants like myself believe Jesus to be the head of the church, not the Pope or Mary. We believe that only Jesus has the power to save sinners. We believe that God gave his only begotten son to die on the cross so that we might live and have everlasting life in heaven. Well, that's our belief, and the Roman Catholics can believe what they want as long as they don't try to push it down my throat. Religion does have a massive influence in this wee country of mine. I can remember as a lad walking home from school, passing a group of guys, there was nothing significant about them, just guys talking. Nevertheless, those same guys were always at the same spot, every day after school. Until this one day I passed them, and they suddenly stopped talking and began to walk behind me. I was a fast walker and was a good bit ahead of them, but they soon caught up to where I was. I again didn't pay much attention to them as I seen them every day. "Hey, mate! Do you have a light?" One of them said friendly enough to me. "No, I don't smoke, sorry." I replied.

"You live around here? I just live down that street." He said as he pointed across the road to a well-known Loyalist estate. "Yes, I live there too," I replied. The guys face changed, and he looked over at his friends and nodded before looking back at me. All of them just started to beat the shit out of me. They were calling me a dirty Hun, black bastard among other derogatory sectarian remarks. I don't remember much after that as the next thing I knew; I was in an ambulance, on its way to Belfast's Royal Victoria hospital. It turns out I was stabbed, and my body went into shock.

My parents were by my bedside in bits asking me what happened. As I was telling them everything that took place, all I could concentrate on, was the tears welling up in my mother's eyes. Ever since that day they wanted to move to another house away from the flash points but couldn't afford to. It bothered them a lot that they couldn't protect me from the hoodlums that visited our estate from time to time. The attack on me did have a positive effect as it toughened me up. I began to see the world through very different eyes and become a less trusting individual. I was hitting the gym hard and took my diet seriously which had me eating every three hours, which in turn piled on the muscle. A year or so later, I started to take the same route again and again, just as I did before hoping the same gang would be about. They were nowhere to be seen, so I went looking for them. It didn't take me long to find them. I would feel more justified for what I am about to do if they came to me. All I needed was a red flag to draw them to me, so I unzipped my jacket to reveal my East Belfast supporters football top. That did the trick. I made sure to bring them to an area that I now could control which was the gates on the peace wall. I went back over to the Loyalist side, and as I planned, they did the same. But this time I had a few friends with me to block their escape as they passed through. I had pre-warned my crew not to step in as I would be taking them all on at once. As I asked, my mates stepped back and made sure they couldn't escape. I informed my Republican aggressors that I alone will be fighting them. One of them recognised me. "Didn't we beat the shit out of this Orange bastard a few years ago?" said the tall Republican to his mate. "Yeah, we did, but this time we will finish the job!" he replied as they all prepared themselves for a fight. A few of the Republicans grinned at as if it was some kind of joke that I was taking them on by myself.

They probably thought the other Loyalists would jump in at some point. They were about to get their eyes opened to what I had in store for them. The built-up anger and hatred I had for them over what they had done to me, and what they put my family through. It was about to manifest itself in blood, their blood. The tallest of the Republican hoods was going to go for me first, I could see it in his eyes, but I needed to gauge who was going next or possibly at the same time for me. Then I spotted him as he was slowly pulling out a blade. Before I knew it, the tall one went for me and just liked I guessed so did the hood with the blade. I had to take a punch from the tall guy to grab the blade from the other and use his momentum with the clutched knife to stab the tall guy. I stabbed him in the chest, and then there were four. The tall guy just slumped over on as side as the look of horror started to contort his face. His mate who was still holding the knife spun around wildly at me as all four came at once which I was prepared for. I found out then and there that I could take a punch or three as I steadily and brutally beat them using my new-found strength and uncontrollable rage.

As my opponents lay twisted on the ground, I was stood over them. I was hurt and hurt badly, but I was nowhere near as damaged as those cunts were. Catching my breath, I slowly hear the sound of applauds building up from my Loyalist brothers and sisters around me. I stood up straight, snorted the blood

45

out of my nose onto the ground, before individually positioning myself on top of the bastards and breaking each of their noses with a devastating forehead smash! I did this so they would always remember today. Whenever the cunts looked in the mirror, they would see their scars; it will be a reminder of the monster they made of me. I ordered the boys to throw the limp and badly damaged Republicans over the wall as I was not going to allow them the courtesy of using our gates as an exit. The peace wall was at least 12ft high in the majority of places, but near the gates, it dropped to about 6ft. It took a bit of effort, but every one of those bastards was thrown over the peace line to their side of the wall, landing in a bloody heap. I felt vindicated and powerful that day!

The next day I was feeling very sore and stiff. I sat down to the breakfast my mother made for me and started scanning the local paper that was waiting for my dad on the table when I came across an article of interest. It was about the death of one of the guys in the group I beat up yesterday. I recognised his name, "A murder inquiry has now been launched by Special branch in Belfast after the death of a local man Doran Aadamsk of no fixed address, Ardoyne. A serious incident took place near the Crumlin road, yesterday at around 1 pm. We are asking for any witnesses to come forward to help with our inquiries. If you have information regarding this serious incident, please contact Special branch on..." Blah blah blah. I put the paper down and continued to eat my toast as I felt totally indifferent to those fuckers as they themselves left me for dead all those months ago. I wasn't worried about the other Republican dickheads touting on me as they would never go to the police. Those type of cunts like to take care of things themselves. Unbeknownst to me at the time, but I would be bumping into one or two of them in the near future. I get up and throw the paper in the bin. "Son, your father never got a read of that paper yet!" my mother scolded. "Nor will he ma", I replied as I kissed her on the cheek goodbye on my way out to the gym.

Presently

Its 4pm and I am minutes away from Portadown when I try to reassure myself that Jason will need me on this operation. I am after all a bit of a silent hero when it comes to working for the agency. I must be of some use to them otherwise they wouldn't keep knocking on my door and giving me more and more assignments.

As I pull off the motorway and head into Portadown, I think again to myself that Jay might be upset and to keep a cool head no matter what he does as he has probably already heard all about me and what happened in Bangor, so I can't bullshit him. A few minutes later I pull into the barracks, and I am greeted with a squad of officers all pointing automatic rifles at me, shouting to see my hands. I freeze and ponder about why they are pointing weapons at me; my mind goes blank. I can't help but smile back at them. What the fuck are they doing? Jason comes around the corner and straight over to my car. He yanks open my door, and before I can speak, he punches me square in the face, which I accept and take like a man. I can see he is a little fucking furious with me. The veins in his throat were bulging as if he was going to scream.

Jason whispers closely to my face. You know Trevor is proposing to scrap Operation REVERT because of you? Do you have any idea how many hours were put into Operation REVERT and the huge risks we had to take to put this together you cunt!" I hold back and take a passive approach as I could easily kick Jason's ass, but that course of action would end badly for me. My mind starts to wonder about all the people I could have affected and start to feel ashamed. Jason and Trevor are right about me; I am a liability. I need to make amends with my team and behave in a more professional manner. I need to prove to all of them that they need me and that I can do the job they expect of me. God forgive me, why did I not think about the bigger picture. We all knew what the agency was like and the littlest mishap could set the tamest of operations back months maybe even scrapped altogether. The armed men started to hold their guns at ease while I parked the car. Jason has already stormed back into the barracks. I could feel the glare of all those officers looking at me while I walked past them going into the building. I keep telling myself I can fix this whilst making my way to Jason's office. As I walk in and closed the door, Jason is roughly opening different drawers of his desk, looking for something. I am starting to feel anxious about what he is going to say next. Jason finds what he was looking for and slams it on the desk. It was discharge papers. Jason looks me in the eye and tells me "Ian you have been relieved from duty." I pretend I didn't hear him, "excuse me?" Jason then repeats "you're fired!" Jason continues, "I heard Trever had to suspend you this morning, then you had the balls to take the agency's sensitive operations data from the compound, jeopardising everything we have been working on over the years. You might not know this but that fuck Trevor would gladly blackball this operation given half a chance as he is a liberal prick! AND YOU, just gave it to him on a fucking plate, ready for his big red pen to scrap. You potentially could have put our agent's lives at risk due to exposing their undercover roles if you lost those papers. YOU KNOW those files never, ever, leave the building!

You're not even an agent, you stupid cock sucker, do I have to continually spell it out for you? You're a fucking temp! I could have a hundred other temps replace you if I wanted. All you do is pull the trigger at who I want, when I want it! I have fucking given you chance after chance, your commitment to us is bullshit as you're a selfish prick!" Jason then hands me my discharge papers and tells me to get the fuck out of his sight. I don't try to defend myself and just leave as asked. My heart sinks as the words Jason spoke cut me like a sharp blade because everything he said was true. As I make my way home to Belfast, my mind is stuck on auto pilot as the journey feels almost instantaneous. I sit down in my living room and stare out the window. I feel and think about nothing. Did that just actually happen to me? Am I really out of a job? Shit! I just came to the realisation that I no longer have a fucking income and I have all sorts of bills that I need to get paid this month. "FUCK! FUCK!" I shout aloud. I pause for a moment. Jason didn't take the brief back off me, did he? I rush out to the car and look above the visor. A smile starts to come across my face; it's still there! Relief washes over me as I can now do some unpaid work for the government and line my pockets with all that RVA money I am going to take off them.

It's a win, win situation but I need to be a ghost and not let Jason suss it's me taking advantage of the situation. Time to put the failed Volunteers feud back into full effect! But first I will make some copies of the REVERT Intel and then return the file to Jason, so he doesn't get into any more shit over me. Ian quickly makes a copy of the entire file, leaving the original with "SORRY" scrawled on the front, on the kitchen counter. Ian knows he has minutes to get out of his apartment before he is arrested. Ian makes his way to a Loyalist safe house in Belfast to start his own plan to reinstate the RVA feud which he schedules for this evening. Ian rubs his face whilst pondering about his first targets, which is definitely outside the game plan of REVERT, but it could pay off big time in the long run.

Chapter 3 - Michael Mordha

Michael is sitting on a cushioned reclined chair in front of a turf fire with a cup of tea in his hand. Michael always liked to keep his house traditionally old-fashioned as his surroundings were almost styled on the house he used to live in as a boy. It reminded him of happier times when his life wasn't so complicated. Deep in thought while staring blankly at the TV.

Another year and I feel like I am spinning my wheels Michael thought to himself. I feel like I am carrying my crew as I don't feel they are giving their heart and soul to the uprising. Do they not want a united Ireland for their children to grow up in? How can they stand having those British fuckers on our land?

I could kill them all and still sleep sound in my bed. They have their own island so why don't they fuck off over home to the Queen. They are like vermin, moving into an area and multiplying like rats. The thought of it makes me want to kill them all the more. I have no remorse or sympathy for them as they shouldn't be here. They are all hell bound anyway, well the ones who are not Roman Catholic. Even then I don't even want Roman Catholic English pricks over here either. To me, they are too far gone being brought up with so called British customs and values. Sure, the fuckers burn Guy Fawkes every year, who to me is a true hero. He would have started a Roman Catholic revolution that would have begot us a united Ireland hundreds of years ago and rid us of a Protestant monarchy and community. I am doing my bit just like Guy and ridding this island of all the parasites that shouldn't be here. We have given them fair warning over and over again so in a way there asking for it. Once Ireland is restored to its former glory we then move to the next evolutionary stage which will be to destroy the Monarchy.

We have already been planning this for years in some detail. With the rise of our popular anti monarchy political parties throughout the U.K, the decent people of this island are no longer going to put up with them. We need more new blood in the ranks of our RVA. We need Volunteers who don't blink and do what needs to be done without hesitation, no matter what the cost. Ah well, suppose the fun jobs will as always be placed in my lap as my kinsmen know I am good for it.

The security forces know I am good at what I do as well as they have been after me for a long time but here I sit unhindered. I don't stay too long under one roof so it makes it difficult for Loyalists and my other enemies to find me. I do however like this new house I am in as I am surrounded with much better security features than my last place. This house has been kitted out with stuff that will alert me to anyone straying too close.

I also have the support and protection of my people on this estate who know who I am and have my back. We have Volunteers all over this estate including watchers who regularly take the reg plates of any cars that come into the area and run them through our connection in the police to find out who they are. Yes, we have a good system going here and at other strongholds across the north of Ireland. I know myself and other volunteers don't always see eye to eye with our political wing but I have to give credit where credits is due. The long lists of demands were practically all given to us and we are still getting even more on top, ever erasing the prods and the Brits from Ireland's history. Little by little, pushing them to the north east of the island and then into the sea where they belong.

Equality is what we want and that will never happen with these types of human beings as they refuse to conform to our Irish way of life, we are actually doing God a favour when we do get rid of this unholy filth. We are taught from an early age we don't have to respect or oblige the hell bound. That's why it feels so easy to kill them. I know some of the volunteers have trouble doing what needs to be done but rest assured they do it! I will always make sure of that!

Michael Gets up from his chair and makes his way into the kitchen to make another cup of tea when suddenly objects all around him start to explode as bullets come screaming in unannounced. He falls fast to the floor covering his head in a blind panic. His face drained of colour as he realises death has come for him. Michael scrambles across the floor over to a set of drawers and takes out a hidden gun taped to the underside of the bottom drawer. As the bullets knock massive holes in the house and tear up his furniture time almost seems to stand still. The house was thick with the dust of bricks and mortar being smashed by multiple rounds thundering through the walls. When the bullets stopped Michael had his eyes focused on the back door as that was one of the many ways killer hit squads entered the house whilst distracting their victims from the front.

They also try to make their victims flee from the back door of the house and then gunning them down as soon as they step out or by strapping a trip explosive to the door. Michael knew to stay put. The bastards will have to come in to finish me off and that will level the playing field, Michael thought to himself. He was a crack shot and knew he had a better chance of taking out his would-be attackers if they entered the house. I have one in the chamber and am good to go, he thought to himself. Smoke started to bellow into the kitchen as the curtains were on fire in the living room due to the glowing hot rounds tearing through them. Panic was starting to step in as he thought they might throw petrol bombs in next and for that he knew there was no defence other than escape.

Michael keeps his back flat on the ground and pushes himself under a table whilst aiming his pistol at the back door. Fuck! I can't stop fucking shaking as he tries to hold the gun steady. "Mick! MICK! Are you there?" Paul shouted while trying to figure out the best way into the bullet riddled house. "MICK, for fucksake where are Ya?" Wee Paul who is a captain in the ranks of the RVA comes into Michael's safe house through the shattered living room window. Michael gets to his feet and shakes the debris and dust from his hair and clothes. Paul and other armed volunteers start to fill Michaels living room to find out if he's OK. Michael walks into the living room and leans on the wall while brushing his hair back with his hand. Then with a big grin, he raises his arm in a clenched fist and shouts "UP THE RVA!" to whoops and cheers from the people inside and outside the house. As he makes his way through the wreckage of the house he stands on his front lawn and pulls a cigarette out and coolly lights it up. Smiling as everyone has now come out of their homes to see the aftermath and celebrate the foiled assassination attempt of their beloved leader. Paul and another volunteer hold Michael's arms high in the air in triumph of the failed assassination attempt. Paul whispers to Michael "We have a number of cars in pursuit of his attacker." Michael nods and continues to take big long draws from his cigarette. Michael doesn't phone the police as they are not welcome on the estate but he does ask someone to get in touch with Odhran who is an RVA sympathiser that works for a well-known newspaper. Michael knows Odhran is not well liked in the unionist community as his views always seem to dismiss the RVA violence and swaps them with reasons as to why the Unionist community is actually to blame for the so-called terrorist attacks. He loves to use the words provoked, dialogue, north of Ireland and situation in practically all his stories.

Odhran is part of the Volunteers media war machine which is responsible for portraying the RVA and its political wing in a positive light. He knows the political wing of the RVA could milk this attack and make it look like, what it was not. The RVA is all too aware of adhering to their winning strategy they use in this fight and to the role each of the Volunteers has to play. This is how my political party always win more votes. This is how we still carry on with our campaign against the British occupation of the north of Ireland using a twin track approach of politics and violence. This is all done with the blessing of our people. Anytime we are attacked, we stand together and blame the British army. It doesn't even matter if it wasn't them, just so long as they are the ones stuck with the blame. You repeat a lie often enough and people started taking it as fact. We make it look like it was an attack on an innocent member of the Catholic community and immediately we have more sympathisers that approve of our cause. Unlike the Loyalists community who would cut their own noses off despite their face.

We continually poke fun at how divided the Unionists are and how they fight amongst themselves. They, however, can be ruthless so this is why we don't engage them and keep our fight to the British army as the law won't protect us from them. Besides, we have committed no crimes nor have we broken any laws as this is a war! What we have done in the past and what we do now is for Ireland and its people. I need to meet with our military council to discuss where we go from here. I believe we should take the opportunity to place a few well-placed bombs at a couple of barracks to show our supporters our defiance and keep them on side as this will be what our people want in response to the attempt on my life. Another dissident Republican group will take the blame for what we did so we can stay in government. I know what you're thinking if the British government are blatantly so stupid to accept these attacks by blaming dissidents all the while knowing it's us then what else could we get away with? The British high elites are so scared of us they would do ANYTHING to appease us and that includes ignoring our non-commitment to this so-called ceasefire!

So not to disappoint my fans, I will be implementing a few more bombing campaigns. Its late afternoon when Michael is overseeing repairs to the house, when Paul shouts over "MICKEY!" from the other side of the road. "Come on over here and meet the new Volunteers." As Michael makes his way over to where Paul is standing he sees two lads along with him aged around sixteen and seventeen. "Dia duit." Michael said to each lad while gripping them with a firm handshake. A little grey haired old lady comes scuttling over and holds

Michaels' arm. "Are you alright son?" she said looking up at him. "Aye, I am," Michael replied. "I have sent over me grandsons to be Volunteers. They are good boys and will do you proud." and with that said, the old girl walked back up the street and into her own house. Casually looking over his shoulder to the two new recruits. Michael asks, "That's your granny boys?" "Aye." they both said. "Priceless," Michael whispers to himself with a grin. As Michael is rolling a cigarette he shouts out. "PAUL, show these boys the ropes, two weeks training at the Tyrone camp and then test their loyalty by throwing them in the deep end. Two dead cops, one for each of them. I want the hit to be plastered all over the papers. You know the score, call it in as one of our dissident groups. Got it?" Michael said. "Done," replied Paul.

Enough bravado, need a new fecken house to live in or do I stick it out? It suddenly it hits me. How the fuck did they find me so quick? Couldn't have been here two months? Running over to his van Michael immediately knows it won't be a Republican that has let him down as everyone is shit scared of the repercussions of helping the British.

He looks under the wheel arches and then spots a little brown and round device stuck under his wheel hub. He says nothing and goes back into his house with a few of the volunteers. "Right! The British fucks have tagged me van, however that has happened? Anyway, I am going to draw these fucks out and kill them." Michael turns to Paul and says, "those new pups will be needed for this one." "Consider it done Mick!" Paul replies. "Meet up at Mass as usual and we will discuss how to make these bastards drop their cover," Michael said to the crew and with that, they all dispersed including Michael. We take the van as normal, but we go and leave it somewhere safe. "Andersonstown?" Paul asks. "Aye, Andersonstown," Michael replies. Paul then drives the van over all the rubble strewn over the driveway as the crowds quickly make room for the van to leave. It's around 7pm when they make their way to Andersonstown, Michael is again in deep thought with that ever-distant stare angrily fixed as he looks out the window of the van. Suddenly Michael shouts "Pull over here." With a confused look on his face, Paul does what he is told. Michael then gets out and makes his way across the front of the van towards the driver's door and asks Paul to jump out before driving off. Paul stands dumbfounded by the side of the road while watching Michaels van driving away from him.

Suddenly Paul realises he is in a Loyalist area and starts to get nervous of being spotted. He knows his face is well known to his enemy. He keeps his eyes low and tries to calmly walk towards Belfast city centre. Ten minutes and I will be safe; Paul kept reminding himself as his pace quickened, he was walking ever faster. Paul was sure people were starting to notice his odd behaviour. Paul pats his jacket where his gun is, in a vain attempt to reassure himself he was armed and could protect himself.

"OI YOU!" A cold sweat creeps out of Paul as he turns around quickly to see four men looking at him. "You alright?" Inquired one of the men who is roughly around ten meters away from him. "Yes, just fine, I missed my bus and I am late for work," Paul shouted back and started to walk away further from the man. "SO, you're worried they might give you the sack then if you're late?" The man continued. Paul, then shouted back "Yes," as he kept walking. "Didn't know RVA cunts could be sacked? Aren't you guys usually shot in the back of the head when your fired, Paul?" The man shouted.

Paul stopped in his tracks when the man called out his name. He wanted to run as he never fought the enemy face to face before. "PAUL! Look at this!" The man shouted. Paul didn't want to turn around but felt he was far enough away from them to pull his gun and still make an escape if he needed to.

Paul turned around slowly finally laying eyes on the man who was doing all the talking to him. He now had his gun in his hand but hidden behind his back. The same man who was talking to him was now making a gun gesture with his hand and pointing it right at him. "You know who I am Paul?" The man inquires. "NO!" Paul replies whilst taking the safety off his gun. The man cups his other hand around his mouth and shouts "I'm the man who is going to kill all of you Republican cunt's!" Paul pulls his weapon and aims it at the man shouting at him. "Are Ya? You fucken Hun bastard? When I finish with you I am going to kill your wife and kids you fuck!" Paul replies. Paul holds his breath as he aims his gun, ready to pull the trigger, the man suddenly shouts "Lights out! YOU CUNT!".

A flash of white light and the feeling of cold air is seen and felt by Paul. Why am I falling Paul thought to himself as everything went dark and the noises started to fade away. Paul is lying in a pool of his own blood with half his head scattered across the pavement.

A man is standing over his kill. It's Ian with a Silenced Desert Eagle in one hand and his mobile in the other. He leans over the body and reaches over to

Paul's right arm and roughly flips him over. Ian is greeted with Paul's mangled face with blood streaming from every orifice. Ian looks up and gives a nod to the men from his brigade. "RFID tracking is a bitch isn't it Paul?" Ian said before quickly walking off towards his car. Ian had been quietly stalking his marks for a few days now with his crew and had been following the van when Michael left Paul at the side of the road. It was too good of an opportunity for the boys to miss as they will bleed Michael for more Volunteer intel later.

Weeks earlier under the orders of Jason we broke into homes of a few of the most prolific Republicans to attach tracking dots to most of their clothing. The unknowing RVA could scan their entire wardrobe and not pick any of these bugs up as they use the kinetic energy of movement when worn to power the tracking devices. So, when they stop moving the bug stops working. My men were not part of Jason's equation but nonetheless, they are part of it now. The men in Ian's Loyalist Brigade quickly start the clean-up of the body; they know they have about nine minutes until a possible police response. They open a trunk of a car to get the equipment they need for the disposal. One man is on DNA scrub, which is by far the easiest job. He has a manual air compressed dispenser which is filled with a liquid blend of Chlorine and Hydrogen peroxide. A quick and thorough spray of a three-meter square area around the body will do the trick. DNA material that could have been used to identify the killer is now useless. The second man has to roll the body into a body bag and wraps it tight in stretchy plastic wrap before lifting it into the waiting van.

The third man has to do the dirty work later which involves the removal of hands, visible tattoos, all teeth and the bullet. He puts the teeth and hands into a grinder and mixes the pulp with lime and disposes of it in small chunks down the toilet. They then cut the body up into six pieces and put each of the parts into one large black plastic barrel. Filling it to the top with Hydrofluoric acid. The barrel is sealed and the metal lever for locking the lid on the barrel is given a few tacks with a MIG welder so it can't be opened again. The finished barrel is given false labels and then mixed with other barrels of toxic waste which come from the likes of car mechanics, fast-food restaurants and dry cleaners. The waste is headed to a big liner in Belfast ready to be shipped to the Ukraine for disposal. Total estimated time of 5 hours from kill to boat.

Meanwhile

Michael is parking up at a shopping centre in Andersonstown. Totally oblivious to the events that he himself caused. Michael was unconcerned about how Paul was going to make his way home. His only motive for kicking Paul out of the van was so he didn't have to put up with him kissing his arse the whole day as he deplores people who can't be themselves. He had things to do and needed to stay focused on how to deal with today's events so having Paul out from under his feet was a step in the right direction.

Where the fuck am I going to stay tonight? He thought to himself while walking down to a car he spotted being packed with groceries. As he approached the car, the woman who was packing her groceries stopped and closed the boot. Looking her in the face and without hesitation, Michael stated "On behalf of the RVA Belfast brigade, you have been asked to provide transport. Do you comply?" Asked Michael. The woman knew refusal could end badly for her so she agreed to take Michael wherever he wanted. Michael didn't want to be chauffeured about as she was just another liability so he took the keys of the car from her and quickly sped away from the car park. Time to head to Dundalk, Michael thinks to himself as he makes his way towards the motorway. As Michael is making his way down the road his mobile starts to ring. Looking at the id on the screen he sees its Paul calling him. "What is it Paul?" Michael said annoyed.

A voice that has been altered, speaks back to him in a deep menacing digital altered way. "Paul, can't come to the phone now but he has left a message for you.... Would you like to hear it?" Michael felt a chill run up his spine as he knows this person is not affiliated with the British Intelligence as he knows the rules of engagement prohibit stealth calls. The person on the other end of this phone is either a Republican or a Loyalist hitman.

Michael quickly disconnects the call as it can be traced and pulls the sim out to destroy later and chucks the phone out the window. Michael knows now that Paul is dead but doesn't understand how it happened. As Michael is driving; he analyses the events of the day and what possibly links them together. The only thing that links them together is me, he thought to himself. The tracker has been left on the van in Andersonstown and this is a bug-free car so what else could they possibly put a tracker on? He then slams on the brakes and pulls over. "My fucking clothes!" he said aloud. He then jumps out to the side of the road and strips all his clothes off in case there are any micro tags. He then jumps back into the car. Turning the heater on and was about to drive off when he realised this was an opportunity for him to kill his shadows. He opened his door and leaned out and grabbed his clothes. He threw them into the backseat and sped off down the motorway. There was only one person that could help him right now with advice and that was the Chief Commander of the RVA, Brendan McMurry.

Arriving in Dundalk he could see different passer byes gawking at him, after all, he was driving around naked. As Michael made his way to Brendan's house he couldn't help but remember how much he yearned for a little place to call his own. To finally have roots and to put the war behind him. Brendan's house was very secluded with no neighbours for miles. A few trees dotted around the house with huge spacious fields surrounding the property.

The fields were filled with all sorts of crops and other plants which were sprouting up in clumps. Michael thought to himself; I bet Brendan's dogs love a good run around in the fields. His mangy mutts are all he needs for his security as they bark like mad at anyone that goes near that property. Better give him a heads up about myself dropping at his door. It was nearly 8pm by the time Michael arrived at the village outskirts. I will use the phone box at the little convenience store before the turn off towards Brendan's house. You don't see too many pay phones these days but thankfully this part of Ireland hasn't changed much over the years.

It's getting dark now with the sun ever slowly sinking behind the horizon with light and dark in limbo with each other, the twilight. Pulling up to the wee shop, Michael parks his car close to the phone booth. Michael puts his old clothes on again despite concerns of tracking before he gets out and makes the call to Brendan. With the street lights dimly lit Michael gets out of the car and makes his way over to the pay phone. Fumbling around in his pockets he discovers he hasn't any money. In a fit of rage, Michael shouts "Mother fucker!" as he smashes the receiver a number of times against the dialling buttons.

Standing in the phone box with the receiver damaged and dangling Michael angrily says to himself "Can nothing go right for me today?" Michael then spots an elderly man walking along the road and quickly walks over to him, all the while hiding a gun behind his back. "Could you spare some change for the phone box kind sir, me cars broke down?" Michael said. "Be away with you boy!" The man shouted at him. "I don't have any money for the likes of you!" Enraged, Michael quickly brings his weapon round and heavily pushes the gun against the old man's forehead before cocking the weapon. "Do you still have no fucken money for me?" Michael snarled!

The look of fear never changes Michael thought to himself as he could see the terrified look on the old fella's face. "Hold on now, just hold on boy and I'll see what odds I have in me pocket, calm yourself now. Look here's a few euros, that's all I have please, please don't shoot me," the old man replied. Michael knew the score even if the old man didn't but took mercy on him nevertheless and let him go. "Go on now, hurry up and remember not a word to anyone or there will be trouble for you and yours," Michael shouted at him as the old timer walked away awkwardly up the road.

Holstering his pistol in his front trouser waistline, Michael went back to the phone booth and put the money in the phone box and lifted the receiver to his ear. As he was about to dial Brendan's number he notices the buttons he smashed in minutes earlier. "For FUCKSAKE!!!! Fuckin proddy scum, hun bastard of a machine! I haven't got time for this fucking bullshit!" He shouted in a rage. I will just go over to Brendan's and he will have to get over himself with his fucken do's and don'ts of contacting him! Fuck him!

Getting into his car Michael spins the wheels of his vehicle and makes his way down the road. He sees the old man that gave him some Euros and rolls down the window. He grabs what's left of the Euro coins and holds them in his right hand.

Slowing the car down beside the old man, he angrily throws the coins at him and shouts "YOU USELESS FUCKER!" before speeding off again. Michael pulls up the road from Brendan's house to assess his situation. He could see no lights were on at his house. This keeps getting better and better Michael thought to himself. I honk the horn and keep honking till Brendan's up as I don't want to be bit in the arse by any of his dogs. The lights in Brendan's house start to flicker on, one by one before his entire property is engulfed by flood lamps. Right now, he will be checking the cams before coming out to me Michael thought. "CLICK!" Brendan holds a gun to Michaels' head. "What are you doing Michael?" Brendan says in a quiet voice. "FUCK ME, that was fast! I am in a bit of a situation and need your help, ok so ease off, I know how it looks". Michael said.

"You better come in but don't think I'm making you a fucking tea! You scared the shite out of me. Pull your car around the back." Brendan replied. Michael does what he is asked and pulls the car around the back. "Is the car clean?" Brendan asks? "No, it isn't," Michael replied. "Then fucking get rid now. Get it to fuck a few miles away and make sure it's lit, just to be safe." Brendan shouts. "Aye," replied Michael. Brendan waits half an hour outside for Michael with only his dogs for company when he spots Mick strolling back down his lane. As Michael is walking up the drive Brendan sees he is in distress. "Mon in and tell me what's been happening," Brendan shouts over to Michael and puts his arm around his neck.

As they were making their way into the kitchen Michael notices Brendan has a two-door entrance to the front and back of his house. "When did Ya get the big fuck off security doors?" asked Michael. "Ages ago, the wife didn't feel safe as the dogs have been barking more than usual lately," replied Brendan. "What if they want to come through da windys? Then you're fucked?" said Michael. "It's bullet proof safety glass Ya muppet, anyway what's this situation you're in?" Brenden replied.

Michael explains to Brendan the events that have taken place. They then start to put a plan together, to kill the shadows stalking Michael by using the tagged clothes that are now in their possession.

Chapter 4 - Compromised

Jason is currently working in the Portadown barracks. He is tired and does not plan to stay any longer than a few hours as he had little sleep the night before.

I don't plan to be staying long here as I have had fuck all sleep last night. I check in for an hour then will head home to bed. I had no intentions of going to the Operation REVERT meeting today in Bangor. I know exactly why Trevor wants to talk to us. He wants to water down our strategic plan even further for God knows what reason this time. He can be a tight bastard when it comes to saving lives and ridding us of the evil RVA. It's like the situation in Northern Ireland doesn't bother him. The heartless fuck will get what's coming to him in this life or the next I thought to myself. I was determined to have a short working day after last night's shenanigans. I have all my shit together so I can go now. As I am walking out of the office the phone rings. I walk right past it as I am desperate to go home but Sergeant Briggs had other ideas. "Hello, Sergeant Briggs speaking. Yes sir, right away sir!" Briggs puts down the phone and enters the hallway. "Major Wright! Deputy Director Hughes on the line for you." I get angry but keep a cool head. "Thank you, Sergeant Briggs!" I replied as I made my way back into the office. I pick up the phone slowly like he was the very last person I wanted to speak to at this moment in time. "Yes, Trevor. He did what? FUCK! No, No, No mate we spent far too much time...Trevor.." I hear a click and then the dead tone. Trevor is threatening to scrap my assignment if Ian is not caught in the next 12 hours. Think Jason, where would that dozy cunt be going with that dossier. I ring Ian's mobile...no answer. Ian will come back to touch base with me. He knows there is nowhere to run. "That fucking loose cannon has fucked up big style this time, this fucking time he has really crossed the fucking line!" Jason mumbled to himself.

Four hours later

"Sir! He is pulling up to the barracks check point, Sir!" Sergeant Briggs stated. "Thank you, Sergeant, tell your squad to lock weapons on the car as it enters the compound and wait for further instructions," I replied. I can't let that bastard leave with that file, a bit over the top I know but I definitely can't let Ian fuck up my operation. As I exit the building and make my way outside, my eyes squint as I was facing the sun. The soldiers are positioned, and I am questioning myself to whether I am going about this the right way as this will get back to Trevor regardless of what I do.

Ian's car pulls into the compound and reality sets in that I have now crossed the point of no return. Adrenaline fills me with rage as I tell the troops to hold fire on the car as I make my way over to Ian. I see the look of confusion come across Ian's face. As I yank open the driver's side door of Ian's Jaguar I bring my clenched fist back and punch him hard in the face. I move in closer to Ian, enough to keep out of ear shot of the troops. I snarl "You know Trevor is proposing to scrap Operation REVERT because of you? Do you have any idea how many hours were put into Operation REVERT and the huge risks we had to take to put this together you cunt!"

I leave Ian in the car and make my way back into the barracks. I now need to fire one of the best men on my team, but he has left me with no choice. I gather my composure as I sit behind my desk in my office waiting for Ian to follow me in. I need discharge papers, where are they? Ah, here they are. Ian comes in and sits down in front of me. He looks at me with those dead eyes but says nothing. The right side of his face slightly red due to the punch I gave him. I could be court-martialled for that, but I am beyond caring at this point and I think everyone would back my corner if it does go to court.

I really don't want to do this, but Ian has left me no choice. "Ian you have been relieved from duty." "Excuse me?" Ian replies. I then repeat myself in terms he couldn't possibly misunderstand. "You're fired." I then continue "I heard Trever had to suspend you this morning, then you had the balls to take the agency's sensitive operations data from the compound, jeopardising everything we have been working on over the years. You might not know this but that fuck Trevor would gladly blackball this operation given half a chance as he is a liberal prick! AND YOU, just gave it to him on a fucking plate, ready for his big red pen to scrap. You potentially could have put our agent's lives at risk due to exposing their undercover roles if you lost those papers. YOU KNOW those files never, ever, leave the building! You're not even an agent, you stupid cock sucker, do I have to continually spell it out for you? You're a fucking temp! I could have a hundred other temps replace you if I wanted. All you do is pull the trigger at who I want, when I want it! I have fucking given you chance after chance, your commitment to us is bullshit as you're a selfish prick!" I then hand Ian his discharge papers.

"Get the fuck out of my sight!" I angrily tell Ian. I radio the soldiers to stand down and let Ian walk out on his own to his car and leave. I feel bad like I could have done something more to fix this situation we now find ourselves in but I remind myself the lives he could have put at risk.

I ponder about how I can remedy the situation as we could now have a possible breach of sensitive material and REVERT could ultimately be binned. I sigh to myself as my chances to kill Michael legally seems to be disappearing before my very eyes. I try to assure myself that we can still make a success of this operation as I am eager to give a few of our well known RVA scum the long overdue dirt nap they deserve. "FUCK!" I shout aloud. He still has the file! I jump out of my chair and run out of the office to try and catch Ian. I forgot to ask him to return the brief! Where is my head at lately? I am never this disorientated. As I run into the car park and scan around for Ian's car, he is nowhere to be seen. This is a major fuck up on my part! A fucking loose Loyalist hitman with Intel on the Volunteers. It's like giving a fat cunt the keys to a sweetie shop! Fuck it! I will inform Trevor we got Ian and taken the Intel from him. He doesn't need to know about this development and recommend we green light REVERT with immediate effect. "Sergeant Briggs! I need four men to find and arrest Ian Stewart." I shouted. "But Sir, you just let him go after the arrest warrant we issued this morning?" Sergeant Briggs said in a confused tone. "Well, it is now in place again Sergeant! Start at his place of residence. Go!" I replied. "Yes, sir!" Replied Sergeant Briggs.

I fill out the paper work and stamp it to make it legal, Ian has been officially fired from the Agency and is a civilian again. I need Ian to be off the radar and what a better place to keep an eye on him than in a cell. I start to calm down and reassure myself this was the best solution to the predicament I was currently in. I mentally prepare myself with what I will go through at the meeting today, I now have no choice but to attend, so we can make amendments for Ian's role as he is now no longer part of this operation. We might not even need the intel taxi role and Mark and Myself could absorb Ian's duties with the ones we already had.

We approach this operation using some fairly new tactics. I already have seven members of the team who are already under deep cover, that basically means they give us information on the ground, which in this case means the pubs and offices these dirt bags meet in. The undercover team is made up of men and women of all ages and backgrounds.

You would never make them out as government agents as we have them so well blended into their surroundings. We teach them how to speak and understand the local dialect and parochialisms used by those people in that area. We also slowly edge our agents into these communities by opening up small businesses and that in itself can make numerous connections for us. We also like to try new strategies like the "temporary tattoos."

We have been getting good feedback from our agents that this added cover adds strength and acceptance to cover stories used by them to infiltrate criminal organisations. The Japanese have been using it to disguise their own agents as soldiers and bosses in the Yakuza for years. They can last up to a year. The specially designed needle of the tattoo gun is a third of the length of that of a normal one. So, our undercover operatives are covered in Republican tats which help them be accepted without questions in Republican circles. It also allows them at times to gain access to most areas the where the normal public couldn't go such as meetings with the Republican councils. All our agents are paid danger money, but we do offer bonuses for agents that go above and beyond and that is definitely the case when some of our agents suffer these temporary tattoos.

I believe it's 2k for each one, depending on the size, as they can claim more for a bigger tatt. You can imagine how this scheme turned out, let's just say the minimum our operatives claimed was around 10k. On the flip side, not everyone opts for the tats as there are other ways to get bonuses. The tattoos themselves look for all intents and purposes, the real deal and can be touched up if needed. The more the agent has the better as they almost always stand out from the crowd and that's what we want. To hide our eyes and ears on the ground in plain sight. Not all our undercovers working on REVERT are tattooed which again makes it very difficult for the RVA to spot them. We have even used foreign agents, as was the case last week. We had a military agent from France last month do an operation for us at a Republican event in Dublin. She made friends with one of the catering staff and from that scored invaluable Intel for us which has been put to good use immediately. So, it just goes to show you that information can come from the unlikeliest of sources. All agents have special hidden software on their mobile phones which have been programmed to stream all video and sounds, even when they have been turned off.

The GPS locations give the agents handlers access to vital information of where and when their agents travel, even voice recognition of who they speak to.

My cleaners work in conjunction with my undercovers. Undercovers never break their cover so this is why we need these faceless assassins (Cleaners) who will eliminate the targeted terrorists/criminals. We only have four cleaners which are Mark, Johnny, Ian and me. Our sole job is to dispose of the HPPTs (High Profile Problem Targets). Basically, we take out the leaders then the sub servants which usually leaves the organisation in a power struggle or the organisation just collapses which suits us either way. BUT, Operation REVERT was different. It was a huge operation that was to happen simultaneously with other agents around the UK and Eire. We were to implement a new shoot to kill policy.

We were going to take them all out, in one bloody sweep, no matter where or who they were with. We were about to make the RVA paramilitaries extinct on a massive scale, unlike anything we ever did before. Why were we not doing all paramilitaries some would ask? It's simple. Take out the ones making the most noise and the others will back down and disband under the threat of being wasted. A bit like the old saying about cutting the head off a snake. We had two hundred and thirty-two legal kills to make and no time to waste. This would be the riskiest operation the UK government has taken on terrorism since the killing of those terrorists in Turkey. It would take a backlash from terrorist sympathisers which include the political lefty lunatics which to me and the majority of others could never tell right from wrong anyway. In this case, God will be our judge but we as a country have had enough! The people are starting to revolt over the weekly RVA killings and the weak excuses our government's police force and politicians keep reciting over and over again. How we the public have to accept that terrorism is now just a part of everyday life we have to get used to. It turns my stomach listening to this horseshit! The government has known about this ticking time bomb of a crisis for over ten years now and still, they are being cowardly about tackling the problem because the EU is part of the problem by making it extraordinarily difficult to legally catch these criminals and prosecute them because of the laws and flaws. That was back then when our hands were tied. NOW we have left the EU and are back in control!

Operation REVERT had 89% favourable outcome prediction which has been verified through a number of our institutes. It's a no brainer really, a once in a decade opportunity to put things finally right.

It's getting late now, need to attend this meeting fast and prepare for tomorrow. "Sir! Trevor on line 7." I froze with fear, please no, I thought to myself. "Jason, JASON!" shouted Trevor down the phone. "Yes, Trevor?" I replied. "Operation Revert has been aborted. The operations have been compromised on two accounts. One of which you have been held responsible for which is losing classified intelligence operations to Ian who most likely will go lone wolf on us." Trevor said. I have the file as I took it off Ian." Jason lied. "The information I have recently obtained would suggest otherwise, I will thoroughly investigate that matter later. The second account is that of a mole who has been working within our team. We already know who it is but we need to follow his movements to uncover any other infiltrators within the agency. This information is on a need to know. Your team will be informed that Operation REVERT has been delayed as to not raise the suspicion of the mole who you and I know as Mark." Trevor stated.

I fell back into my chair as I felt dizzy. My fucking childhood friend? Mark, the one I personally vouched for to be employed on our team? I feel enraged and heartbroken at the same time. "Jason, are you still there?" Trevor asked. "Yes, yes, how do you know this about Mark, what evidence? TELL ME!" I shouted! "I knew you would be too close to this problem Jason. You have left me no choice but to reassign you. Come to my office and we can discuss this unfortunate situation in further detail." Trevor said in a calm voice and then disconnected the call. I still hold the phone to my ear listening to the dead tone and stare into space. Northern Ireland's last hope of a real peace compromised by ME?

I rip out the computer on my desk and smash it on the floor. Tensing every muscle in my body I scream at the top of my lungs, "FUUUUUUUUCK!!!" Everyone looks into my office through the huge windows that surround me. They stop work for a few seconds and quickly look busy again as I barge out the door and make my way to the car park. Once in the car park, I start to compose myself. Whilst driving to Bangor, I remember what Trevor said about the mole. If it is Mark, he will pay a very dear price for this. I'm at HQ and once out of my car I start to straighten myself up and make my way to the operations room where my Operation REVERT team are waiting. I am aware that my face talks before I do and try to put on a calm and cool front, remembering to show disappointment at the delay but also emphasising what a brilliant team we have. I can easily do this.

I walk into the room with my usual stern look. Everyone stands to attention before sitting down after me. I mustn't look at Mark right away and can't give him any indication we are on to him. I don't even know myself how the agency knows this Intel? I come straight to the point.

"Good evening, Operation REVERT has been put on hold due to technicalities beyond the agency's control. I can tell you that it's not from our side as we have a strong team here. I want everyone to assess each other's work for weak areas and see what improvements can be made for the time being." "Lauren!" I called out. "Yes, sir?" Lauren replied. "I want you to take the lead on this and submit a report to me in three days' time on any tactical changes we could make to Operation REVERT." I ordered. "On it sir!" Lauren answered. I stand up and salute the team and leave the operations room.

A very quick meeting I thought to myself. As I make my way upstairs to Trevor's office I cannot help but think about all the questions I will put to him. I walk into his office, without knocking and see Trevor in conversation with a new face that's sitting on the couch.

Trevor looked at me disapprovingly as I just rushed in and took a seat. "Robert, this is Jason the man who you will be replacing command with," Trevor stated. I shake Roberts' hand and exchange greetings with him. Trevor then asks Robert if he could have a private word with me and states he will be in touch. As Robert leaves I jump in and ask Trevor "What the FUCK are you doing?!" "If you're going to take that tone and be so ignorant as to swear in front of me, your senior commanding officer. I can assure you it makes me feel better about the difficult choices I had to make. As you are clearly in no fit mind to handle the current situation!" Trevor replied. "I am sorry Trevor, you are right. I was out of line" I replied.

Trevor brought out a bottle of Black Bush and put two glasses in front of him. As Trevor was pouring a hefty shot of whiskey in each glass I felt a little more relaxed and was not thinking about grabbing Trevor by the neck and beating some sense into him. I grab a glass and we toast the Queen. "I'm now going to talk with you informally and I invite you to do the same," Trevor said to me. I nodded my head in agreement whilst trying to sip my whiskey like a gentleman.

Trevor leaned back into his plush black leather chair. "Mark has been on our radar for a while now due to the friends he was knocking about with. I don't need to tell you about these friends do I?" Trevor asked me.

"No, you don't. I didn't think for a moment they had any influence over him as it's always good protocol to have a mix of friends from all sides of the community as it looks like you're a neutral person that doesn't hold any strong political views.

Mark WAS in my mind hiding in plain sight of the RVA which all good agents should do as it actually keeps them safer and less likely to be targeted. Wouldn't you agree?" I said to Trevor. He nodded his head slightly but didn't look wholly convinced. "How do you know he is leaking information to the RVA?" I added. "Do you know about the latest woman in Marks life?" Trevor said. "Yes, this saddens me as he is married to a good girl but unfortunately he has gone back to his old ways and is secretly seeing a woman called Brook. What has she got to do with it? From what little I know, her dads in the Protestant lodge and she lives in a Loyalist estate in Portadown. I don't understand how that family could have anything to do with the RVA?" I replied.

Trevor went on. "Brook has been secretly seeing a well-known Republican called Colin Murphy and she has been doing so for years." "Colin?? That piece of shit!" I blurted out. "Her father doesn't know her ties to Colin and is unaware of her allegiance to him. Colin is as you know a very attractive and wealthy man who has used his charms on Brook to benefit the RVA by using her as a spy for the Republican movement.

She has infiltrated her family's connections within the Loyalist community and passes back whatever information she gets to her so called beloved. Brook is utterly besotted with him and has no real idea of the immediate danger she is putting herself and others in as she's a bit fucking thick that way. Mark must now be known to the RVA as I believe their relationship was purposely set up by Colin to gain information about our agents through him. Mark would obviously introduce Brook to his friends and colleagues whilst socialising, not realising he was making them targets. We have had Brook shadowed for over a year now and know exactly when she and Mark met up. We are using this situation to our advantage to gain a better insight into what Colin actually does for the RVA," Trevor continued.

"Classic honey trap. Mark, you stupid FUCK!" I said myself whilst holding my face in disbelief. Brook was indeed beautiful. Tall girl, around five feet eleven, six feet in heels. Long dark hair and steamy green eyes that would put you in a spellbinding trance that would be hard to break away from. Any man would give her what she wanted, and she knew it! No harm to him but he would be an easy meal for that girl. Mark would definitely be the type to try and woo her with tales of heroics but what exactly did he leak to Brook was unknown. I couldn't interfere now otherwise I would be court-martialled along with Mark for impeding a government investigation, but I can't just leave him to the wolves. I needed to give him an indirect heads up, so he would snap out of it and cut ties with this bitch but with tits like hers, this was not going to be easy.

I ask Trevor if there was anything I can do to assist the investigation and to my surprise, he said yes! "Jason, I need you to compile evidence of fuel laundering in South Armagh. The RVA is making significantly more money these days from it. We estimate in the region of fifty to sixty million pounds has been made over the past five years. This is an embarrassment to her Majesties government and local law enforcement. We need arrests and hard intelligence on their whole network." Trevor said.

"Ok, Trevor," I replied. GREAT! He's fucking side-lined me! I knew deep down I wouldn't be allowed anywhere near this investigation as Mark was not only my friend but on my team. I was absolutely gutted as well that I had to do this shitty assignment but those are the breaks. I swallow back the rest of my Bushmills and make my way out of his office. I don't even look at him or give a goodbye just to make my feelings clear about the decisions being made for me. Before making my way out of the building I check to see if Ian has been caught.

I walk into the ready room where our police and military live in the building. I phone our Portadown barracks.

"Sergeant Briggs!" I shouted while scanning the room to see who might be earwigging my conversation. "Yes SIR!" Sergeant Briggs replied. "What updates do you have for me on the whereabouts of Ian Stewart? Is he in custody yet?" I asked anxiously. "No sir, we have yet to locate him but will inform you the minute we arrest him. We however recovered the missing dossier you were looking for. It was on his kitchen table" Sergeant Briggs replied. Trevor is going to find out I lied to him about Ian but it hardly matters now. "Ok, thanks for the info!" I replied. I put the phone down and walked out and smile to myself as I am not surprised they can't find him; after all, we trained him to be a ghost. I now make my way down the stairs through security and into the car park. I lift my head up to see the evening sky above me and listen to the gulls. What a perfect evening I thought to myself. Pity I won't be able to enjoy it. My first task; phone the wife.

I haven't been home during sociable hours in ages. I take my mobile out and scroll down to (Olivia X) it's a bad habit I have kept through my adolescent years where I place an X beside their name to show I was romantically involved with them if they called. Let's just say I had a number of names with an X beside them. To be young and stupid again, I chuckle to myself. I press Olivia X and wait for the ringing. It goes straight to voice mail. She is always on her phone, I rage to myself. (Mobile automated voice)"Leave your message after the beep." "Hi sweetheart, I have a major problem to take care of tonight, really really really sorry I am working late again. I haven't forgotten about our talk and I do miss spending time with you and Daniel. I wish we could get on top of things at work but new jobs keep adding to the pile I already have. I Love you loads, give Daniel a big kiss and hug from me. Also, double check the doors are locked. See you in the morning. Night." Then I push disconnect.

I will hunt down Mark first as Ian could be anywhere in the country. I get into my car and make my way over to a pay phone I know near a petrol station outside of Lisburn. I turn on my little spy gadget called the Pulsar and slide into my pocket. This little gadget that runs on a small watch battery produces enough white noise and static to fuzz out any working CCTV cameras in fifty-metre circumference. In layman's terms, it makes all the video camera footage fuzzy and unusable while the signal is on. I have it on me at all times but only use it when I need to even though I am permitted to use it wherever I go. Little did I think that I would be using it against the agency to get in contact with Mark? As I drive into the forecourt of the petrol station I can see someone on the pay phone already. I wait about three minutes before walking over and start standing behind them. It's a mental move to unnerve the person using the phone. It works as seconds later he hangs up. I quickly grab the phone and dial Marks mobile. As I wait for him to answer, I give the area a quick scan before concentrating on the call again.

We have this code we use if the other is in trouble and a meeting point. "Hello?" Mark answered. I then hit the number nine button three times and hung up. The nine button has a unique tone that Mark and myself can instantly recognise from the rest. I get back into my car and head off to the meeting point. As soon as I am fifty metres away from the station the cameras can start to see images again. Nothing links me to the call I made to Mark. I make my way to an underpass near the river Bann and park my car.

My little rowing boat I use for fishing is moored among the reeds. The shite thing about having a moored boat is getting cold a wet trying to retrieve it. I ungracefully climb into the little row boat and direct it towards our meeting place.

Our meeting point is at a small wooden dock just across from the shopping centre we like to fish at from time to time. As I am rowing closer to it I can see Mark is already there. We both know how to spot or lose a tail, so I didn't even ask if he thought he was followed. Fucker can pick me up at times and I consider myself above average at the agency.

As I start to line up the boat with the dock I can see Mark grinning at me as he thinks I am shite at anything to do with boats or driving. I ignore him and try to steady my little row boat so I can climb up onto the dock without falling into the water. "Having a little trouble Jason?" Mark gleefully shouts at me. "Feck off" I shout back at him. I clamber out of the rowboat and onto the dock and sit beside Mark. "What's up big man?" Mark asks me. I don't turn to face him, I just stare across the river and reply. "I hear you have a big mouth?" "Whatcha talking about Jason?" Mark replied sarcastically in a deep Ulster accent. "That bitch with the big tits you don't think I know about... BROOK! Did you know she has another boyfriend? Her real fucking boyfriend who she has been seeing for years is an RVA! Did you know that?" I said to Mark whilst trying to hike my jeans up around my waist. Mark looked worried but said nothing. "AND to top it off it's NOT just any fucking volunteer, it's Colin (Three Holes) Murphy! They fucking made you and sent in a honey trap and we all know how that went! Have you been slobbering Intel to this bitch? You do know in reality it goes back to Colin! HOW could you do this? It's not like your fucking stupid, YOU KNOW BETTER! Never mind the most important fact that your FUCKING MARRIED you twat!! That wee girl deserves better than you as you're only just lucky you patched things up the last time you did this shit! I bet you were making yourself out to be the big man because that fucking turncoat cunt was getting her panties in a twist over it, stop me if I am getting it wrong!" I said to Mark. "I fucking vouched for you.... "I can't even look at you as you have really

70

made me, your commanding officer and best mate look a complete dickhead in front of the agency!" I continued in an angry voice.

"Do you have any idea of what that looks like to them when you don't even know what's going on in your own team? To have a fucking rat give our Intel to some scummy RVA loving bitch?" I stood further away from Mark and scanned the horizon as the last thing I needed was to be caught talking to him. It was very dark now and there were no lights anywhere near this little dock so it kept us hidden. Seems clear for now I thought. I am waiting for Mark to speak but he just sat there silently, looking into the dark and murky waters of the Bann. The blood had drained from his face. He knew deep down I was right and the reality of the situation became more and more unnerving to him. I left him for a few minutes more to gather his thoughts.

Mark then perked up and asked; "What will happen to me now?" The way he said it was hard to hear like he was already a broken man before the shit had even hit the fan. "You broke your MI6 official Secrets Act contract. The agency will appoint your commanding officer as a judge to investigate if you best fit the description of the Treason Act. If you are deemed to be a best fit for the act you will be court marshalled at a special hearing and be tried by a military jury of your peers. I will be honest; they won't go easy on you. You could be looking at fifteen to twenty years in prison," I replied.

"I never gave her anything information related to any of our missions. The only thing she knows which is true is that I work for MI6. I fed her a pile of shit because she put out over it. I haven't compromised anything, I swear!" Mark answered.

"Listen, we can try to use this to our own advantage!! You're being watched by the Agency now so you need to look like you are infiltrating the RVA through Brook to bleed intel on Conor. We need to make your shit look legit so they can clearly see what you are doing and where you are going with this side line mission of yours. You will still be reprimanded as it will be deemed an illegal assignment but at least it is a much lesser charge of insubordination. I need you to continue meeting up with her and keep feeding her bullshit.

Keep in the back of your head that these people know who you are and will be ready for anything you could throw at them. I will see if Trevor has a file on you so we can actually see what they know about you and Brook. When are you meeting her next?" I asked. "Next Wednesday at 6 pm." Mark replied. "Cool that gives me enough time to plant a few seeds with our commanding officers with regards to your motive with Brook. Don't worry about this as I think I can put it right" I said, before getting myself up and making a wobbling return to the row boat. "Speak later kiddo" I shouted over to Mark as I started to slowly row away.

Mark then got up and turned around to face my direction "Cheers mate, safe home." Mark replied. I could see the stars fading and rain clouds drifting in, I need to hurry up and get to the car before I get soaked. Another fucking night evaporates before my eyes! No rest for the wicked I thought to myself.

Ian can wait till another night as I needed my sleep. I know there is a row ready to erupt with the wife when I get in and my little boy who will be awake in the early hours, will want to play with his daddy.

I get into my car after securing the boat and start to make my way home. I keep looking at the clock in the dash of my car, eyes fixed on the time. It's 2 am! I drive past a hotel and it hits me like a ton of bricks, the idea that I could use a hotel room to catch up on my sleep. I use the roundabout to make my way back to the hotel and pull into their dimly lit and surprisingly empty car park. As I enter the hotel, I get sucked into the posh surroundings. I walk over to the check in desk, my shoes are making sloshing sounds as they got wet during the boat ride. The sparkling marble floor in the lobby looks amazing as it reflects the lights of the huge crystal chandeliers hanging from the roof. The hotel stings me £120 for a room. If I can get a solid nine hours sleep here, then it was worth every penny.

I make my way to the elevator and hit floor three. I looked around the halls for signs that point to room 304. As I stick my key card in and open the door I am greeted by a fairly posh looking room with a 40-inch TV on the wall and a king-sized bed with crisp clean sheets and a mini fridge which undoubtedly was brimming with over price alcohol. As much as I would love to indulge myself with a drink and a movie, I don't bother as my reserves are running on fumes. I just strip down quickly and collapse into bed. I was about to go to sleep but remembered I didn't say my prayers. I did this every night from the age of ten.

It was a struggle trying to say them tonight as I kept dozing off but I eventually finished them and went out like a light. 3:45 am my phone abruptly wakes me when it rings, Olivia's name is flashing on the screen, so I quickly hit the answer button. I'm not prepared for what comes next.

This would be the start of where everything went wrong in my life.

"Olivia, you ok?" I ask. I get no answer, but I do hear the smoke alarm and my son crying in the background. "OLIVIA! OLIVIA!! CAN YOU HEAR ME? WHAT'S GOING ON?! OLIVIA!" I shouted. Panic is starting to take over me and I quickly put my jeans and shoes on and run out of the room holding the phone to my head. I am making my way down to the car and I can faintly hear someone's muffled sniggering. "WHO IS THIS!" I shouted as I was starting my car.

"So nice to finally meet Ya Jason, I would hurry home as your other half doesn't look so good...click" the line goes dead. I speed home taking every corner to the limit without rolling the car. As I drive closer I can see a flickering orange glow. "Please God, no! Please GOD, NO!" I can now see my house with flames coming out of the windows. I speed up my driveway and notice my front door of the house is lying open, I hear my sons cry as I run into the hallway and up the stairs shielding myself from the flames and gagging from the smoke. My son is not crying anymore as I find him hugging his mom who is lying lifeless and bloodied on the bedroom floor of my son's room. "OLIVIA!" I shouted. I need to get them out of here now! The flames were nearly coming into the room and I needed to get them both out now as the fire was already starting to eat at my son's door frame. You could hear the snaps and whistles of everything the fire was consuming as I was moving Olivia's body into a position I could lift.

I lift Olivia's battered body over my shoulder and then pick up my son. I carefully take them out of Daniel's room and begin to slowly stagger down the stairs, careful not to drop them as I need them out first go. Anxiety is starting to set in as my lungs are struggling to function due to the thick smoke that is overwhelming us from every direction. I began to notice that the fire was starting to burn my face and arms, it feels like my skin is bubbling and peeling off my flesh but still I hold on to my family. I just make it outside.

I struggle with my footing and drain every last bit of strength out of me to make my way over to the grass and away from the smoke. I vigorously try to wake them both up. I shake their faces and am reluctant to slap them as even now I would never intentionally hurt them. I have no choice, they need to start breathing! I slap my wife around the face to try and wake her "OLIVIA, OLLIIVVIIAAA!" I scream. I then slap my sons' cheeks gently to try and rouse him. Nothing! The adrenaline is pulsating through me like a train; I am barely keeping it together. I then lay Olivia in a recovery position, I then immediately work on my son.

My little man is not moving and going blue. Panic is starting to pull her twisted evil veil over me. I quickly blow into his mouth and try to clear the lungs, and then check his vitals. He has no pulse! "Fuck, Fuck, Fuck, no you don't, I'm not going to lose you, son, come back to daddy, I love you, Please God no! Don't DO THIS TO ME! Those FUCKING BASTARDS ARE DEAD, FUCKING DEAD!" I scream! I have to be careful not to push hard and break his little ribs as I start CPR on him. I get a few breaths in and pump his chest twice and Daniel starts to cry. Tears fill my eyes as I have my son back again. I hold him close and kiss him then put him down again on his tummy to let him cough up the smoke in his lungs.

I now turn my attentions to Olivia and realise I can do no more for her as three little holes in her chest suddenly start to slowly glisten in the fire light. I am fixated on them; she has been shot three times. I knew immediately who shot her as the bullets make out a small triangle around the heart. It was Colin! That was the sick fucks well known calling card to show he did it. They want a calling card; I would fucking give it to them! Their fucking head on a pike to know, I DID IT! I hold Olivia's lifeless body in my arms and call for an ambulance at the same time. Her eyes were still opened, looking at me. I am awash with guilt staring back into those beautiful brown eyes. This was my fault, if only I went home. I squeeze her even tighter and lose all control of my emotions. I did this to my family, I did this! My home was engulfed, and our cherished memories were now turning to ash. I sit down on the grass cradling my crying son in my arms while cuddling his mummy closer to us. I just waited there, lost in a horrible dream that I cannot awake from. I hear the fire crew and ambulances coming closer and closer. Everything starts to drown out and I find myself in a daze.

I jump out of it when someone grabs my arm, I instinctively pull my gun on them and quickly realise it was a fireman. Thank God, they are here. I explain to the startled Fireman I am with the Police. I holster my weapon and hand my boy over to one of their medics. I pick up my wife's body and follow behind the medic who has Daniel. The Fire crew were running all around me trying to put the house out. I didn't care about the house. All I could now think about is how I am going to tell my sweet boy that his mommy is dead. I place Olivia on a stretcher they pulled out for me. I lean over her trying to rub the soot off her precious face; I then closed her eyes and give her a long kiss on her forehead. I then whisper in her ear how much I love her and make a vow that I will protect Daniel from these evil people.

I then cross her arms and stare at her rings on her little hand, remembering when we first went looking for them together around the different jewellers. It brings a weak smile to my face as those were the good times we had together, one of the many good times. I leave Olivia and make my way over to my son, he keeps trying to look over at his mommy, but the medic wants Daniel to keep his oxygen mask on and let him attend to a burn on his wee arm. I lift the mask over my son's mouth and nose and hold him tight while the medic works on him. He hasn't realised yet his mummy won't be coming over to comfort him. A pain in my chest is getting worse as my heart feels like it's actually breaking. These moments have been burnt into my memory and I will never forgive or forget what they have done! Before I can start killing the bastards responsible, I need a secure place for my son to live. I promised Olivia I would keep him safe from all that is evil.

This is the time when I decided Daniel and I would move to Canada.

Mark and Ian arrive unexpectedly. "We got Olivia's text messages," Ian said. I looked confusingly at them both when I suddenly realised the RVA used her phone for further sinister motives. The cunts used her phone and her contacts to lure more agents out into the open using my family as the bait. They have now probably made Ian out even though he is not an agent, just like they have done with Mark and me.

They would almost certainly be watching their hellish handy work from afar. The fuckers seem to be all over the agency like a rash. This in itself was unusual. "You just got fucking made by those cunts!" I said to Ian, whilst looking at Mark in disgust as this fucking started with him. I pulled them closer to me. "The fuckers got Olivia and nearly killed Daniel" I continued in a shaken voice. I wanted to scream that I was going to kill them all but I knew better. The rage welling inside me could be seen on my face. "Everything will be Ok Jason, we have your back. We will get these bastards. I swear it!" Mark said. "We will get them Jay, every fucking last one of them!" Ian quickly added.

Both Ian and Mark now knew they were compromised and needed to act quickly to implement safety measures to protect themselves and their families. I let them get on with that and went back to my son. At the hospital, my thoughts were with my son who was lying in a bed sleeping in the children's ward. He looked exhausted. I was sitting close to his bed, holding his little hand. I couldn't stop tears rolling down my face as this was my fault. If I wasn't in this line of work I wouldn't have exposed my family to any of this shit. I hear a muffled commotion as I turn around to see Olivia's parents, Amanda and Thomas Wilcock's being escorted into the ward with a look on their face that I wish I could blank from my memory. If they hated me, I couldn't blame them. They went to either side of Daniel's bed and in turn kissed him gently as not to wake him.

Amanda didn't even look at me. After a few minutes, she left without saying a word, but Thomas put his hand on my shoulder as to say sorry for everything you are going through. He then followed his wife out of the ward. I needed that assurance as I was gutted for them losing their only child, whom I had promised vehemently to protect and shield from this side of my job. I look into my son's face and see a little bit of his mommy and couldn't help thinking about the day and hour he came into this world. How he looked about in silence for a few minutes and then let out an almighty roar. I get distracted from my thoughts again as I hear hard heeled footsteps coming towards me. It was Trevor. "I am so sorry for your loss Jason.

I have personally made sure you and your family are now under the government's protection. I have also given you a fully paid six-month leave of absence," Trevor said. "Thank you, mate," I replied. I was grateful for the support from Trevor, but something didn't sit right with me about his body language. It felt like he was almost disappointed to see me.

You could tell he was in a hurry to go and my gut instincts were going mental, screaming out at me to look deeper into his odd behaviour. I kept telling myself not to be stupid why would I get bad vibes from the main man running the show. I asked myself. What possible motive could he or anyone in the department have, to be involved with my situation? Trevor stayed for about three minutes and left after having a long look at Daniel.

I don't know why but that bothered me.

Chapter 5 - The two faces of Trevor

Trevor Hughes; people would describe him as sophisticated, late forties with a thin build. He is about six-foot-tall, Caucasian male with short black hair and wears thin tortoise shell spectacles. He always dresses smartly and in reasonable priced but nonetheless fashionable suits. He is the deputy director of MI6 Northern Ireland and currently in charge of three projects at the moment with one of them being Operation REVERT.

The British are so cocky in how they think they can meddle in other countries affairs. A bit hypocritical of me to say as I now work for the war machine. Ever since I was a little boy and was old enough to understand what my mother and father taught me about the Brits interference with my ancestral home of Ireland, it infuriated me. I never thought of myself as British even though I was born in England as my father immigrated here to work in the coal mines near Cumberland. I always thought of myself as Irish like my father and grandfather before me. I can't stand the way the English think they are above everyone, like the rest of the world is stupid and desperately needs their advice. The bastards cause nothing but destruction wherever they went throughout history by waging war and conquering weak nations. They built their Empire on the corpses of the indigenous people of the foreign countries they invade so they can stick their flag on a pole and claim the land for their King and country. Well, the tides have turned, and now they are losing their precious Empire a little piece at a time. Over the coming years, God willing, they won't even have an England to call their own.

I am one of many people of influence that want HRH the Queen and all her sprogs to be expelled from this country and Britain to be a republic which will make Wales and Scotland free to govern themselves. It will also leave the doors wide open for a united Ireland. My ancestors fought long and hard for this, and many of our brave boys died not seeing this dream fulfilled. To be honest, I don't give a fuck about Scotland or Wales. They've nothing to do with me. My heart will always be with Ireland and the native people that live there. The quicker we achieve a united Ireland, the quicker we can legally rid ourselves of those awful planted unionist people by outlawing all their parades and medieval sectarian traditions.

Hopefully, then they will march back to England where they belong, or we will start getting rid of them ourselves. The unionists are like old dinosaurs, they fear change and are twisted in their cultural identity.

Those people have no place in modern society. A modern society is one that works for the good of the country, it changes with the time and adapts to what the people want. We just need to eliminate the culture and history attached them and then we will be truly free of the British once and for all. I mean how can you develop a modern society in the U.K if you still have people that celebrate the torture and execution of Guy Fawkes or those that celebrate the Royal family in any way? This is why I support the Irish Republican rally's and enjoy seeing the RVA and their political representatives gain more and more power. I am one of the many Republican revolutionaries who fight by whatever means necessary.

Every Republican revolutionary has their part to perform; mine is using the media and the legal system to influence politics, and I'm doing it right under their noses. It was no secret thousands of years ago nor is it a secret today that the population of any country as a whole is more exceptive of change if the change to society is consistent and slow. Even if they venomously oppose what's happening, they eventually accept it.

Our united Ireland has been many years in the planning. We've created a huge political party in the North and South of Ireland called "An Streachailt" that helped put men like me in positions of high government, especially in England. I and my fellow revolutionary comrades will rewrite the history books showing we had a duty to rise against the British warlords. The bombs and killings were justified as a necessary evil. We will hammer that message repeatedly until the children hear it enough times that it becomes the utter truth. My part in the revolution is to take the blame off our warriors "The RVA" and the dissident groups. That means having a two-tier policing system put in place that will pardon the Republican dissidents and hammer the Loyalists.

To make it more accepting to the Loyalists and the general public we use the media to concentrate their efforts on reporting every Loyalist incident and only fractionally covering any Republican violence. This perceives the illusion to the population of Northern Ireland and abroad that there is vastly more trouble and violence caused by Loyalists than by Republicans. Thus stories of ethnic cleansing of Protestants from the west of Ulster becomes an urban myth. This then, in turn, helps with our fund raisers and seminars we hold all over the world to raise money for the RVA and our Republican Party An Streachailt, as the media perceives us as the victims. By focusing our young Republicans on jobs in the media and in politics, we will, in the long run, win the war by covertly creating a biased reflection against the Protestant scum living in the occupied counties of Ulster. These young Republicans were taught from an early age what they need to do to regain a United Ireland.

We point them in the right direction, and they do the rest. The mainstream public would identify them as socialists or of the political stance of the extreme left. Because of the effective use we've made of the media, we already have the public convinced that there are at least several different Republican dissident terrorist groups. Though the RVA does the actual terrorist activities, the blame gets shifted onto another made up dissident group so the RVA can stay in the peace process. Utterly brilliant! It's a bitter pill these stupid unionist dinosaurs have to swallow, and we love it. Even their own British government knows it can't afford to go after us as the whole process would seem a farce to the public if they all of a sudden started to arrest and convict RVA members on a regular basis. The people would start to question if the peace process ever existed. The British will do anything to stop this peace process from collapsing which includes royal pardons, light jail sentences for major crime such as terrorism or as we like to call it "Freedom Fighting." They will also put politically motivated high-ranking officials in top police and military roles to down play terrorist incidents in the hope of the public buying into their distraction strategies of blaming other dissident Republican groups.

Everyone is aware of this, but no one wants to speak out about it as they could be seen to be anti-peace process or be called a sectarian bigot. This is why we know we've little left to do to push the British out of Ireland once and for all as they are practically on their knees. As long as we stick to the long-term plan and our sympathetic friends in America keep funding us through Irish Republican marches and rallies across America. We can go the distance, guaranteed! We use Saint Patrick's Day parades all over the world as a platform to shout out to the public our cause. That the RVA are freedom fighters struggling to break away from British colonialism of their homeland of Ireland. Which at the end of the day is the Gods honest truth in my eyes anyway?

Presently

I'm sitting here at headquarters waiting for my meeting to start. I am nervous as we are close to our political goals. Even so, any day I could be exposed as the mole, but still, I press on and turn up to work for the Brits. It excites me whenever I sit down with them in the same room to discuss national security; I can't tell you how smug I feel knowing every step the enemy is about to make. The government think they developed a devious strategy to undermine all the progress we made under the camouflage of the peace agreement by incapacitating the RVA army and political wing by causing multiple divisions within their organisations. The old divide and conquer strategy that works so well for England over their decades of colonialism.

I'v been feeding this information back to my handlers in drips and drabs, so it doesn't look like they are suddenly reacting to leaked info. If that were sussed by the Brits, our office would be closed, and myself held and interrogated at her majesty's leisure. I am all too well informed what they do to obtain information from people. I rather put a bullet in my head than divulge sensitive information against our cause. Nevertheless, I need to water down this Operation REVERT, or it will fuck with our strategy. I have already done this twice for no good reason, so I suspect a few people may now be wary of what I am doing so I need to play it smart and make sure eyes are off me. I need to shift their attention onto one of their own to give me the time I need to put REVERT on the back burner.

Maybe if I can make a few of the team members, disappear that should shift the focus off me. The RVA already obtained my detailed file that outlines the members of my team and other British agents in this building. My Irish companions like to fuck with them to let them know they could kill them or their family at any time. This mental game of cat and mouse drives most undercover agents mad and common consequence of this is a mental disorder called PTSD which is a medical term for Post-Traumatic Stress Disorder. They lose all self-control and are made vulnerable which means they are no good to the British intelligence, but for us, it means one less Brit in Ireland. The same strategy worked for the British government when they wanted to keep their spy's from being discovered. They just kill a few low rankers in a suspicious manner thus creating your smoke screen.

The RVA started to analyse and learn from their mistakes in such a way that whatever the target was now, our men were only told what they needed to know, never given the whole plan which started to create devastating consequences for her majesties secret service. We killed a few of their top staff a few years ago, and the Brits soon realised that we could get to them and thus thought it would probably be better to play ball with us instead of being our enemy. I predict the mighty Brits will soon have their tail tucked between their legs and start to give us everything we want and more. We even got compensation for our boys who were injured from the British army; their victims from our campaign didn't even get that. It's hilarious if you think about it. Well, I think it's funny. Just recalling these things put me at ease. The Great Britain we all once knew, was no more. I'm still waiting on a few people to start this meeting. Ah well, let's get this meeting started. I hand out the new and further watered-down specs for Operation REVERT. I also talk in a mono tone to disinterest the other agents, and I don't even ask them to put away their laptops or phones as I like to encourage them to multi task. Which promotes mistakes and disarray.

Unbeknownst to the agents, I am destroying Operation REVERT from within. Slowly, ever so slowly are the keys to change. "Good afternoon team," I said while taking a seat at the head of the table. I begin the meeting by reviewing the Operations boundaries and what we've accomplished and the things yet to finish. Agent Joanne immediately pointed out a few inconsistencies. "Sir, it appears that there are fewer field agents than before, and money for temps has nearly been cut by a third. These two vital cogs in our network are needed for Operation REVERT to work. There is far too much ground to cover on what we have now. There are too many RVA operatives working on the mainland never mind the rest of the U.K." Joanne said anxiously. My revolutionary comrades and I know this I thought to myself while looking at her with my perfected false look of concern. I start to gently nod my head in agreement and begin to speak. "We've far too many other threats to our country at the moment. With radicalised Jihadists to home grown Anarchists, never mind the problems we already face from the dissident Republican and Loyalist military groups. Our Government is stretched to breaking point. We must implement these cuts and make the most of our limited resources. You've been allocated your assigned roles, and we will expect results regardless of our new fiscal position. No other option I'm afraid." I stated to the group as a whole.

Joanne who originally addressed the issue of the cuts just sat back in her chair and said nothing. I then scanned the table for any other agents who wanted to say anything else about the changes and again it was accepted as an inevitable change in Operation REVERT, its potency ever diluting to the point of it being something that is no longer important or given much thought about. Then before you know it, it's scrapped.

Well, well, well. The behemoth that is Ian arrives late as usual. You couldn't meet a bigger bigoted Neanderthal idiot, even if you tried. He is a ruthless killer, that I will give him. I will however eventually leak his details to the RVA like I have done before with Loyalist temps, so they can kill this piece of shit and weaken his protestant stronghold in East Belfast. I know it sounds awful, but when you see an opportunity to better a situation, you mustn't shy away from it. I do need him for my plan, at the moment, as he is an all too easy pawn to play with. Look at him; the lump is ignoring everything around him. We are supposed to be having a meeting but he never takes part, he just sits there looking about the room or playing on his phone. This time, however, he has picked up the brief and is reading it. Casually flicking through our new Operations dossier like he understands what he is looking at. Fucking twat. I'll ask him if he understands the changes to REVERT. "Ian..IAN!" I shout over to him. Ian eventually looks over at me. "Well?" I ask him.

"Well? Well, what the fuck do you want?!" Ian replied. "Can I see you in my office", I ask Ian in a semi angry voice. We walk into the office, I ask Ian "I take it you like your new assignment?" "Yeah, it's alright," Ian replied. Now to rile this big idiot up I thought to myself. I know he is jealous of Jason's position in the agency as he has more experience. I use this to my advantage. "I would like you to go through the assignment with Jason to see if there are any changes that we need to make to the mission to reduce detection as it will be largely an intelligence gathering operation before we need you to clean up what needs to be cleaned up," I said to Ian. You can see Ian's face contort with anger when I was asking him that question. Ian then blurted out. "Once again my years of experience overlooked by you, you bureaucratic knob heads. Why do I need... You know what, if you can't trust me to do a fucking mickey mouse recon job you can go fuck yourself as I have more experience and prowess over the years in the Para's than that wannabe COCK Jason!"

"Did you even look at the file I gave you? It's not just a recon mission!" I replied angrily. "Right... I will have another look at it again." Ian replied. "That's a bit of tough shit now you fucken moron. I have had enough of your fucking mood swings to last a life time, and in this unit, your antics are becoming more of a liability every day for this agency." I said sharply to Ian. Now to drag the other agent, I need rid of into this escalating and heated situation. "Furthermore, any fucking wonder Jason keeps you on a short leash with your fucking tantrums ever ready to shit all over our operations that's been methodically planned out for months on end. You're a fucking liability and are suspended until further notice." I shouted at Ian while he started to walk out the office.

Ian will compromise this operation, I can feel it, but I don't know as yet how he will do it, but when he does, I have a very good chance to officially quash operation REVERT for good. If I can remove Jason off the team as well, I could grind this operation right down to a halt as the rest of the agents on the team are easily led by me and could be placed on operations elsewhere. Then our movement will have nothing standing in its way to start Impeachment of the government ministers who are still loyal to Queen and country. We will then further embrace the EU with our laws and politics till the U.K will be only recognisable by its name alone. We could also throw in a couple of false flags for good measure, accusing parliament of sanctioning an illegal war against the Irish people. We could also reward our Irish warriors with large compensation packages as a thank you for their vital services. A British Republic with no crown attached and a united Ireland to boot. My dreams and goals were finally in reach. One little problem called Jason still stood in the way of progress.

I go back to the meeting and apologize for the unfortunate incident that just happened. "I'm sorry everyone for that unfortunate incident with Ian, but as you and I know, it was a long time coming. He wasn't a team player, and for the moment he has been placed on suspension without pay pending further investigation." I stated to the group. Before I could sit down, I noticed Ian's file was not on the table. Fuck, Ian still has the file with the names of our volunteers and where they live. PERFECT! This would be my smoke screen. I thought to myself.

"Lynne, I need you to get that eyes-only Intel off Ian quickly before he leaves the building. If he doesn't cooperate you pull your weapon on him and call for back up. Do you understand me?!" I shouted. She looked nervous as she nodded yes. "Do you want me to go after him, sir?" Mark said. "No, you just sit there. Lynne is more than capable of handling this!" I replied. I wasn't counting on the big dumb shit taking Intel out of the building after being suspended. It seems opportunity has presented itself with what I need. "Lynne, hold on. This is a large building; we don't want to lose him." I shouted across the room to her.

I was stalling for time. I wanted him out of the building. "Where does he frequent in the building?" I ask the others. "We are wasting time!" Lynne shouts out.

"Go to the control room and scan the cameras, that's an order" I shouted over to Lynne. That should allow Ian some more time to exit the building. I look out the window to the car park and spot Ian's Jag. Fuck he is still here, Wait! It's him. He walks over to the car with the file under his arm and gets in. He is reversing. Come on you dickhead get out of the car park. Shit there's Lynne. FUCK she caught his attention. Yep, he handed over the file. That opportunity was a big fucking gift wrapped in a bow. Now it's fucking gone! I quickly dismiss the agents from the meeting and head into my office to come up with a new strategy to remove these two thorns out of my side. I will have them nutted, I could get a team... I am interrupted in my thoughts as Lynne comes storming into my office with a worried look on her face. "What's wrong? " I asked. She hands me the file. It was empty. I get excited, but I can't reveal myself. "What the FUCK Lynne! Do you really mean to tell me you didn't check what Ian gave you? What an amateur mistake. A fucking MI6 agent can't retrieve a file that was still on the premises? Get out; you're a fucking disgrace!" I angrily told her. As Lynne left in tears, I was grinning ear to ear. I quickly grab the phone "Operator, put me through to Portadown barracks!" I said with authority. I explain to Jason over the phone the situation which I now lay in his lap. He has 12 hours to arrest Ian and recover the Intel, or I will be scrapping the operation. I ignore Jason's pleas and reasoning's of the situation before disconnecting the call. I presented him with a near impossible task as Ian could be anywhere in the country. Maybe this will go to plan after all.

Chapter 6- A Painful Goodbye

It took a few days, but Jason and Daniel have had their Canadian citizenship rushed through and approved. They received their new Canadian passports and papers by special courier on the day of Olivia's funeral. They were about to start a new life together on the other side of the world, but Jason knew he had a job to finish. He couldn't just run away from the people of Northern Ireland who were themselves hoping for a better life without the constant fear of terrorist attacks. He knew that the little time he was to spend in Canada was for settling his son into a strange house, in a strange land, with a person he has never met face to face, to keep him safe while his daddy silences the guns that have been waging war against the innocent for so long.

The painful memories that lurked in our hearts and the feeling of being unsafe in our beds continued to be far too much for us to bare. I made the decision to move to Canada as it would be number one, safer for both of us and number two, Daniel wouldn't be exposed to sectarianism which is rife within Northern Ireland. I promised Olivia when Daniel was born only seconds into this world that I would always keep him safe, no matter what came. I keep thinking about Olivia and often reliving the times I could have made an effort to come home to be with her and Daniel, those moments that are now forever gone. I knew we still had to bury her and that was going to be the single hardest thing I have ever had to do. A loving mummy and caring wife was about to be laid to rest in a quiet church yard where we once got married, not so long ago.

After a short chat with the fire chief about the structure of the house and the implications of re-entering the property. I was given the green light with a word of caution on some parts of the house hold. The house was structurally sound, but areas needed to be rebuilt as the fire weakened some support structures. I wanted to gather what mementoes we had left which was not claimed by the fire. We departed from the in-laws and made the short drive over to where we used to live. We make our way into our estate, we could see the corner of the house far away through the trees. Closing nearer to our house, the swaying blue and white police tape could be seen skipping in the wind. Thankfully someone has boarded up the windows that were smashed by the firemen which has saved me a job to do. I pulled the car into the driveway; the car breaks the police tape which in turn falls gently to the ground. It would be typical of the RVA to hide an explosive device on the expectation of my return to the property, but I already had the house checked by the agency. Saying that I always like to check things myself two or three times in case anything was missed. It gives me peace of mind.

I step out of the car first and ask Daniel to wait with his granny as I want to check the place out again before they enter. I brought with me this time a little invention the Israelis made a few years ago that sends out a multitude of frequencies which in turn trips detonator switches that are within a fifteen-metre radius. We've used this technology many times, and it was indeed flawless. The RVA don't know about it, well I assume they don't as we have been using them for a while and they haven't changed the build of their IEDs.

Nothing triggered to my relief. I didn't feel right exposing Daniel to the house, but I knew he needed closure as this was a very traumatic and tragic experience for him. I went inside and did another check of Daniel's room as well as my own because they were the only rooms we were going to enter which I deemed safe.

I make my way back outside and got Daniel out of his car seat. Amanda got out as well and came into the house after us. We made our way upstairs which was badly smoke damaged. I needed to collect Olivia's favourite dress and make sure she was to wear it along with a few mementoes to keep by her side. I asked Daniel what he wanted to give mommy and he went into his bedroom and came out clutching his favourite bedtime snuggle rabbit. "I want mummy to have this" Daniel said to me in a quiet voice. I tried my best to hold back the tears as I bent down to hug him. Holding him close I whispered in his ear "your mummy will love it." I held him tight, and we both cried together as we missed her so much.

My mother in-law Amanda came up stairs and took Daniel in her arms. "You are a very brave boy, "she said. Daniel slowly nodded his head in agreement. I had grabbed my dog tags from the top drawer of the dressing cabinet. I remembered that she loved me wearing them. I put them in my pocket and continue to rummage through the bedroom picking up what I needed. The house was gutted by the fire with only a few rooms having escaped with smoke damage. The strong smell of damp smoke was overpowering, and light fog that hung in the air was only visible when looking down the hall or when you were at one end of a room.

The beams of light cutting through the cracks of the boarded-up windows added to the unfamiliar eeriness of our once humble home. I felt angry, pathetic and useless. How could I not have seen this coming? It's my job to know what the enemy is doing before they do. Amanda took Daniel out to the car, and I started to finish up gathering what mementoes I could in a duffle bag. I took my hard drives out of my water-logged computer tower and prayed that they would be unaffected as I had stored all of our photos and videos on it. Making my way out I could help but recall that night in great detail.

Staring at the stairs and how I ran up them with the fire licking the walls and roof around me. Seeing Olivia's lifeless body with my son lying on top of her unconscious. Tears started to stream from my face again. I needed to quickly gather my composure before chaining up the front door and clamping a padlock on it.

That would be the last time the RVA would emotionally break me.

I got into the car and made our way back to the in-law's house where we were staying. Olivia's body was there too, in her old room. The coffin was on two props at the bottom of her bed. When we got into the house, I took Daniel in to see his mummy. I asked him to put his little blue rabbit beside her. I lifted him up, and he said quietly "Here you go mummy, I am giving you rabbit. Mummy, wake up. Mummy..." I reminded Daniel to place the rabbit beside her. He stretched out and did just that, then immediately moved it again closer to her face. I put him down again and explained to him "your mummy's body is asleep, but your mummy's soul is in heaven right now. She is always going to be with you" I said to him. Daniel didn't say anything and just kept trying to look in the coffin. I knew we needed to leave the room as I didn't want him to remember his mother this way.

I quickly put my dog tags and a family photograph of us in much happier times beside her. She loved this photo as we had it blown up and put in our living room. We both left together and closed the door behind us. We buried Olivia the next day. It was a big funeral and many faces that haven't been seen in years make themselves known to me and the immediate family once again. After a poignant service, I carried my beloved one last time to her final resting place. I helped lower her coffin in the ground and made sure Daniel dropped the first flower into his mother's grave. The sky was over cast, but the rain stayed away, and as the crowd started to dwindle away Daniel and I stood fast.

I didn't go into the church hall for the after procession as I had nothing to say to anyone and didn't feel like eating. I took Daniel with me and texted Amanda we were going home. It was a few days later before Daniel and myself got onto a Boeing 747 from Belfast Aldergrove to travel to Toronto Pearson's Canada. We were sitting in our seats getting ready for take-off, you know the part where the plane taxis up to the main run way and stops before juicing up the jet engines. The high-pitched whine of the engines got Daniel excited, and we both started to count down, "five, four, three, two, one, blast off!" we both said simultaneously. The Plane raced down the runway with the view of blurred scenery going past the window at a furious pace.

The best part of it was the g-force pulling us back into our seats just before the wheels left the ground. Awesome! I had planned for the seven-hour flight to Toronto so that Daniel wouldn't be bored. I had a backpack with a pile of children's comics; you know the ones with the free crappy toys attached but he loved them. I also had enough sweets to keep him satisfied but not enough to put him hyper during the long flight. I sit back in my chair and stick my ear phones in and scan over my carefully selected stockpile of mp3s, which I stuck on my mobile phone the night before.

I start to relax and listen to my tunes all the while watching Daniel eagerly chomping away on his sweets and pretending to read his comic aloud to me. The flight itself goes like a dream. As we were approaching the weather clears, and it looks like it will be a glorious summer's day in August. The vast city of Toronto stretches out before us as far as the eye can see, even at this height. I show Daniel the massive CN Tower and tell him we are going up it in the next few days. The flaps pop up, and the noise of the aeroplane's hydraulics could be heard as the wheels punch out with that familiar robotic whine. We are ready to land, so I make sure Daniel's belt is on and adjust my own and pray for a safe landing. Drifting down fast we bump off the runway a few times, and then the engines begin to reverse thrust, slowing the big jet to a trundle. A few whoops and hollers with the sound of half-hearted clapping could be heard in the cabin. We make our way out of the plane and just as I expected the humidity hits us with a sweltering thump. Wish I didn't put my jeans on this morning.

We continue into the airport and make our way through the maze of corridors that lead us to luggage pick up. Once we got our bags, we walk over to the hire car company and pick up our wheels for the next two weeks. A man in a smart looking navy blazer comes walking forward to the reception desk and greets me at the counter. "Good afternoon sir, how may I help you today?" he said. "I've a car booked under Helpelstien, Edward Helpelstien" I replied. The sound of clacking keyboard buttons fills the room. "Yes, I have those details here. All paid for by your company I see. You over for business I take it?" He asked.

Keeping it short I replied "Yes." I took the keys and went to find my car. Which was conveniently parked close to the building. I check the back to make sure they provided me with a child's seat, tick. A quick look around the vehicle to make sure nothing was out of the ordinary, tick. I strap Daniel in and then make my way around the car to the driver's side. I nearly get in. What a tosser I was, forgot that the driver's seat was on the left-hand side of the car. We then drive out of the multi-story car park and make our way downtown.

I start to take in all the changes that have happened around Toronto since I moved away all those years ago. I turn on the air conditioner while I was coasting in the busy traffic and switch on the radio. "You hungry Daniel?" I hear nothing. "You hungry Daniel?" Still nothing. I raised my voice, "DANIEL!" "What?" Daniel answered. It was like I was interrupting him from whatever he was doing. My funny boy, I laugh to myself. "Do you want lunch or are you not hungry?" I asked him "My tummy says it wants sweeties," he replied. Why do I bother asking when I always know the answer? I keep my eye out for a chicken restaurant that I use to go to when I was a kid. It had the best dipping sauce. I can remember when I finished my dinner; I use to drink the sauce to my parent's disgust. I chuckle to myself.

I see another restaurant I recognise which makes amazing steaks and killer homemade cheeseburgers. The only problem is that they don't have a car park as they are located on the main street. I start to scan up and down the street for a place to park and find one not too far away from the place. I park up and begin to feed the meter. I feel myself start to smile; it feels good to be somewhere safe. I bring Daniel out of the car and take his hand as we begin our walk towards the restaurant. The sound of the busy traffic and that familiar smell of city air brings back childhood memories. We walk through swinging saloon doors into the steakhouse.

It's just like I remembered with the old mini juke boxes at the end of the booth tables. It also had huge cow skulls and buffalo horns adorning the walls with black and white photos of Cowboys and Indians. Daniel was impressed by the place as he couldn't stop asking me questions about all the dated adornments. A very chirpy young lady comes over and cleans an already spotless table. "Hi boys would you like to order any drinks while you look at the menu?" she said in a strong Canadian accent. "Yes, thank you. Could I have a pint of Diet Coke and glass of apple juice? Cheers." I replied. "No worries. That is an interesting accent you have if you don't mind me saying, are you Australian?" She inquired. "No, from Northern Ireland but I have lived in Canada for many years before I moved over there," I answered. I do get fed up of people asking the same question over and over again. I know it's not her fault as this is the first time we've met. "Oh, that's very different, isn't it? I like it!" she said. With that, she was away again. Looking at the menu, I see some of my old favourites I use to order. It hasn't changed much, but those fucking prices have! "Fucking Hell!" I said under my breath, so no little ears could hear. I then realised it was in Canadian dollars so basically half the value of the sterling pound. That made me feel better as I can be a bit of a tight ass when it comes to spending money. I don't mind paying for something if it was worth it.

The same chirpy lady comes gliding over with our drinks and puts them down in front of us. I detest the way restaurants fill your glass to the brim with ice, it's a cheap restaurant trick to give you less of the drink you ordered and more of the free ice. I ignore it as I give my order to her for Daniel and myself. I show Daniel the mini juke box and ask him to pick a song for us to listen to. He carefully studies the pictures on the on each one the flip tabs and makes a choice. "I want that one!" he shouts. "B5? Good choice." Daniel chose a track from Phil Collins, "Two Hearts." I haven't heard it in ages. I put a dollar coin in the slot and select his song. As we listen to Phil, our order arrives. That was quick I thought. I help Daniel cut his food up and then got stuck into mine which was a monster cheese burger. They don't make them like this in the U.K. We are too full for after's and decide to make our way out of the place and back to the car. I leave a five-dollar tip and thank the waitress for a pleasant meal. Little did I know the tip was already added to my bill, the sneaky fucks!

We start to make our way back to the car, and my mind is working out how to get to the hotel we were booked at. It is getting dark fast and looks like it might pour out of the heavens at any minute. I quicken the pace as I start to feel the rain faintly hitting my face. I pick up my wee man as his little legs can't move as fast as mine. We just make it to the car before the rain comes teaming down. Daniel is dry, but I am getting soaked trying to strap him in. He finds it funny that rain is bouncing off daddy's head. I turn on the satnav and programme our route to the hotel. FLASH.....RUMBLE. We are in for a treat as the lightning storms over here are amazing due to the high humidity. Surprisingly Daniel finds the experience as interesting as I do as he leans back in his car seat looking out the window.

The sound of the rain beating on the car was deafening, and I counted myself lucky we got to the car in time to miss the worst of it. Driving through Toronto was taking some time to get used to as I never really drove anywhere in Canada as I left at 17 and my second-hand car I was given by my parents never left the driveway. It was actually gifted to my Dads Masonic buddy as it would cost way more than it was worth to export it to Northern Ireland. Trying to adapt to a left-hand drive car was fine but driving on the road and obeying the Canadian traffic laws that was another thing entirely. I was pulling into the underground parking of the hotel and noticed a lovely pub across the road from it. I would so love a drink right now but had the wee man with me. It was going to be an early night, so the plan for both of us was a shower, little snack and drink, then bed.

I park the car and unload our stuff. I take out the huge black roller case and a duffle bag. Daniel immediately runs over to the roller case and climbs onto it. I lock the car and begin to trundle myself and the case with Daniel on it over to the elevator. It was all brass and polished within an inch of its life; it was quite elegant looking. We enter the elevator, and I push the lobby button. The doors glide gently over and then a little jolt from the lift which carries us smoothly up two floors. Daniel suddenly let out a little fart and giggled to himself. "You dirty munter" I blurted out and began to laugh with him. The doors glide open at the lobby, and we make our way over to the check in desk. Daniel continues to sit on top of the roller case as I drag it clacking over the marble tiles. The check in desk looked busy with six members of staff scuttling around quickly checking in guests. They were all very proficient at their jobs as it took no time to reach the front of the queue. "Good afternoon sir and welcome to The Royal Edward Hotel" a clerk shouted over to me. "Good Afternoon" I replied as I made my way over to where he was behind the desk. "Have you made a reservation with us?" he inquired. "Yes, under the name of Edward Helpelstien. One adult and child for a double/ twin room." I replied. "One moment....... Yes, I found your details. You're staying with us for a week and paid your bill in advance. I just need to programme your key card.........OK, here you go, room 304. We hope you enjoy your stay at The Royal Edward." He said with a smile. "Thank you!" I replied.

We make our way back to the elevators and once inside hit the third-floor button. As we exit onto the third floor, we pass some vending machines with everything and anything you could ever want. I will be paying them a visit later. We arrive at our room which is located beside a fire exit as I requested as I like to be prepared for any eventuality. I turn on the TV for Daniel and find the kids channel for him. I then begin my meticulous search of the room looking for bugs or things that are out of place. I disconnect the phone as it can be used as a listening device, even if I don't use it. I open and close the door a few times to confuse the data logger which is a small magnetic connection on top of the door frame. It alerts staff to rooms that are opened but not occupied. It also can be used to alert staff to when you leave or enter the room. Curtains are drawn, so surveillance is scuppered. The window opened, and air conditioner turned on to try and distort any heat signatures we are giving off. I take out my extendable heavy metal door jammer and place it over the handle of the door and wedge the bottom of it against the carpeted floor.

The spiked metal pad at the bottom of the jammer makes sure I have a secure grip on the floor. "KNOCK KNOCK KNOCK!" went the door. I quickly pull out my loaded 45 and sit Daniel against the wall far away from the view of the door.

I then begin to approach the door not worrying about my foot steps as the TV was drowning them out. I've yet to place my external cam outside so at the moment the only way I can ID a threat is by looking through the key hole which will give away the position on the other side as my head will block out the light. I cock my gun slowly and carefully point the barrel at the key hole making sure my body is tight to the wall. "Who is it?" I asked. "Mr Helpelstien, sorry to disturb you.

I couldn't phone through to inform you about your visitor waiting in the lobby. A Mr Mark Thompson." He said. "Please ask him to come up to my room," I replied. "Right away sir." He said. I could hear his footsteps walking away from the room and down the hallway. Nevertheless, someone else could be waiting outside, so I move the barrel of my gun side to side across the eye piece to make it look like I was looking out into the hall. Nothing. I hold my breath and slowly move over to look. I see an empty hallway. I quickly unlock

92

the door but leave the jammer on. Nothing...I was being over cautious, but I will apologise to no one about my mannerisms as it's kept me alive this long. So, Marks flown over, probably on the same flight as me to try to make me look like a dick for not noticing him tailing me.

I quickly stick my mini sticky cam to the back of the hallway, making sure I have a clear view and a good connection. I test it on my video receiver. Perfect! I return to my room and lock up again, waiting for Mark. A few minutes later I can see Mark swaggering down the hall and to add injury to insult he finds my camera on the wall and waves to me. Mark then knocks on the door in his usual manner of one hard knock. I keep my gun on me as my nerves have been spooked and open the door to let my old buddy in. "Come on in mate; I bet you've come to gloat about how you found me," I said. "You know me well. I was sitting two rows behind you, followed you to your rental car place at the airport. I already had a Kawasaki bike booked and used that to follow you to a restaurant. I ate a few hot dogs while waiting for you and Daniel to finish and then got soaked trailing you to the hotel. I've now just booked myself a room down the hall from you." He replied. "Fucking smart arse, glad it was you and not those other cunts. I was ready to give that hotel porter a new arsehole in the middle of his forehead! Ha ha!" I chuckled. "Hello, Daniel," Mark said. Daniel didn't reply as he was too engrossed in his cartoons to have taken anything under his notice. "Daniel!" I shout over. "What?" Daniel replies. "Say hello to Mark," I ask him. "Hello, Mark," Daniel said in a quiet voice.

"You know how he gets when he is watching something," I said to Mark. "Definitely do mate, ha ha," Mark replied. I go over to the small fridge and pull out a few mini liquors and ask Mark to get some ice. We had a few bevvies and talked about all the shit that's been happening. I order some room service for all of us as we didn't feel like going to the restaurant to eat. I get Daniel off to sleep, I remember the promise I made to Olivia. I say quietly to myself that I will always keep Daniel safe and that we both miss you very much. I sometimes find myself talking to Olivia even though I know she's not there. I tuck Daniel in and make sure his little tiger is snuggled close to him. "He looks just like you," Mark said. "Thanks, bro," I replied.

"Want to come to Moose & Bears Theme Park tomorrow with us?" I ask Mark. "Sounds like fun! Count me in! ... Jay, I'm going to head back now to my room for some shut eye and maybe check out the talent at that bar across the road. Night mate." Mark said. "Have fun, and we will see you in the morning mate," I replied. I lock up after Mark leaves and then flop on the bed. I was out for the count. Hours pass, and I wake up to morning traffic noises. The room was lit up in a glorious golden yellow colour with the beams of light almost bursting through the curtains.

Daniel is already up and using the bathroom. "Morning poo head!" I shouted of over to Daniel. "I'm not a poo head!, You say that again, and I'm going to smack your bum!" Daniel said in a stern voice, his little face was very serious. I laugh aloud as I find him extremely funny. He is just like his mum and takes no nonsense from anyone. I get us both showered, dressed and out the door for 8 am. We walk down the hall to wake up Mark.

I hammered out a couple of big knocks on the door and waited for Mark to answer. No answer comes so as I was about to give the door another rattle I hear this voice shout down the hall at me "Good morning!" Mark bellows as he comes strolling down in the same clothes he had on yesterday. "Well dirt bag, I see you had a productive night," I shout back. "Give me two minutes to get a wash, and I will meet you at the restaurant for breakfast," Mark asked. "No worries mate, we will see you down there," I replied. We make our way down the stairs and to the restaurant on the main floor of the hotel. Daniel runs in and selects a booth seat for us. We leave our coats at the table and help ourselves to the breakfast buffet. I love buffets! Chinese, Indian or even a salad bar as it means no waiting. As I pile the food on my plate, I can see Daniel just picking at the fruit which was fine until he sees the chocolate chip pancakes and chocolate sauce.

"Daniel don't fill your plate will that junk, eat some fresh fruit or get some bacon and sausages!" I ask him. It's like he's on auto pilot and doesn't hear anything I say as he continues to pile on the junk food. Well....he doesn't eat crap all the time, so I will let it slide. Mark comes jogging over and plonks himself down at our table. He quickly grabs some bacon off my plate and starts eating it. "Oi!! Get your own, pleb!" I tell Mark. He smirks and makes his way over to the breakfast buffet. We spend the next half hour filling up for our busy day in Toronto. First stop for the day was the world-famous CN Tower. It was completed in 1976 and stands at an incredible 1,815 feet high. I remember going up the tower when I was a kid. The lift going up was amazing, the speed of it was like a carnival ride in itself. Then the glass floor! It was by far the scariest thing I had done as a kid. People just freeze near the edge of the glass floor.

You can't blame them as it's only natural not to walk on glass, never mind glass that has a gigantic drop underneath it. The tower looks like it bends when you look down, and every ounce of your common sense will just not let you walk normally over that glass floor. It's funny watching people freeze over it or on their belly, with just their face peeping over the glass. I try not to let my past experiences get in the way of today's events as Mark and Daniel have never been here before. We leave the hotel and make our way over to a multi-storey near the tower. The Dome where the Toronto Blue Jays play was directly below the tower which we could visit later. We all walk over and make our way into the building which was at the base of the tower. The tickets were reasonably priced, and there wasn't a big crowd today. After a short introduction from our guide, we get into the elevator that will bring us to the top. I watched Daniels face as the Elevator starts to ascend faster and faster. He had an excited smile on his face and looked up at me as to say this was great!

The elevator slowed and the doors opened, we could see the huge windows in front of us with Toronto expanding as far as the eye could see. The beautiful weather only added to the picturesque scenery. Daniel and Mark were straight over to the windows, no fear of the incredible height they were at, unlike me. I can ripcord jump out of a plane or engage in military fire fights but fly a kite or look over the edge of a building, no chance. We drop the car off at the hotel after the tower and use the sightseeing buses to see the rest of Toronto. As the day goes on and we make our way around the city and visit the usual tourist destinations and find ourselves robbed of time. We say goodbye to Mark and get a taxi back to the hotel. After being dropped off in front of our hotel, I had a very odd feeling that we were being watched. My brain had picked up something my eyes were not yet seeing. I purposely make my way with Daniel to the fire escape. This will tell me if someone is trying to tail me.

I unholster my 45 as I carry Daniel quickly up the three flights of stairs and pause to listen on the third floor to hear if anyone was following. I put my finger over my mouth and Daniel did the same, so I could listen out for the door opening and get a glimpse of what my tail was wearing. The door opens, and someone quickly clambers up the stairs. They keep to the far right so I can't see them. I'm not waiting; I rapidly check to see if the hallway is clear and quickly open my room door and lock it with the bar. I then scan the room and check the bathroom, empty. I place Daniel in the bath and give him my phone to play with. Curtains are already drawn, so I turn on the TV to mask the sound of our movements. I can see the shadowy movement at the base of the door as I turn on my video receiver.

Just as the picture comes onto my little screen, I see two men with weapons drawn in front of my door. The door receives a wallop which would of put the door through only for my bar holding it. Daniel drops the phone and covers his ears. The poor pet's eyes said it all; he was terrified. I cock my weapon and line up on the monitor where I need to shoot through the door as I only have one shot at ending this quickly. I wait for the second kick of the door and open fire on the two of them. I empty eight rounds through the door going left to right in secession. My hollow points shatter massive craters into the wooden door and make mincemeat out of the would-be intruders. The dust settled and the wheezing and groaning sounds quietened down. I checked my video receiver again. My eyes are fixated on the blood-spattered walls behind them. They had no bullet proof vests on. Daniel was screaming due to the noise of the guns. My shots incapacitated the men before they could open fire, so I knew he was uninjured and just scared. I can't see their hands or their weapons clearly so I carefully make my way into the hall to disarm them. I want to go to Daniel to comfort him, but I need to make sure these men can't hurt us. I check to see if they are dead. Check! Then investigate their necks, arms and chest quickly for tattoos that would show me who they may be affiliated with as Canadas got quite a few dangerous organization's and street gangs. Both of the dead men had quite a few Russian mafia tats. Why would they target me? This makes no sense? From the corner of my eye, I see the fire door slowly open and a police officer cautiously entering the hall way before shouting at me to drop my weapon. "PUT YOUR WEAPON DOWN ON THE FLOOR AND PUSH IT AWAY FROM YOU, NOW!" The police officer screamed as he began to find a position of advantage. I complied and carefully slid the weapon down the hall. "GET ON YOUR KNEES AND PLACE YOUR HANDS ON YOUR HEAD!" the officer continued. I complied with his instructions. "CROSS YOUR LEFT FOOT OVER YOUR RIGHT AT THE ANKLES!" He screamed again. I was getting fed up as I could hear Daniel crying, but I complied. "DADDY, DADDY, DADDY!" screamed Daniel!

As the officer approached me my anger grew as he was stopping me from seeing if my son was alright, I knew Daniel was scared, and he needed his daddy, I snapped! As soon as he laid hands on me, I grabbed his fingers, which I twisted to expose his wrist which I then quickly got a hold of to flip him over. I twisted too fast and too hard as a crunching noise, not unlike a carrot would make when snapped in two, came from his wrist. The officer was screaming out in pain, I lined up a punch and hit him square in the mandible part of his jaw which immediately knocked him out.

I rushed over to my son and calmed him. I kept thinking of my promise to Olivia. I gently kiss his head and whisper "I thought we would be safe here, daddy is so, so sorry." I quietly held him tight till he stopped crying. I picked Daniel up and gathered our belongings and quickly left the room, past the bodies and to the elevator. I pushed the button to call a lift, I noticed a lift was about to open on my floor. I stepped in-between the two vending machines to keep out of eyesight of anyone coming out. It was a cleaning lady. She walked over to the bodies holding a bunch of towels under her right arm. She was calm and collective as she was examining the bodies on the ground. I got into the lift with Daniel, but my eyes were fixated on her as she started to pocket the money she pulled out of their wallets.

"Scumbag," I thought to myself as the doors of the lift closed over, not even considering it was me after all that put them there in the first place. We got into our car, we made our way to another branch of the same car rental company. I wanted to change our wheels in case the car was tagged. I also bought new clothes, shoes and travel cases to rid us of any tab trackers using Piezoelectricity. Hateful little trackers as they don't need batteries to operate and they are very tiny, extremely hard to spot if you're unaware of what to look for. Now to dispose of my mobile. I keep my memory card and smash the phone. I then use my mini stun gun to whack a few thousand volts into my tablet to blow any bugs that were placed in it as the voltage tolerance will be much lower than my tablet. It would definitely cure my tracking problem, but the damned thing might not work again, nevertheless, that was a risk I was willing to take. We needed to be clean before I could consider travelling to our next stop.

This was the secret place where Daniel and I were going to start over again. Feeling more secured we travelled by car for fifteen hours into the northern part of Canada to a place called Thunder Bay. A trusted family member is living there. Gerard is his name. He is my mother's brother and a retired SAS captain. He's had many tours of duty in and around Northern Ireland during his long career.

This was the man who was going to help me take down Northern Ireland's rapidly growing cancer, the RVA. I take out my map book and read over a few

97

helpful instructions drawn hastily onto the pages the night before to help me zero in on my meet point. I follow the instructions closely and end up at the docks overlooking the Sleeping Giant.

We spot a mobile café and get some snacks while waiting on Gerard. We didn't wait long when Gerard rolls up in his black Bronco truck. The wheels on the thing were enormous. He pulls up beside us and jumps out of the truck like he was still a young pup.

He was in very good shape for a fifty-five-year-old man. Gerard makes his way over to us with a huge smile on his face like someone who has won the lottery. "You boys alright, thank God you made it!" He then proceeded to give us awkward hugs. You must understand that Gerard is a man's, man. Being all touchy feely or showing emotion was alien to him so I knew he was trying with us, God bless him. We pack up the truck with what little belongings we had and made our way to Gerard's cabin which was located a further two hours away into the northern Canadian woods.

Chapter 7 - A killer plan

Jason and Daniel are settling into the outback way of life in rural Canada. They start to relax and enjoy their time together with Gerard, something they both needed after the life changing events they both been through.

Two incident free weeks past and we were settling well into our new way of life in Thunder Bay when by chance I came upon a news broadcast on my tablet that was covering the incident in Toronto that I was involved in. I shouldn't have hurt that officer, but my son comes first regardless of what was right or wrong. "Morning Jason, Coffee?" Gerard asked. "No thanks" I replied. The news broadcast has put me in a bad mood as I thought we would be free from worries over here in Canada. "What's up mate? You can tell by that mug of yours; you ain't happy." Gerard added before plonking some Bush Mills Whisky onto the table. "How bouts that, stop being a moody fucker and get that into you! Whatever you're worried about, we will sort it." Gerard continued. "I hope you got friends in high places over here as I'm now one of Canada's most wanted," I replied.

I took the bottle and necked a few gulps out of it. "Daddy?" Daniel said. I nearly spat the whiskey out as I thought Daniel was in the other room and he surprised me. I didn't want my son to see me drinking. He would have no idea what it was anyway. "Yes, son?" I said. "Can I please have a fizzy apple juice please?" Daniel asked. "Of course, give me two minutes, and I will bring it up to you in the living room."

I go over to Gerard's big stainless steel American fridge freezer and pull out a carton of apple juice and a bottle of carbonated water. He loves this drink and it's good for him, unlike those high street drinks that are unnaturally full of sugar and other chemicals. I mix it fifty, fifty in a glass and walk down to the living room to give it to him. "Can I borrow your tablet to watch my instructions?" he added pointing and looking hopeful. "Yes mate, I will get it for you now," I replied. As I made my way down to our room, I was hoping that the tablet would be working as I haven't turned it on since I zapped it. I rustled around in my duffle bag on the bed and took the tablet out and turned it on. It was fine. I connect it to the WIFI and found some videos he would like before handing it over to him. He was a content little fellow after everything that has happened to him. I pray that these events will be forgotten about as he gets older. "JASON, come back into the kitchen for a minute." Gerard bellowed. "Sit down, son. You are in a nasty predicament that's for fucken sure.

You and I both know these cunts won't go away. Being up north will only keep you off the RVA radar for a little while as they have recruits in all parts of the government, including the military and police. You can't reason with them son! These scumbags wholeheartedly agree with their method of systematically ethnically cleansing everything that is British from Northern Ireland which includes men, women and children. Look at the demographics of Northern Ireland; they are literally pushing our people ever Eastwards into the sea. All they care about is their fucking cause, a so called united Ireland of equals which do not include the likes of us. They won't give two fucks about killing you or the boy if you're a threat to them." Gerard said.

I wish he would stop harping on about this. I know I am in the shit! "We need to start killing these cunts now and on their home turf before they spread more of their brainwashed philosophy to those whom would be easily swayed." Gerard continued. "You're not telling me anything I don't already know. I need help as I am over my head. There are too many of them!" I replied. "STOP FUCKING WHINGING LIKE A LITTLE GIRL! You have the upper hand. You know where they live, where they work, what they look like! Stop worrying about the fucking CUNTS you work for as they don't give a shit about you or your family! The RVA seem to have free reign over the country almost like they already got their united Ireland given to them as you can't even wave your own flag in your own fucking country for fear of being jailed on trumped up charges. Ulster been politically corrupt since those terrorist bastards were elected to government by the brain-dead lefties who thought putting killers in suits would be a good idea? For a terrorist organisation that put their arms beyond use how come we are regularly finding hordes of weapons and semtex? Why are they still killing and carrying out paramilitary shootings? Why are there still bombs being made and used if we have a working peace process after all these years? Nothing has changed except the withdrawal of British troops and giving in to every fucking demand that evil, corrupt Republican Party wants! Why has there been no investigation into a party that only seems to hire ex RVA terrorists! I wonder do they have anyone of the Protestant faith working for them, unlike the other parties who have a wide range of people from different cultural backgrounds!" Gerard snarled. "GERARD!" I shouted, to snap him out of his rant. "Can you listen to me and keep that gob shut for a minute? I haven't been able to tell you or the family the extent of my involvement in the military until now. I am part of an operation called REVERT that the government has put together to fix the mistake of putting terrorists in politics. I believe the British secret service has a number of RVA sympathisers working within it that are directly responsible for the deaths of our agents and of the leaked Intel that would be useful for terrorist groups.

I am certain those dirty fuckers were solely involved in the death of my wife and near death of my son." I continued. "I understand and agree with your assessment of the situation; Northern Ireland finds itself in. Whatever possessed the powers to be that a democratic society would derive from people who killed and bombed thousands of innocent civilians because they didn't conform to their twisted beliefs? What the government failed to realise is now that they've bent their knee to terrorism, the terrorists have shown other militant groups around the world that you can take what you want if you are ruthless enough AND keep demanding more on top! Under the new government, we have now; understand this was a GROSS ERROR of judgement by past government officials and have created REVERT to erase this monumental mistake and finally be on the right side of the history books. The execution of the REVERT operation was to be carried out over a long period of time to disestablish the Republican Party who the RVA is associated with. We can't just kill all of them, just enough to cut off the head of the snake, the leaders!" I said.

Gerard leans in closer to me with a deathly look in his eyes. "We kill within the group and start a war with the other Republican movements. They won't know who to trust and become too paranoid to regroup or make any noise for fear of death. We need to kill them in such a way that it would put the fear of God in them. It must be public, it must remain anonymous, and it must be excruciating. That is how we got rid of the Ba'ath party in Iraq" Gerard replied. I smile and never let on that we were already doing that under Operation REVERT. I thought I would let him have this moment. We both lived for this type of hunting. Hunting the hunters using their own stinking tactics against them. Gerard was already prepared for this plan as he had a huge map of the UK and Ireland on his wall in the office. "This is where we start!" Gerard said in a triumphant voice. "Ok, let's do this," I replied. We create a detailed plan of attack that was already pretty much finalised back in Bangor, Northern Ireland. I give over my eyes-only folder to Gerard who will get an insight to in Operation REVERT. Gerard starts to look over the pages, we begin to make calculations on man power, weaponry and possible points of attack. We have a short window to do this as the iron curtain is closing in on me and making life difficult. I only have three false passports, and four connecting bank accounts left I can use before they too are compromised by MI5. This puts me in a tough position as money greases the wheels for any operation. I can't afford to make this a political war by letting these terrorists become political hero's as it will do nothing but ring a dinner bell for more RVA recruits. I can't just arrest them as they will use social media to highlight their cause and be eventually let out after a short custodial sentence which does nothing but fuel the fire even more. We must be ruthless and fast, so there is no time for them to think. That this cause they kill for will ultimately lead to their own death.

We want them to feel vulnerable that the corrupt laws they twist will not help them against this vigilante army which cannot be bought or bartered with. I want the government officials who secretly support these types of organisations to feel utterly terrified and know undoubtedly, they too could be killed if evidence was ever found connecting them to terrorists.

I start my plan off by putting my most trusted and battle-ready captains in charge of a team, we have seven teams altogether. I now need highly skilled foot soldiers that are already combat hardened as the RVA will outnumber us at least three to one. I know the very men and women to pick. My old battalion that I trained with overseas in Israel had the best of the best amongst its ranks. From these fine soldiers, I will select the deadly skills needed for each group to be successful for their individual missions. It suddenly dawns on me that I need to talk to Ian Stewart to make sure he is in on this. I know he is a temp, but he would make a good agent. I try a number of times but eventually get a hold of Ian and apologise for the way I behaved. He was understanding and reconfirmed he would be part of our plans. I tell him I will see him soon and that I would be informing the others of his full reinstatement regardless of what Trevor thought.

As I hang up the phone, I realise that things were starting to fit together nicely. I then get stuck back into our plan of attack. Those who are going into hot zones such as Belfast, Armagh, Lurgan and Dublin will need armoured transport with demolition, sniper and heavy artillery soldiers who will work together in two squadrons that will attack heavily protected RVA areas simultaneously on two different fronts. I will also need several lone wolfs to take out political leaders who are incontestably part of the RVA movement and directly involved in killings. This could be falsely seen as an attempted coup which will put British Special Forces against us within an hour of our campaign starting. There will be no negotiations as the use of deadly force will be authorised at the cost of eliminating the potential threat in the least amount of time. If we pull it off in time and are successful after these events, those socialist M.Ps will be made to reconsider their affiliation with known terrorist organisations. Timing will be essential to this operation as we are not only facing the RVA but also law enforcement and military intervention. I know from working in MI5 all these years that the reaction time of police in Northern Ireland is considerably slower than that of American due to mitigating factors of possible terrorist ambush.

So each call is scrutinised and methodically planned out before any police enter the area to investigate the emergency call. This gives us roughly a 25-minute window.

The helicopter will be issued first to give Intel on the situation from the air and advise local police authorities and if a situation seems too risky, the military will get involved which brings our time frame up to 50 min's as police will not intervene until the odds are stacked in their favour. We need to be fast and disappear quickly from each attack. The only way to disappear without being followed is to kill all cameras, and that has been already covered. My man on the inside will take the entire grid down with one click of a button. Then rewrite and scramble the security algorithms which will take the government computer geeks hours to fix. Next, I need communications to be intercepted so we can keep one step ahead of the authorities and avoid them. I will get Mark to add our communications relay to the military tower on Black Mountain. From there we can access on our GPS map systems where all the government vehicles are in real time as they are all wired into the grid. The tower is unmanned with an electric security fence and three CCTV cameras. Mark can do this job blindfolded, wee buns.

Next, we need to steal the vehicles needed to carry out the attacks and store them without being traced to our temporary HQ. We pick cars that are in abundance in Northern Ireland with the most popular colour being red. That way we can just blend in with the civilians. The cars would need to be at least 2.0lt, but we also needed a few vans as they hold more men for transport. Once we acquire the vehicles from second-hand auctions or as a last resort stolen. We replace all the tyres with run flats; windows are upgraded with blast proof laminates. We also bolster the chassis and weld armour plating to the inside of the vehicle's weak points. This will take at most approximately five hours to accomplish with a team of twenty as we already have the materials needed on standby. Now to strategically place our HQ. There was already a place I knew we could use as I scouted for an HQ months ago and kept the findings to myself. It was a disused farm I could rent in Castlewellan, just off the Clonbadre Rd which had two huge industrial buildings I could use to put REVERT into action. It was rural and secluded with high terrain almost on all sides which would mask our visibility and noise. This was crucially important as it would be a hive of activity over the next couple of days and we needed to keep a low profile. I forwarded the funds to Mark in the tune of 100K, so he had payments for our operatives and money left over to lease the farm and purchase the transport we needed. I ordered seven estate cars; seven high performance cars which would be blockers. We also needed five black transit vans.

Mark was making the purchases for me in my absence, and my captains were organising the day to day operations until I arrive in Northern Ireland 4 days from now. My team is utterly efficient as they complete the checklist in three days.

They had a whole day to rest up and prep for action. The time to initiate REVERT in T minus 32 hours and counting. I dismantle the war room and everything we have done and squash it onto one memory stick. Gerard and I burn everything out the back that could incriminate him in any way. I'm up to my neck in it, so it doesn't matter about me anymore. If things go to plan, I will be exonerated. If things don't go to plan....well I don't want to even think about that as I am all too aware what happens to people like me behind closed doors. "Well Gerard, we've done it!" I said to him while holding my wee man up on my shoulders looking at the bonfire we created. "Told Ya son, have confidence in yourself. I can't wait to see these scumbags finally wiped out!" Gerard replied.

"I appreciate you looking after Daniel while I am away. I know babysitting is a waste of your talents, but I couldn't have thought of a safer place for my son than with my hard as nails SAS uncle. If they got to Daniel, it would be over for me; you know that don't you?" I said to Gerard.

"Aye, I do Jason. That I do know for sure. Rest easy as Daniel, and I are going to be safe here. The house is fully stocked for a month, so we won't be going anywhere to bump into anyone and my house is like Fort Knox so even if they do find us they won't be getting in. Stay focused as your mind needs to be sharp for tomorrow." Gerard replied.

With that, we locked up and went to bed. I let Daniel sleep in my bed that night as he said he saw monsters in his room. I didn't mind as this could be the last time I spent with Daniel. I started to well up but caught myself on as I was again not having confidence in my abilities. Just remember who you fight for, I thought to myself. I then drifted off to sleep. The next morning, I was awakened by a knee to the chest. It was Daniel doing his usual tossing and turning. I look at the time on my watch, 6:30 am. Time to get up. I lean over to Daniel and whisper "Do you want pancakes, poo face?" "Poo face" is an endearing term I use for Daniel as he can't resist to fight me after I call him it. Sure enough, "WHAT!" said Daniel. He rushed at me with a volley of punches and kicks. I'm going to miss our play fights together. "Alright, you win! You want pancakes or what?" I said. "Can I have a sandwich?" Daniel replied. "Of course," I said. With breakfast agreed upon we both got up and went to the kitchen. I opened the fridge, and my business phone started to ring. "Fuck!" I said loudly. "You shouldn't say that daddy, say sorry!" Daniel scolded. "Sorry darling." I replied as I answered the phone in haste.

I knew something was wrong as they never phone unless there has been a change of circumstance. "ID authentication please," A computer generated voice asked. "45035XXA " I answer.

After what seemed to be a long pause, I hear a familiar voice. "Jay? We need to put your flight forward by three hours as the weather will be too dodgy of the west coast of Northern Ireland at the time you will be arriving. For your flight, not to be rerouted or cancelled you need to leave now. We have people who are on standby for you." Captain Rodgers explained. "Understood Captain, on route," I replied. I end the call and look down at Daniel. I see his sad eyes looking back at me. As I kneel down, Daniel could see there was something wrong by the look on my face. "Sweetheart, Daddy has to go out and do some busy work now, but I will be back later. I might be even gone overnight, but I will be coming back with presents and sweets for the best boy in the whole wide world!" Daniel's eyes didn't look sad anymore, and he leapt up and gave me a big hug.

"Uncle Gerard, uncle Gerard, Daddy is buying me loads of presents and sweets cause I'm the best boy in the entire world!" Daniel shouted as he ran out of the kitchen towards Gerard in the living room. "Are you now? What's your da getting me?" Gerard asked Daniel. "Nothing!" Daniel replied as he ran giggling away from Gerard who was chasing him.

"Gerard, it's time" I shouted over to him. "You got the keys to the bike?" I asked Gerard. "Yes son, on top of the microwave. You got everything you need?" Gerard said. I gave him a big hug and said "Yes." Then I shouted for Daniel. "Yes, Dad?" Daniel said. "Give me a big hug and kiss. I will see you as soon as I can. Be good for uncle Gerard, won't you?" I said to Daniel. "I will," Daniel said before running off again. I'm glad I am leaving on a happy note. I closed the door and make my way over to the back of the garage. Gerard has a dirt bike that will be perfect for me to use to get to the landing strip. I can use off road tracks which will allow me to avoid any main roads that may now be entertaining checkpoints looking for yours truly. Gerard knew what he was doing when he bought this dirt bike as it goes like the clappers in all terrains and this is exactly what I need to get myself out of any unwanted encounters with the police or special agents looking for me. I whip off the canvas covering the bike, and there she was, a 53.6 Stroke engine with five speeds. The wheels on it were massive enough to tear into any terrain. I walk it around to the front of the house where Gerard and Daniel were on the front porch looking over at me. I hop on the bike and try to balance myself with my heavy gear bag weighing me down. Once I had balance, I turn the ignition on and kick start the engine. "Roooooooooarr!!" couple of accelerated twists of the gas before putting it into gear and taking off. Daniel was covering his ears as the bike was making such a racket and Gerard gave me the thumbs up. I waved goodbye to them and spun the back wheels out as I was speeding down the long lane to the roadside. I make it to the airfield in less than 30 minutes with no encounters with the law after taking a few short cuts across fields.

I see the hangar I need to meet my crew at. I drive over and park the bike inside the hangar. "Major Wright! Major, over here." Captain Rodgers yelled. "Hello my old friend, you came all this way yourself for me!! I'm honoured." I shouted over to him. "I didn't trust anyone else to get you home on schedule. We are just going through the pre-flight checks; go on in as we have food and drinks waiting for you. We leave in 20 mins." Captain Rogers said. "Good work, see you when you're done," I said.

Flight checks are done on our Gulfstream G650. I strap up and look out the small windows as we taxi along to the main runway to wait for our turn to take off. The plane comes to a slow stop and waits for clearance from the tower. I can hear and see the pilots as they have the door open. "Gulfstream, XPT56, Regan Tower, cleared for take-off, runway 09. Repeat" The Tower continued. "Gulfstream, XPT56, Regan Tower, cleared for Take-off, runway 09.

Acknowledged." Captain Rodgers repeated. "XPT56 you are clear to proceed." The tower said. The engines started to whine and get ever higher in pitch before the plane started speeding down the runway at a fantastic speed. The Gs' were pushing me right back into my seat as it took off the ground. I watch the ground below me get ever further and further away, and all I could think about was my son was down there, away from his daddy.

The anger builds up in me again as the reality of the situation becomes clear. The RVA doesn't know it yet, but death is only hours away from them tonight.

Chapter 8 - Reassessing the situation

Michael explains to Brendan the events that have taken place over the last few days. They then start to put a plan together to kill the shadows by using the tagged clothes that Michael is now wearing.

"Yes Brendan, we will use that chip shop down the road from St. Mark's church just outside Newry to set up an ambush. There are about five routes out of the place into highly populated areas where we can get lost in the crowd." Michael said. Brendan was pondering the idea in his head while closely studying the map. (Mobile phone tune plays) "Sorry Brendan, I need to take this," Michael said while Brendan didn't take much notice of him. "Hello, whatcha want now? I'm trying to lay low here after that attempt on my life or didn't you know that? You're the last person I want to speak to now. How the fuck could you let that happen to me, Trevor!" Michael said. "I am really sorry about that, but I can't get that fucker, Jason, to back off the Operation, so we tried to take him out a few days ago with Colin Murphy, using that orange bitches Intel on Jason. We fucked up." Trevor said. "No, you and Colin fucked up. Don't be fucking bringing me into your shit!" Michael snapped back. "Ok, Ok I will rephrase it, Fucksake, you're a sensitive bastard. I have a big problem that needs to be fixed ASAP! Jason will have this who, what, where and why sorted in the next few days, guaranteed, which leaves me fucked! I need you to tie up some loose ends for me. Jason has taken his son to Canada today, and I need you to kill him and the boy" Trevor said.

"My associates over in Canada would be happy to take on this job. They won't be cheap, about £15k each plus my usual fee of 5k for setting it up. Were you able to obtain any other Intel on him, place where he is staying?" Michael asked. "I'm confused Michael; you sound like more of a greedy business man than someone who wants to fight for the cause. You're a fucking leader in the RVA, and I have to pay you to do shit that your fans think you do for free. If I didn't pay you or advise you, where would the RVA be?" Trevor said. "Well Trevor for one thing, you're an English prick so never confuse yourself for one of us. The second thing is we would be doing our thing with or without you. You're not the only one that gives us money and intelligence reports. We are everywhere. You want to play with the big boys; it costs you, you understand you fucking prick!" Michael said angrily. "Fuck you!" Trevor replied before hanging up. Michael walks back into the kitchen and sits down with Brendan.

"Who was that?" inquires Brendan. "Nobody, a fucking bullroot! All sorted now, so it is!" Michael replied. "Ring, ring, ring!" Brendan's house phone went. Brendan gets up and walks over to the phone and answers it.

"Hello...Yes...He said what? Paul? Ah no... not Paul! Listen leave it with me a wee second will you and I'll sort it out and call you back? I can't apologise enough for these events. I assure you there will be no repeat of them. That's grand...bye." Went Brendan's conversation. Brendan walks behind Michael and places both hands on his shoulders before landing a heavy right hook across the back of his head which knocks him to the floor. Michael furiously shouts at Brandon "What the FUCK did you do that for?!" Brendan pulls out his gun and points it at Michael. "Who are Ya?" Brandon shouts. All the commotion alerted Brandon's wife who comes rushing into the kitchen. "What's going on here?" She demanded. "Shut up you stupid woman! Fuck off to the living room, NOW!" Brendan's wife did what she was told and went into the living room and closed the door behind her.

"Who are Ya?" Brandon shouts again. "You know me, Brendan, what the fuck are you doing?" Michael replies. "The Michael I know is a smart man who is loyal to the cause. Loyal to Ireland! Who is this bastard I see before me who does not follow orders of high ranking commanders? That's punishable by death!" Brendan said while getting closer to Michael on the floor.

"Trevor rang you?" Michael said. "YES, he did! He informs me you've ignored orders and got wee Paul McMahon killed by complete incompetence. He says that big fucking oaf Ian from the Agency most likely nutted him as wee Paul was put out of your vehicle in a loyalist estate. IAN'S ESTATE OF ALL FUCKING PLACES! You might as well of shot him yourself! Let me tell you this now. You're on very fucking thin ice! You ever ignore a commanding officer like Trevor or ask him for money again I will personally bury you where no one will find you! That man is the keystone to our operations, we should be paying him, but he is a loyal Republican son of Ireland who fights for his people and not for what he can fucking scobe off his fellow kinsmen!" Brandon angrily scolded. Michael shamefully nodded his head and got to his feet. "Now you ring Trevor back and do whatever he asks, or you're a dead man," Brendan said, still pointing the gun at Michael.

Michael got his mobile out and rang Trevor. "Hello, Trevor? I just wanted to say how sorry I am for not giving you the respect you deserve. I don't want your money, and I will sort that wee problem out for you in Canada when you forward me the rest of the details I will need to locate that man. OK, will put him on now."

Michael said to Trevor. "He wants to speak to you Brandon," Michael said while handing him the mobile. "Yes, Trevor....Yes.... Hold on. Michael, come you here next to me." Brendan asked while he holstered his gun. Suddenly Brendan punched Michael in the face while still holding the phone in the air.

That knocked Michael to the floor again. Brandon then lined up a weighty kick to the ribs. Michael was wheezing in pain. Brendon put the mobile close to the heavy breathing of Michael then back to his ear. "Yes, no problem. Speak to you later, bye-bye." Brandon said to Trevor before ending the call. Brandon throws the phone gently on top of Michael. "That punch was from Trevor. The kick to your ribs was from Paul's family. That fucking ambush you wanted to do is no longer happening. You take care of that fuck Jason and his kid in Canada now!" Brendan said sternly. "I'm sorry Brandon, my heads away with it, so it is. I love you like a brother, and I hate the thoughts of you seeing me in a different light. I will make things right. I am a true brother to the cause. No more fuck ups from me," Michael said as he got up and walked towards the back door holding his side where he just got booted.

"Sit down you stupid cunt. Cuppa tea I think is in order after all that shite. We need to keep the head clear and figure out your next moves." Brandon said. Michael came back from the door and sat down where he was before. He had a smile on his face as Brandon said "We," indicating he would help him with this situation he now finds himself in. "I know a few mates that would take care of the problem, just for the fun of it. They are friends to our struggle, but they are not Republicans, they are Russian and would expect a token gesture of money to keep face if you understand me." Michael said. "Just how much of a gesture would they want?" Brendon asked. "About 30k for the whole lot. Just need a place for them to start looking, and they do the rest." Michael replied. "Beep!Beep!" Michael grabbed his phone as a text message arrived. It was from Trevor with the information they needed on the whereabouts of Jason. He opened it up and read the contents aloud to Brendan. "Trevor contacted the mobile phone provider for Jason and inquired about any overseas calls to Canada.

We got a number for a five-star Hotel called The Royal Edward Located in central Toronto!" Michael said excitedly. "Well, what are you waiting for? Sort it out now with your little friends." Brendan replied while putting the tea bags in the cups. Michael phoned his contact in Ottawa Canada, explained the situation, and wired the money over to them through his mobile banking. This was looking like a straight forward job, and Michael thought no more about it. Michael stayed overnight at Brendan's and left after breakfast in the morning. He had to phone for a cab into the nearest town to TWAC some new wheels to go home. While in the back of the taxi he was thinking of what would have happened if he had lost his temper and killed Brandon last night. Brandon is one of the RVAs eldest commanders and has great respect and contacts not only in Ireland but across the world. I wouldn't have gotten away with it. I would have been tortured and shot for definite, he thought to himself.

As the taxi drops Michael off at the nearest village to Brandon, he starts looking around the cars like we would in a car show room. "Ah, there it is!" Michael said to himself as he starts walking towards a grey beat up looking truck. "Easy to break into and solid looking for those times when you need to ram your way through a road block. I'll take it!" Michael said and chuckled to himself. As he got in, he twiddled with the wires which tripped the trucks alarm off. He didn't even blink, Michael just kept on striking the live battery wire across the exposed ignition switch and "Brrooooooom" the engine started. Michael pulled out from the parking space and started to drive towards the border and on to Belfast.

It takes about two hours for Michael to travel home. As he pulls up to his house, he can see people have already been hard at work patching up the house with new windows and revamped brickwork. He also notices lights on in his house, which made him happy as he will have someone to talk to and update him on the latest goings on. Two of Michael's friends come out of the front door of his house and down to the truck to greet him. "We've the place practically looking like new for Ya," Robbie said to Michael. "Well show me what all you've done," Michael said as he exited the truck. The house did look well, in some cases better than before. Michael had a good look at him and examined every room before heading to the kitchen. "Cuppa tea fellas?" Michael said to his friends. "Yes, yes, that would be great" they all excitedly said.

All of them stood around the kitchen without saying a word. Michael read their faces; they wanted to ask him something. "Well spit it out, GO ON!"

Michael said breaking the silence. A few of them started to stutter "Well..." and could say no more until Robbie spoke up. "Where is wee, Paul? He was last seen with you and his family are very worried about him." Robbie said to Michael. "What are you trying to say, Robbie, that I had something to do with it? Well, I didn't! He is however dead. He was probably killed by that big fucker Ian Stewart. Well, that's what Brendan has told me anyway." Michael said while looking at the kitchen ceiling.

"Robbie, you go around to Paul's house and break the news. Take this as well; there are about...five hundred notes in there. Tell them we are sorry for their loss....and ... we can't locate his body at the moment, but we will in time. You got all of that Robbie?" Michael said. "Yes, Michael. I will do it now." Robbie replied. Robbie left the men in the kitchen and left the house to deliver the bad news to Paul's family. Michael knew because of that incident his popularity would go down and someone might challenge him for his position he now holds. He was getting nervous as the men in his kitchen didn't want to look at him.

"We are having a social gathering in Belfast next week to bring our brothers and sisters together and discuss new ways forward to uniting Ireland. We all know that killing Brits will be involved, but we just have to agree on whom." Michael said with a grin as he held his tea cup up in the air. The rest of the men smiled and clinked their tea cups together in a mocking gesture of a toast. "To Queen and country," One of the men said. "No surrender!" Said another as they all laughed. Michael relaxed after that tense meeting and was focused on a renewed war footing that would take his name even higher in the ranks. Maybe even further than Brendan's he thought.

For the next few days, Michael delegated tasks to his supporters and comrades to organise a kick ass meeting with loads of booze, music and triumphant speeches designed to motivate the RVA recruits for another push against anything British. He would organise the RVA youth to interrupt British marches and festivities which would incite riots which he could operate in for his next kills. Michael liked nothing better than a huge group of loyalists gathering together. If he was careful, he could take out many of them at once if he were to predict where the Loyalist mob would go.

Michael knew this would bring him back into favour with his supporters if the nights' events went off without a hitch. What he wasn't going to be expecting was Jason planning an attack at the very venues he was about to use.

112

Michael had everything in place. The VIPs accepted their invitations to speak or just to attend. These VIPs included high ranking political party members, Irish celebrities such as the comedian Doran Davis and German pop singer Pumpter Vixin. Michael put the squeeze on a few alcohol suppliers to supply the drinks free of charge. He also had a local DJ organised for the after-party disco. After a long busy day getting his party partly organised Michael sits back in his chair and closes his eyes. I wonder how those boys are doing in Canada he thought to himself. "Ring, Ring" went Michaels land line. His eyes immediately opened looking at the phone, almost sensing it was trouble.

He could feel the bad vibes with every ring it made. As he grabs the receiver, he leans forward in his chair and holds his head with his free hand. "Michael, we lost two of our own today trying to cap that Jason fellow and his son. This guy took two of my best and slaughtered them before they even got into his hotel room. Who the fuck is he?! Why did you not fore warn us this guy had tactical skills?! We expect a further deposit of 50K for the loss of our men and their replacements due to bad Intel on your part!" The voice said.

"Ha ha ha, yeah, I won't be paying that! You, however, will honour our contract and get that fucking job done before I jump on a plane and fucking kill you myself instead! Wanker!" Michael replied as the line went dead. Brendan can't know about this as that was the absolute last mistake I was allowed to make. My life is now on borrowed time. I hesitantly phone the jack ass back I was speaking to as my contact for Canada was now one of the deceased. "Hello? Don't hang up. How about 40K to finish the job?...You want it wired today?? I need some time to gather that kind of money...No, No, No..hold on, yes it will be done tonight. Same account? OK, bye." Michael ended his conversation with the new contact. Anger and frustration were creeping over him as Michael knew if he tells Brendan they didn't kill Jason he would be tortured and killed as the RVA can't show any weakness when it comes to missions. It is either get the job done by any means necessary or never show your face again under penalty of death.

There was another option, but Michael didn't want to do it. It just kept repeating over and over in his head, kill Brendan, and take over as Chief Commander of the RVA. After all, he was considered the face of the movement. If it worked, he would have to answer to no one. That fuck in Canada will be waiting for a long time on that 40K, he smirked to himself.

The decision was made, Michael would take out Brendan. He thought long and hard how he was going to kill him and then it hit him. He would leak information to the Loyalists to do the job for him. That was it, the perfect take down that would never have a trail leading back to him! Now all he had to do was wait for an opportunity to present itself.

Chapter 9 – Vengeance is mine

The plan is flawless, everything's ready and in place. REVERT was covertly given the go ahead unbeknownst to Trevor. Even with the odds stacked against him, he would carry out his mission to the bitter end. Remembering that this mission was not just about vengeance, it was about making the world a safer place. Killing his enemies by his own hand was just an added bonus.

"God forgive me for what I am about to do." I quietly pray to myself. If this goes right, two hundred and thirty evil souls will be extirpated tonight. These cunts say they are at war with the British government? Then I say let them have their war and let's be done with it! In one 110-minute block, all Operation REVERT teams will have solved a problem that has been consuming Northern Ireland like a cancer for over 50 years. It's a bit poignant when you look at that soon to be fact. These people have been compiled from a long list of key personnel who are involved in all areas of the Republican movement. We even got a few radicals that are from different denominations who are killing civilians and spreading their poison which is included in that number. The Murphey twins, Eion & Douglas and their comrade Paul Watson will be my squads first hit.

Again, a dreamlike feeling engulfs me as I sit in the small cabin by myself staring at my equipment. All I can hear is the whining of the jet engines and the sound of my foot tapping on the floor of the plane with my black steel toe boots. I take out the photo of my family from my inside pocket and just gaze at them. I love you guys so much! "Time to keep my promise sweetheart," I said softly to myself. I place them on the table along with my wallet and other personal belongings. I waited a long time for this and have prepared myself mentally and physically at the gym through weight training, aerobics and Krav Maga over the years which is an Israeli martial art which is shown to be very effective in urban warfare.

I pull out a black velvet satchel and put it on my table. I unravel the ties and expose two black handled Wakizashi swords. I hold one by the handle and extend it in front of me, twisting it slowly, watching the cabin lights refract up and down the blade. It was a magnificent bad ass sword! The blade on this type of sword is one of the sharpest and most durable you can get. I place both of them in holsters which are attached to my ballistic vest. Now I pull out my special razor wire garrotte which I intend to use on the worst of the killers. It was also a thing of beauty.

I made it myself from the bits and pieces I ordered from the internet, but this is not what I am going to use to kill Michael. I have something much better in store for him. As the hour's pass, we finally enter the airspace over Northern Ireland. The plane lands quietly at a small air strip outside Enniskillen. It was practically deserted for our arrival. As the plane, gently trundles to its parking spot I put on the rest of my combat gear, I checked my weapons at least twice, I am good to go. I test my ear piece to make sure we receive constant communication throughout this mission. As the jet comes to a halt, three black armoured Land Rovers come quickly rolling up to the plane. I have to put my game face on now. I finally throw my pack over my shoulder and make my way out and down the steps, over to my squad.

Ian is part of my team and has everyone prepped for combat. I greet the team. I wait for a moment before addressing my squad. "All of you tonight are here because you love your country. You want your children to grow up in a safe environment. Free from terrorists, radicals and sectarianism. You are here because you believe what you are about to do will ultimately make that dream of a free and safe society a reality. I, LIKE YOU, am certain, that every one of these targets is not only legit but deserve the repercussions we are about to deliver onto them. These repercussions were brought by their OWN hand, because of their OWN actions." I now bow my head and my team follows.

"Lord make our hand steady and our aim true. Protect us this night and make our operation a success! AMEN." I prayed. "NOW, WHOS WITH ME?!" I shout. "WE ARE!" the squad replied. "WELL LET START KILLING THESE FUCKING TERRORIST SCUMBAG BOG RATS!" I shouted as I made my way over to my group. My team of 12 bang their clenched fists against their body armour over and over again. Making an almighty racket that can only be compared to the warriors of days gone by, banging their swords against their shields to frighten the enemy. Working themselves into a frenzy. Whooping and cheering as they get into their jeeps, ready to make history. The one fact about history is that it is always written by the victors. This is why we can't fuck this operation up. The people, not the government are going to take back control of their country from the corrupt grip of the politicians that let this happen in the first place. The clear night was cold and the bright moon, lit our way down the road. It reminded me of a passage in the bible, Revelations "And I looked, and

116

behold a pale horse: and his name that sat on him was Death, and Hell followed with him." I have no doubt that for their sins these RVA scumbags were going first class straight to hell. Our first six teams split off and go to their assigned areas in County Londonderry, County Antrim and County Fermanagh. We were still far off our first targets.

As we drive into Belfast the weather seems to be on our side, giving us a cool, clear night. Which was welcomed as our tactical gear was making it very warm for us. I hate driving through Anderson's town as the place has that many hidey holes and vantage points which makes it ideal for cowards that like to keep their distance when trying to riddle you with bullets. Here comes the propaganda shite, all strewn across the walls were murals, posters and flags blaming today's British people for killing their innocent volunteers who want a free Ireland of equals. Some people actually believe their bullshit but it's like I always say; there is no medicine to fix stupid! Another five vehicles split off again and head to County Tyrone and County Armagh to their assigned destinations. It takes another fifty-nine minutes to reach our destination in County Down. We park the vans about five car spaces away from a well-known RVA supporter's pub in Warrenpoint, Intel reported that three of our targets are known to frequent the place. Our spotter confirms that they are all there as we pull up. I pull my balaclava on and bring it tight down over my head. The van stops and the side door gets jolted open. We all quickly pile out and stack up, making our way over to the building. My tech man jumps out of our stack formation and makes a B-line to the main transformer power box at the back of their building. To my surprise, the power cut took out some of the surrounding area lights which put the entire place in a blanket of darkness. Our team is prepared for this as we have special light reactive contacts that allow us to see 35% better in the dark than those without them which gives us one of many tactical advantages against the enemy. Night vision goggles are only beneficial in wide open areas where there is no light from street lamps or houses. Plus, they are a nightmare to shoot with, fucking liability to be honest.

We now divide ourselves into two teams. One for the front and the back of the building. Our spotters are now authorised to engage the enemy with their suppressed sniper rifles as well as giving us updates in real time. My desert eagle tightly gripped in my hand, the safety is off, and my blue laser sight is turned on ready for carnage. As we approach we can hear commotion in the pub. We have all memorised the faces of our targets and understand that we are taking no prisoners.

117

Making our way to the front, we pause at the entrance. My heart is beating really hard with excitement and fear at the same time. "ENGAGE!" I commanded over the comms. Ian busts the front door open and takes into the building to the left, I go right and see Eion at the end of the bar, without hesitation I take him out. POP! POP! Double tap to the head, "target one down." I updated over comms. The back wall was spattered in his blood which covered the majority of the RVA hall of fame photos, the shameless bastards.

I smirk to myself whilst trying to stay focused. Eion should be actually thanking me as he will be up on the wall now soon enough, next to his hero's. His lifeless body lay in a heap beside the bar stools. We stopped stacking and took up positions of strength, in case there was going to be a fire fight. We quickly make our way into the back room when we heard gun fire. POP! POP! POP! POP! "Target three down," Ian states over the radio. Fuck! That sounded messy. I thought to myself. As we enter the back room we saw the left overs of Paul Watson. Another one for the wall I thought. I ask Ian's squad to cover the ground floor while we sweep upstairs for target two. "Yes, sir!" Ian replied. We approach stairs and check to see if it was safe to proceed. "Clear!" I said as I lead my squad up the stairs and into the hallway. We buddy up and take the rooms in tandem. First two rooms empty. Where the fuck is target two? It's hard to concentrate with all these bastards screaming in panic. "target two spotted on the roof, engage?" whispers sniper one into our ear pieces. A sense of relief fills me "Engage!" I reply.

Sniper one lines up his sights as Douglas hides behind a chimney with his piece drawn. Sniper one can't see him anymore, so he turns on his thermal scope and changes his round to a high-velocity bullet. It's a beautiful looking bullet with a light weight red ballistic cap which is shaped around a steel alloy penetrating shell which has a desensitized packed charge. Basically, it will punch a hole through that concrete chimney block as if it wasn't there! BOOOMMM! A small hole instantly appears through the chimney bricks and a bloody mist is created by the missing half of Douglas's head.

His body slowly slumps over and then slides quickly down the roof tiles on his back and off the edge of the building. He has a death grip on his gun as he smashes to the ground into a bloody mess. "Target two down." Sniper one states. "Fallout!" I shout over the radio as we all regroup and stack out of the building, back to our transport. The whole thing took less than five minutes but guaranteed the rest of our targets have been informed of the situation, so time was against us now. My data comms man looks at the data streaming in, our percent calculator updates our live status. We are at 10% with the first wave of attacks. So far so good I think to myself. Our Data man updates us seconds later from our teams in Londonderry and Strabane, "19%! The lads in Derry & Strabane took them out with no fuss!" he announced. We are informed by our target spotter at the second site in Andersonstown, that the RVA are on the move. He is closely monitoring the situation, unbeknownst to the enemy. Back in the van, we rock around in our bumpy transport speedily driving back to Andersonstown. It shouldn't take more than fifty minutes as we know the scuttled RVA will regroup in Belfast.

As we pull up to a building close to their RVA strong hold, we immediately spot the RVA guards placed all over the area. There were at least seven, but they have scarfs covering their faces. We can't just shoot them before getting a positive id. FUCK! Data man announces "Dungannon was successful and stats are at 23%!" We all are grinning, but the good news doesn't help us with this new turn of events. I was not going to be the team that fucks the plan up! I get the squads attention and inform them of the situation. "We are in a bit of a predicament now that the RVA are spooked. They covered their faces and they appear to be unarmed which throws a right fucking spanner into the works when it comes to legalities. The operation is still a go but we need to take each one down, and if it's a positive identification, we kill them. Those who are not a positive hit, cuff and secure them. Make sure you take any credentials they have off them. We can't afford any fuck ups on this one, ARE WE CLEAR?" I asked. "YES SIR!" the squad replies.

We all get out and stack up and make our way to a hedge clearing to analyse the current situation further. It became quickly obvious that they are waiting for us. Our advantage of surprise was now gone. Twenty-five minutes is all the time we have left to get this done or we've failed. We got enough people in our squad to take everyone down at once, but I don't want to be in a fire fight with them as they would just bunker down and ride it out which we do not have time for. So right now, they are spooked as they do not know the situation they are in yet. We will attack by stealth with our suppressed weapons. Everyone gets assigned a target. I pick the biggest thug, loitering near the entrance of the supporter's club. "Move out, take targets down," I instructed. Everyone began to silently make their way to their targets. We all get into position carefully not to get noticed. There is little to no cover for me to hide so I run around to the back end of the building and approach from the bottom of the road which is a steep hill. I need to be quick or this will end badly.

As I move silently ever closer I notice a small automatic gun peeking out from under his shirt. Your fair game now my son I think to myself as I unholster my blades slowly. Making my way stealthily behind him. "You fucking cunt," I whispered as I slowly insert both blades into his back, through his lungs and out the front of his chest. His body started to stiffen as he went into shock but not a sound was made as his lungs no longer had the air needed to speak. Muffled take downs and sporadic pops echoed in the square. Everything was going to plan until the gun fire started bouncing off the ground near our positions. We were made! I scream "ENGAGE FREE FIRE!" We had multiple gun fire coming from all directions. I yell "What in the FUCK are you waiting for sniper one and two?"

As I scramble behind a low-level wall with bullets narrowly missing my legs. I know this as I could feel the sharp sting of fragmenting pieces of concrete hitting them. Keeping my head down I repeat "Sniper one and two, come in!" No one answered. Comms may be down, I thought to myself. I grit my teeth as I feel the operation starting to unravel around me. I quickly holster my blades and take out my automatic rifle lovingly named; "Arsehole", as it can make you a new one! My rifle was already locked and loaded. I switch off my safety and return fire on the upper floors across the road to those who were trying their very best to send me straight to the morgue. I had loads of ammo with me so I didn't need to be tidy about it. I was enjoying myself in a way as if I had to die in this battle at least it was going to be on my terms as no one dragged me here.

BOOM! BOOM, "YES!" Jason shouts. My little angels were still with us as I watch chunks being punched through the second floor. A couple of windows on the second floor were spattered red with blood showing me that the snipers had hit their marks. Using the covering fire, I try to find some of my crew on up the street. I find Ian and Conway, they inform me that some of the comms are down. I signal the squad to disengage and fall back by numbers to the transport. Back at the transport I regroup and organise our new approach. No casualties, they all came back. I was going to get my team a second bite at the cherry. "Well, it wasn't that big of a surprise the twats took up positions on the higher ground and made use of the square. We are going back in but this time through the houses." I said. "You got those door charges Ian?" I ask. "Yes, Sir!" Ian replied. "I am splitting the squad into "A" team and "B" team. You know which

120

one you are in. "B" team start from that house at the end of the square and we will start on that house across from you and meet in the RVA compound.

My eyes in the sky will seek high ground and support us where needed. Questions?" I said. "Sir, What about the back gardens of these houses. They could escape Sir", Lieutenant Shields asked. "Lieutenant, excellent question, there are a few reasons we are doing this. Firstly, there is a high level of civilian houses around here, so we need to minimise our free fire outside this square. Secondly if one or two escapes, we will catch them later. Our prizes are in the supporter's club which is walled off at the back at the height of fifteen feet. They are cornered that's why they are making it hard for us to approach the front. Bursting through three or four houses to get into that compound is our only goal at the moment. Any other questions? No? Fallout!" I stated.

As we headed back into the square we had the odd bullet ricochet in our direction. Couldn't hit the side of a barn some of these volunteers I laugh to myself.

We break down the door of our first house and secure the property with no resistance as it looked like nobody lived here in years. "CLEAR!" Ian shouted. That was my cue to place the door charge on the wall. "COVER!" I shout before detonating the charge. BOOOOOM! Instant door way. We toss three flash bangs in at different directions to make sure we got the whole place covered. BOOOM!! BOOOM!! BOOOM!! We rush through and again prepare to secure the building. I check in to team "A" to monitor their progress. "Team "A", Status?" I called. Nothing. I forgot we don't have comms working. YOU FUCKING MUPPET, I thought to myself.

I look out the window carefully to see if they have made it to the next house. I know they have set the charge off as the brown smoke is billowing out the entrance. They will be fine. They WILL be fine. I keep reminding myself. "CLEAR!" Ian shouts. I am up again, pack and whack the wall. "COVER!" I shout. "BOOOOOOM!" Wow, that was messy. The stale smoke of thousands of cigarettes fills the room as the nicotine laced walls released its' payload. Gun fire erupts through the opening and makes everyone dive for cover. Corporal Chris was hit in the shoulder but his ballistic armour took the impact. "You OK bro?" I asked Chris. Chris gives me a quick nod of the head and gets his game face on.

We quickly find cover as we have no idea how many of those RVA cocks are next door, nor their position. "Fuck it!" I say to myself as I quickly grab two frag grenades from the back of my belt and toss them individually through the hole in the wall.

I was saving them for Michael but they will be put to good use here. I throw one near and the other one further away for maximum damage. The RVA know not to try and throw them back as it's a safe bet we cooked them before we lobbed them. "BWOOOM!.....BWOOOM!" The shockwave of the exploding grenades shook the entire building. I started to listen out for the quiet moans which let me know it's sort of safe to have a look inside. "Yes!" I shouted. "Do my eyes deceive me? You're on my list sunshine." It was Conner Duffy lying on the floor behind the sofa. He was coughing up blood which to my guesstimate means he has approximately 40 minutes to live if he doesn't receive medical attention right away. This bastard has a lot of blood on his hands. Look at him writhing in pain. I wonder if he is giving any thought to all the good people he has nutted over his lifetime. His last campaign of violence consisted of civilians being terrorised and killed off in both Protestant and Roman Catholics areas. Ethnically cleansing Protestants from the West of Northern Ireland and Killing Roman Catholics that disagreed with the RVA. "Any last words?" I asked. Before he could utter any Republican drivel, I shot him five times in the head. Closed casket for you me thinks.

He didn't give any of his victims a chance to defend themselves, let alone speak. So, I wasn't going to entertain it! Now Conner Duffy can be crossed off the list. Fuck? It was only him in the room as we started to clear it. Fucking good with a rifle, I will give him that, the cunt! Ian makes his way up the stairs to investigate the second floor. "CLEAR!" He shouts down. "WINDOW OPEN SIR, TOP FLOOR CLEAR!" "USE YOUR VIDEO PROBE TO INVESTIGATE OUTSIDE THAT WINDOW, USE EXTREAM CAUTION!" I shout up the stairs. Ian takes out an extendable video probe out of his vest and extends it about two feet. He then uses the mechanisms below to manoeuvre the video cam which his handset sees in real time. Making his way slowly to the opened window Ian has his side arm drawn and ready to use if needed. The video probe slowly peeps out of the open window. Suddenly and without warning the probe gets snatched from the other side of the hole it was trying to peer through. "BRAAAAAAPPPPPPP!" Gun fire then viciously disintegrated the glass in the windows and peppers the hall we were in with bullet holes.

Ian responds by letting loose his own clip as we all rush upstairs to support him. "I can't see them, Sir!" Ian calls over to me. "They must be on the lower roof, they grabbed the fucking probe out of my hand!" Ian continued. I signal Ian to take cover in the doorway behind him in the hall. I reload my rifle and so does Ian. I signal to Ian to shoot through the walls on my mark. I am listening to hear if the bastards are outside or trying to get closer to the window. "Crunch!" That's the sound I wanted to hear. Both of us unload our heavy calibre rounds through the wall.

Shooting in a zig zag pattern all over the area where the unfortunate RVA once stood on the shattered glass outside. The walls were falling apart as disintegrated bricks were blasted into dust, creating large gaping holes in the wall which allowed more light into the dimly lit and now very smoggy hallway. I run over and use one of the holes in the wall to look outside and see what we hit. We hit nothing? Not a fucking dicky bird? "UPPER FLOOR CLEAR!" I shout to the rest. I twirl my hand in the air to get my crew to regroup. We all meet in the kitchen and get prepped for the final wall into the compound. "This is not going to ...." The windows are all blown through. I am disorientated and confused. Everyone is frantic around me as I am on the floor. Bright flashes of automated fire fill the room along with muffled gun fire and shouting. I can't see more than two feet in front of me as the room has dust and debris floating everywhere. My ears are wet from the blood seeping out of them. Ian comes over and shouts in my face "WE'VE BEEN HIT BY A MORTAR ROUND!"

Reality starts to focus around me again when another explosion shatters through the wall to the back of the house. "WE ARE GOING TO DIE HERE UNLESS YOU MAKE A FUCKING MOVE!" Chris shouts over to me. "WALL CHARGES ON SUPPORT WALL, NOW!" The crew attach two wall charges to the wall. I signal them to get to the back of the building. "Beep!" BOOOOOM!... The power of the two charges takes out the supporting wall as the second floor comes crashing down. It looks like a war zone now, but the job was done. We now have access to the RVA compound.

I check over my team for injuries before we stack up and push through. Everyone has been hurt in some shape or form, but no one is dead. I signal for flash bombs and frag grenades to daze and confuse before we explode some frags to thin them out as we will almost certainly be under heavy fire. Sure enough, before the dust has a chance to settle there was a barrage of automated gun fire. It was like fireworks going off with all the muzzle flashes, pure carnage! The firing was sporadic and in all directions indicating the enemy's sense of defeat and unwillingness to rise up from their hiding places and engage us. Basically, they were shitting it. If I was them I would be too if they knew what was coming their way. As we had gaping holes to the first and second floor, we threw Incendiary Grenades first, so the enemy couldn't see where we were going and would be choked out by the chemical compound in it which is similar to pepper spray.

We put on our masks and all threw together our Incendiary Grenades on the upper and lower floor. It was like a symphony of decimation going off one after the other. Next, we armed and cooked our high explosive frag grenades which would definitely, without a shadow of a doubt put a severe dent in their numbers as the painful chemical smoke would force them from their defence positions in a desperate bid to breathe. So almost immediately after the flash bangs we lobbed our frags and took cover. The noise was deafening as each frag detonated. You could feel the shockwave pound against you. The ringing in the ears was part and parcel of using these bad boys but is soon wears off. Due to the explosives, we had a fire on the upper floor which to be fair would help us root out any RVA still alive up there. Unfortunately, because of the layout of the compound, I knew our grenades would only do so much.

This was going to be a tough job clearing this place as it had eight rooms with a basement and attic and because it was an older building it was made of dense stone blocks which makes good cover for anyone behind them. Only our snipers had rounds that would penetrate them. We also know it's been modified with a few safe rooms and two tunnels. The silence was deafening as we waited to hear movement before going forward.

We would normally follow straight in after the frags went off but were playing on the safe side. I fire a few rounds through to the other side of the building. Nothing, no sound, time to move. I take the lead and signal the team to advance behind me. I have set one of my crew to keep guns trained on the openings on the second floor with another one covering the bottom hallways. That leaves three of us to clear the first hurdle. I keep an eye on the second floor as I make my way into the building as I don't want another section of floor to land on my head. So far so good, I see some body parts on the floor and a lot of blood which was to be expected. but no full torsos to be seen. I tactically enter the first room which was the bar, to discover fifteen RVA men and one woman lying down

124

with their hands behind their backs and few of the men propped against the wall with severe injuries. I call out "ENEMIES SITUATED FRONT ROOM!"

Poor sods are going to get a taste of their own medicine in a minute. "ROOM SECURED!" Ian shouts as he and two other men cover the cowards. I proceed to lead the rest of the team and make our way to the next rooms. The first bedroom to the right looked clear, there was a bed, side table and a closet. A few places to hide, unluckily for me as I had to clear the area without causing harm to innocents. "MAKE YOURSELF KNOWN OR DEADLY FORCE WILL BE USED!" I shouted, hoping they wouldn't call my bluff. The closet creaks open and an RVA man in his readies makes his way out slowly into the middle of the room. I didn't need his ID as I recognised him immediately. Finton McGuinness. This piece of shit has slipped numerous times through the judicial system even though we had concrete evidence linking him to several murders and the massacre at the Brownwell Inn. This was due to RVA sympathisers in the police deliberately mishandling arrests and corrupting vital evidence which under law collapses the case against them. I signal the rest of the team to continue searching the building and unclip my rifle and side arms. I place them to the side. You could tell Finton knew what was coming next. "You have to arrest me!" He said. I don't look at him as I take off my helmet.

"What you're doing is illegal and against the Geneva Convention of warfare!" He added as I continued to ignore him and prepare myself for hand to hand combat. "I surrender; I have a wife and kids! I FUCKING GIVE UP YOU CUNT! YOU FUCKING HUN BASTARD, THIS IS MURDER!" Murder? It's funny how the minds of killer's work? I prepare my razor wire Garrotte and throw him one of my swords and back up slowly, so he had room to pick it up. I remember those who Finton slain in cold blood. Those crying and pleading for mercy, he and his comrades ignored. "I'm not picking it up. FUCK YOU!" Finton Shouts. I don't respond to him. I stare into his eyes knowing what I am about to do is legally wrong, but it was justified. That was good enough for me.

I run towards him and punch him over and over again which awakens the devil in him. Finton fights back like his life depended on it, and it did. I was but toying with him, when I quickly wrap the razor wire around his neck and turn my back to him. As I start to lean forward and could feel his full weight on my back as I pull harder on the razor wire. Each pull of the Garrotte handles cutting deeper into Finton's throat. I am oblivious to his gasps and death moans and concentrate my efforts on keeping my balance. The one thing that did catch my attention was the blood stream starting to gush down my shoulder. I grasp the handles tighter and tighter till the wire loop snaps free and his head falls quickly past my face, gently glancing it before hitting the floor with a thud. His limp body then slides off my back and onto the floor behind me.

When I picked his head up, his eyes were already closed. I spot the sprinkler on the ceiling which a use to smash through his skull and wedge his stinking head to the ceiling. I don't know why I did that. Maybe it was to send a message to the rest of the RVA. I pick up my Wakizashi sword and holster it again. I shake my Garrotte free of blood and put it back in my vest. His blood was starting to get cold as it was seeping through my vest which was irritating as I didn't want his dirty fucking rebel blood anywhere near me. I join the rest of the team in scouring what remains of the building. I check our time and we are over by ten minutes. The fucking police and army will be outside by now, I remain calm. "BUILDING CLEAR!" Christian Shouts. I make my way back to the room with the RVA captives. "We have ID all of them but one" David said as I entered the room. "David, take the one we don't know out now!" I shouted. "SIR!" David replied. Ian guides David and the woman out. "Close the fucking door!" I shouted at Ian. "SIR?" Ian replied. Ian then shut the door as directed. These fucks were all on the list and had their own hands dripping with blood. Now it's time to pay for their cause and it was going to cost them dearly. I take out my swords again and give them a chance to fight back.

"COME ON YOU COWARDS, FACE ME!" I shout at them. I pulled my balaclava off, so they know who I am. "SIR! WE ARE OUT OF TIME!" Ian shouts through the door. I ignore him; these fucks have evaded death for far too long. I hear the helicopters hovering above the building. Looks like I am going to be late for my next meeting. I untie each one of them one by one and give them a fighting chance. They were all beyond useless at hand to hand combat, but I didn't hold back until everyone was dead. I open the door and ask calmly "Where is the woman you took out Ian?" "She's in the next room Sir," Ian replied. "Could you bring her in please?" I add. "Yes, Sir," Ian said. I am covered in blood and out of breath. I place my hands on my knees to recover my energy. Ian pushes her into the room. I sit her on top of one of the bodies.

"My name is Jason, I work for the military and have been asked by the government to kill all the RVA I come across. I don't know you. Why don't I know you?" I asked her. Whilst I was talking a loud speaker can now be heard in the background, shouting my name. It's sounds kind of garbled. I can almost make out something about me being under arrest. The woman is still not talking

126

so I unclip my side arm and fire two rounds at her feet. "How's your memory now? Why are you here? Who are you?" I asked angrily. You could tell she was very afraid now that I am holding the gun instead of her RVA mates. "Trevor Hughes has sent me!" I stand up in anger and hold my gun to her head.

"Talk to Trevor, Talk TO TREVOR," she said trembling. "I'm not talking to him, I am talking to you, you fucking piece of shit! Why don't I know you? You don't work for us!" I aggressively state. I take her prints with my phone and send it to my cloud storage. "David, get her the fuck out of my sight!" I gather my team quickly before they bash down the doors. I update my end of the data and data man bring back a tally of 90% of our targets are verified dead, 10% outstanding. "Congratulations team, you have changed the course of history. We may not have got them all but Northern Ireland is forever changed.

It won't stop here as we still have people of influence playing to a political agenda. We will never stand for terrorists in our government again!" I announced. We cheered and hugged each other and threw down our weapons before heading outside with our hands on our heads. We knew we could face jail but the prospect of this didn't dampen our spirits. I led them forward to a squad of jeeps and police cars. We got on our knees and waited to be put in custody. "You knew they would be coming, don't panic. They're actually here to protect these scumbags. Little too late, ha ha!" I said aloud to my crew. I now see "B" squad coming out with their hands on their heads. It looks like we are missing one? "MARK!" "MARK!" I shouted over to them. They still had their goggles and helmets covering their heads. One of them looks over at me and shakes his head. My heart sank, they got him? I look over again and the same guy flips me the bird. "What the fuck?" I said under my breath. It was Mark taking the piss as usual. I feel much better now we have zero K.I.A's "Killed In Action."

I smile back as the cuffs are put around my right wrist, "click" and now my arms are brought behind my back and left wrist is fitted and locked into place "click." Everything slows down, and I just go with the flow. The army man, with his face covered brings me to my feet as another soldier takes a hold of my other arm and marches me in a line with the rest of my team to a number of vans which are lined up and waiting for us, their prisoners.

When the soldiers suddenly break from the rest of the line and guide me alone towards a Land Rover. They put a hood over my head and I am thrown into the

127

back of it. I wonder to myself, why are they separating me from my group? There is loud music being played. As we travelled they kept playing the same song over and over again during the transport to wherever we were going. I was keeping a mental count of how long the ride was so I could get an estimate of my bearings. The Land Rover stops near enough bang on 16 minutes. I, unfortunately, had a good idea of where I was as the van pretty much went straight north. I am at the docks. I really hope I am not because if I am right I am also a dead man. That's how the agency gets rid of people who cause constant complications with regards to the stability of the peace process. The "MISSING" and I say this word loosely, as they usually turn up as bodies appearing around the docks from supposedly jumping off the ferries trying to escape to England or Scotland. You see it on the news from time to time. The back doors of the vehicle are whipped open and I am man handled to my feet. I can hear water and the seagulls. I'm still walking on the tarmac until I hear the thumping of boots on wood. FUCK, they are skipping the interrogation, think fast! I get ready and take a very deep breath before grabbing the soldier to the left of me and whip us both into the soldier to the right of me which knocks us all into the water. I still have a grip of the soldier and use my leg to lock onto the other one. Now I wait for them to panic and use up all their oxygen.

They both thrash around wildly hitting and punching me which doesn't hurt as the water slows their blows right down. I concentrate on being calm. They will stop in a moment. I'm nearly there. Small convulsions indicate they were unconscious. I let go of them and shake the hood off my head underwater and swim up using just my legs. Air, beautiful sweet air. I go under again and scoot my cuffed hands under my bum and bring my legs through until my wrists are in front of me. Now I bring each soldier up and snag each on one of the many rusty nails protruding from the dock beams. I check their pockets for the keys and uncuff myself. I look about and know that my guess was right. Suddenly a metal door swings open which was my cue to get tight to the side of the docks. I unholster one of the soldier's guns and hope I don't need to use it. They walk past and end up standing close to the Land Rover we just came from. It's Trevor! He has twigged that they haven't signed in yet with me. Trevor walks back to the metal door and slams it behind him. I had to resuscitate these boys I have hanging up, I understood they were definitely going to kill me, but I also knew they were just following orders.

I need to act fast to save them. I swim up to the ladder and climb up casually. I start to shake the water off myself and take off my top which gets the other soldiers attention. "Oi YOU!" one of them shouts over drawing his gun. I shout at them "Help me get these men out now!". Two immediately jump in and start to hand the lifeless bodies up to me.

We put them on their sides and start to work on them draining their lungs. One starts coughing right away which relieves me but puts me in a panic. I have seconds to escape. I make my way to the Land Rover which should still have the keys in the ignition. They don't notice till I start the engine. I back out quickly and make my escape. Making my way towards Bangor at high speed, I start to rip back the roof lining to expose the installed tracker the vehicle has fitted. They are in all government vehicles and funny enough in the same place over the driver's seat. As I rip it out and toss it out the window my location becomes immediately unknown. I now change direction and head out of Belfast to Larne in an old fashion double back avoidance technique. I am aware of the ANPR cameras and take the back roads to my destination. I have a safe house in an abandoned basement underneath a castle ruin. It will take me a few days to organise myself to fully see the bigger picture of where we are at this point in time. I hope my team are alright as I wasn't expecting the government to nut me right away, which was a complete surprise.

Before I get to Larne I hide my vehicle in an abandoned warehouse on the outskirts of the town. I know a Loyalist group that will strip this puppy down and have it sold the same night. I let them know where it is and ask them to bring me a clean car. I take out my personal gear from the back and strap it on again. I found a hand-held tablet that was stuffed into the back seat. I'll have that. I took back my weapons and checked about the cab for any other gear that could be useful. I found another two guns, some ammo and a mobile. I stop my search as I hear a car approaching and quickly get out of the Land Rover. I take cover behind some crates and ready my side arm. The car stops and a man gets out of the vehicle. "Yoohoo, Jay, Jay, where are you??" Ryan calls out. It has only taken them twenty minutes to arrive to do their thing. "Alright, Jay!" Ryan shouts over as I walk out from behind the crates. I holster my weapon. "It's been too long mate!" he continues as he throws his arms around me and gives me a few slaps on the back. I slightly reciprocate as it's unusual for him to be so friendly. "Yeah, it has been a long-time bro" I replied. "How did you get my number?" Ryan asked inquisitively. "You know what I do for a living... do we have to do this again?" I replied as I knew what was coming next.

"Why are you getting in touch with us when you wanted out? You're in a bit of shit and now you want to be friends again?!" Ryan said angrily. "Did you know I did three years in jail because of your unit and I know it was your unit before you spout your bullshit as MARK WAS THERE!" He continued getting closer to my face. "I did know"... "SMACK!" Ryan landed a punch on me. I know I deserve it as he could have touted on me for the killing of the RVA bros Gabe and Paulo McCleanne. "I kept my mouth shut for you, fucking CUNT!" Ryan continues as his crew come closer. "FUCK OFF!" Ryan shouts over towards them.

"Get that truck sorted NOW!" he continued. "Your file was already made and handled by another team; we just carried out the raid," I said to Ryan whilst sitting crossed legged looking up at him. I needed him, so allowed him to let off his vented-up anger towards me. "Three FUCKING YEARS YOU CUNT!" He was going to wallop me again but didn't. "Where was my warning, my heads up, anything? You did nothing Jay!" Ryan continued in a softer voice. "My kids resent me; my missus divorced me, three long years in that bastard Maghaberry hole. You left me in a right mess!" he continued. "I did owe you a heads up, but I did also get your sentence reduced if you remember. I am not responsible for your life choices mate. I still know a lot of shit you have done and have kept it locked away. I was only following orders if it wasn't me it would have been someone else and you would have got double the sentence." I said calmly to him.

You wouldn't know this, but Ryan and I have already had this very same conversation before. Sometimes he chooses to change things in his head and then convince himself it's the God honest truth. He is a good man but has a wicked temper. "Am I forgiven?" I ask Ryan. "Sure, just transfer 50k into my bank and we will call it quits." He said. I didn't see that coming. "Where the fuck am I going to get that!?" I asked Ryan. Ryan just stared at me like he knew I was lying. "Fuck it!" I said. The man knows everything about me. "20k and not a penny more you robbing bastard! consider it wired" I said. "Thanks, you're not all bad are you Jay?" Ryan replied. "Oh, and by the way, your wheels are behind our car on the trailer". I get up and make my way over to the trailer and pull off the tarp. "Fuck me!?" I blurted out. It was a banged up old baby blue scooter. "What the fuck am I supposed to do with that?" I called over to Ryan.

Ryan got into the Land Rover and drove past me slowly with a smile on his face and an arm hanging out the front passenger window with his hand clenched with a fuck you gesture. Which I interpreted as payback for what I did to him. He was quickly followed by his lads who took my new wheels off the trailer. I didn't care if I fell out with him. Who the fuck does he think he is? "Fucking Dick!" I shouted after him as I walked back over to the scooter.

I just stared at it like it was going to change into a Supra or any other three-litre engine car that could have been useful in my hour of need. Hang on a minute, maybe it was a smart move as they wouldn't expect me on this piece of shit. I got onto the scooter and bounced up and down on the seat testing the shocks. It squeaked every time. I then turned on the engine and listened to how it ran. It chugged along with no hiccups. I then tested the lights, all working. It had a cloned southern plate which was still working as the details stuck to the seat matched what I ran on the tablet.

Everything was working well, and the bike seemed in good working order but I knew it wouldn't outrun jack shit. I drove it a short distance to my place and got ready for a long night of prep work. Tomorrow was going to be a busy day. I stopped the scooter inside the castle ruins and rolled it around to face out in case I need a quick exit. Then I paused for a minute. "FUCK! You have forgotten to give me a helmet you prick!" I said aloud as I didn't realise I needed one at the time. I would definitely get pulled for that, especially in Northern Ireland. I will try to get one tomorrow but I have to make new cash cards. I hope I got everything I need in my stock cupboard I thought to myself. I will test a cash machine tomorrow at a secluded place where I can easily avoid my comrades if I trip the withdraw money alarm. As I settle in for the night I break into another WiFi account, it was one of my neighbours so I don't get traced using the data roaming on the tablet. I quickly video call Gerard to check on Daniel.

BEEP BEEEEEEP ..... BEEP BEEEEEEP .....BE. "Hello?" Gerard said. "It's Jason, how is Daniel doing?" I inquire. "He is doing great, got him a game system and he hasn't put it down since it was hooked up. You want to speak to him?" Gerard said. "Of course," I replied. I can hear Gerard in the background calling Daniel. Gerard picks up the tablet again and brings it into his living room. "Look who it is! It's Daddy!" Gerard said. Daniel didn't even look away from the T.V "What?" Daniel said. "Daniel, Daddy is on the tablet." Gerard is trying to convince Daniel to pry himself away from his game to talk to me with little luck. "Gerard, just stick the tablet between him and the T.V," I asked. Gerard did just that. I can see his precious little face again. The picture was a bit dark and blurry but I could see him. "Hi sweetheart! you ok? Daddy misses you!" I tell Daniel.

Daniel then grabs the tablet and begins to talk to me "Hello Daddy, when are you coming home?" "I will be coming home soon darling. Make sure you behave for your Uncle Gerard and do what he says." "I will daddy, I love you," Daniel says as he kissed the monitor. "I love you too son, more than you will ever know." I kiss the monitor too and ask to speak to Gerard again.

"I miss him, please look after him if anything happens to me as I have had a few close calls today from the enemy and our own people. I am going to wire you some money to your off-shore account and some money for Daniel when he gets older. Call it insurance if the worst is to happen. You're one of the few people I trust. Thank you for everything you're doing for us." Gerard looked sad. "Keep your chin up Jason, this won't be for long. You will be back here with us in no time." Gerard said in a sombre voice.

I smile, "thank you for everything mate. I couldn't have done this without you. From what I have quickly glanced at on the tablet, the news over here is making out that it was an internal feud within the RVA from what I have seen in the headlines so far. How is the media taking the events over the pond?" I ask. "It's been quiet so far, give it a few more hours." Gerard replied "My data man compiled the information on the success of the operation. We are at 90% of the list. I really thought we would have got through more, but it is what it is. 10% still lurking in the shadows and most likely will regroup. Any suggestions?" I ask.

"Kill the remaining 10%," Gerard said. "I knew you would say that! Anyway, you have a good night and keep safe" I replied. "You to mate," Gerard said. "BYE BYE DADDY!" My little man shouted. I put the tablet down and draw up my solo plan to finish what I have started. I transfer £300K for Daniel's account and £100K for Gerard. Now I transfer £20k to Ryan's account with the reference "Froot", I laugh to myself. It's 3 am and I hear a car driving slowly over loose stones outside. I dim the lights and check my sticky cams feed.

One car, one male occupant, unarmed and making his way over to my neighbour's house. Nothing to worry about I thought to myself until I hear the screaming! I check the sticky cams feed again and see that this twat is trying to rob next door. I carefully exit the building and stealthily make my way over. I don't want to make any noise, so I take my Garrotte with me. The silly fucker was a right armature as I walked right up to him while he was trying to interrogate the scared old dear of the whereabouts of her money. I quickly wrapped the garrotte around his neck and immediately tightened which made him instantly drop the knife.

"Go back to sleep gran, this is nothing but a bad dream!" She slowly nodded her head and I dragged the choking burglar out the door. I left the knife, so she would give it to the police for analysis. I had to loosen up my grip around his neck as he was starting to lose consciousness and I wasn't about to carry him. I open his boot and realise that I like his car. A BMW 3 Series beats a shitty scooter any day of the week. Then it occurred to me that he didn't fit the profile of a smack head burglar with this car as his wheels?

I knock him out with a well-placed punch to the lower jaw and tie him up in the boot of his own car. I quickly grab my tablet and lock up my safe house. I then get into the BMW and inspect the ignition, nothing has been messed with? I then open the boot again and grab the cars fob off him and throw my weapons and gear into the back seat before closing the boot again. I hope the old lady lays low so I can leave before she can see this car. I start the engine and make my way over to a Crispy Chicken fast food restaurant which is close by.

I order a three-piece chicken select meal which is my favourite and make my way over to a secluded part of the car park. I eat my meal and clean up my greasy hands before getting my tablet to scan my sleepy passenger's fingerprints. It takes a few minutes as I am too far from the WIFI I hacked earlier so I have to use the open link that's available to me from the fast-food restaurant. "Flash Red!" Yugoslavian born Andrija Horvat. A migrant to our beautiful country and this is how he thanks us for letting him stay. I drive the car to the end of the car park beside the ditch and quickly exit the vehicle. I open the boot and take his wallet which is flush with cash, at least a couple of grand. I then untie him and throw him into the ditch behind me, he just lies in a heap.

"So, this is how you can afford your flashy car you cunt, topping up your minim wage with a few burglaries a month. I hope the police deport your ass back to where you came from. They probably will when they connect your prints to that fucking knife you used at that old woman's house. You're lucky I don't gut you, you fuck!" I suddenly realised I was scolding his unconscious body. I didn't want to kill him but my rage was lit, so I threw my finished contents of my fast food at him. That did the trick, I was slowly calming down.

Now to do my nice deed for the day. I drive back to my neighbour's house and see a police officer is already there, fuck. So much for giving her a few notes as an apology from Mr Horvat. I knew the police had to come, just surprised they arrived that quick as they usually take their sweet time. I will give her the money another day. Now to check if my wheels are stolen. Please don't be stolen, don't be nicked...... I say to myself as I wait anxiously for the plate check. CLEAN, no outstanding offences but it's not coming up showing Mr Horvat as the owner? Mr Bernie Andrews...DOB 16/07/68...address 16 Maple View, Donacloney... I must remember that name, date of birth and address if I am pulled over. Another cloned plate on another stolen car. Yes!! Mr Horvat had done the hard work for me and he can't say it's stolen because they will contact the owner with the details on the DVLA database, ha ha. Loving it! I park the car in the street behind my safe house and sneak back into my bolt hole for the night. Finally, something is going in my favour for a change!

Chapter 10 - The uninvited

Finton McGuinness is a long-standing member of the RVA and has a lot of blood on his hands. Not that he is worried about it as he is convinced what he is doing for his country is justified. He is in Belfast, drinking at a well-known RVA compound in Andersonstown.

I love coming here on an afternoon for a drink. It feels safe. It won't be long now till all the pubs and social places will be a worry-free zone as soon as we push those British bastards out. I believe great things will start to happen after Michaels gathering tonight. I'm getting too old for this war as I used to have glorious locks of hair, now it's a number one all over, due to me receding hairline. Ah well, old age is a blessing as some never see it. Still, I am a handsome fella and if I play my cards right at the gathering I could pick up a bird or two.

Look at Nula, running around like a blue arsed fly. You would think Michael would be down here pitching in but knowing him, he would believe that's beneath him. "Hold on Nula, give me and end of that streamer," I said. "Ah, cheers Finton, you're a lamb," Nula said while she handed the end of the streamer to him along with a tack. "Just stick that end in that far corner and I will stretch this end to the top section of the bar." Nula continued. The place was looking well, I thought to myself. We just need to make more of a fuss with the pictures of our fallen. "Nula...What are you going to do to dickey up those pictures on the wall of our fallen heroes?" I said. Nula tried to turn around to face Finton to answer him but was trying to keep balanced on a stool whilst pushing a tack into the wall to hold up decorations. "We are going to put a table below them with some candles and whiskey shots for the usual send off," Nula replied. I nod and sit back down at the bar to finish my drinks. This place is empty tonight, you would think people would come early to get a seat and get a few down them to start the night off with a bang. "Alright Finton, you're looking jumpy tonight you wee shit!" Andy said as he slapped his hand down hard on my shoulder unexpectedly. "SHIT! Trying to give me a heart attack, I'm nearly fifty Ya dickhead! My ticker can't the stress it used to, ha ha!" I scolded. Andy was a friend and a fellow RVA man. Me and him have been through a lot together. We even killed together. I remember arguing who was to shoot this fucking prod in the head behind the cinema and neither of us wanted to let the other shoot him as we liked killing vermin. I shot him first in the head and Andy was fuming as he wanted to do it so he just ended up emptying his clip into the poor sod. "Well, you looking forward to tonight? You think we will get a mention?" Andy said.

"They amount of orange bastards we put in the ground, I would hope so!" I replied. "Just think, if there were twenty of us, we would own the North!" Andy said. "You, ever regret killing some of them the way we did? You know, sneaking up on them at their homes or when they leave work. They never see it coming." I asked Andy. "Hell No! That was our job! They knew the score by staying in Ireland, they have no fucking right to be here. You know this, are Ya going soft or something?" Andy said with a strained face.

I agree with him and nod my head. I daren't tell him that I have regrets about what we did. He simply wouldn't understand why I was fretting about it as he doesn't see Protestants as human anymore. This war has twisted his mind and for a while, it did the same to me. "Listen you moping wee fuck! WE did a good job and this movement would be years behind schedule if it wasn't for the likes of us. Now, what are you drinking, or do I even need to ask?" Andy said. "Vodka Chaser, with ice!" I replied. Andy tried to get the bar man's attention to order the drinks. I knew he wouldn't understand, there something's that are better left unsaid. I'm an atheist but for some reason, I still think I'm going to Hell and I can't shake it. I know what I did was wrong, but it had to be done. The British don't fit our social values, nor do they want to. The more I thought about the British the more I felt better about the lives I took.

"Here you go, get that down your neck." Andy said whilst pushing a double round my way. I raise my glass towards Andy. "Fuck em!" I said. "Fuck em!" Andy replied back. "Finton! Come here!" The bar man said nearly breaking the toast we were having. I get up and go over to talk to the bar man. "What is it?" I asked. He just hands me the phone and I quickly put it to my head. "Yes, hello!" I quickly hear someone shout down the phone. "Finton...they are coming...Fint...".
Muffled sounds echo down the line before it cuts off to the dial tone. What was that? What the fuck is going on. I quickly reverse call to find out the number of the person who rang. The computer automated voice read out the number to me. It's a Warrenpoint dialling code.

That's all I knew as I didn't recognise the voice or what the fuck he was talking about. I'm the senior ranking officer in the building so it's my call and if I get it wrong it's my neck. "CODE YELLOW!" I shout. Everyone in the bar area who heard me then immediately tells the rest of the building. I just ordered a perimeter watch and gave warning of a possible attack. "Someone phone Tim the peeler and find out what the Police are doing. I also need someone to phone Brendan to inform him of what's happening; maybe he can shed some light about Warrenpoint." I instructed. I unholster my gun and make my way up the stairs to the second floor. I see a captain and take use of his radio.

"Attention, do not have any weapons on show as we don't want law enforcement to disrupt the festivities tonight. This alert is purely precautionary. Do you receive?" I asked the sentries. "Understood, sentry leader out!" said the captain of the perimeter guards. I watch the men hide their weapons and walk the parameter of the building. I give the radio back to the captain and proceed to the armoury to lock and load a rifle. I pocket a few magazines in case I need to put down some covering fire. I'm watching out the window on the second floor as I am prepping for the worst when I notice some cunt sneaking up on one of our guards. I don't get time to open the window, just lock, load, aim and fire. I fired a whole clip at him as I knew our poor sod was dead, I just hope I clipped him. I can't believe that fucker .... put a sword or something sharp straight through his chest. This is definitely not the army or police. It must be the Loyalists. I didn't have time to ponder over what happened as the windows and walls were being peppered with automatic gun fire.

I put a scope on to get a better idea of the situation. I can't see any of them... wait I see that fucker again hiding behind the wall. "Chhhakka, Chhakka!" I fired two rounds at his exposed legs. I take cover and wait for a response. It didn't take long. The second-floor room of the armoury was being lit up like New Years. The walls were disintegrating before Fintons eyes. He knew he had to get out now! Andy comes rushing into the room and sits down on the floor behind the desk that I am using for cover. "Who the hell are these guys?!" Andy shouts as he cocks his rifle. "No idea but they are coming in hard and fast!" I replied firing a few more rounds at the incoming intruders. Andy gets up to do the same but gets two massive hits to his body which practically tears him apart, causing his blood to spatter everywhere. I freeze and stay put, not daring to move. Fuck it, I am out of here. I thought to myself whilst crawling on the floor covered in Andy's blood to the door and down the stairs.

I make my way cautiously back into the bar area. "Nula! Nula!!" I shouted with no response heard. "She ran out the back with a few of them, so she did", one of the men shouted over at me. "What's going on, do you know? They are not shooting anymore." I ask. "No idea, has anyone called Brendan or Michael to bring reinforcements?" The man asked. I didn't know if my orders were carried out so I decided to make the calls myself. I check in with the soldiers around the square and find out they don't have many men left in high ground positions and was warned to fortify the building as they believe the intruders were going to try to gain entry. "HAS ANYONE CONTACTED MICHEAL OR BRENDAN YET?!" I shouted down the hall.

"No one can get through to him as it keeps going to his message recorder!" a voice said. "KEEP TRYING!" I shout. I then phone Tim who is our man in the police. "TIM, major fucking situation happening at The Pen Supporters Club, we need assistance right now!" I said to Tim in an irate voice. "I will send someone now down your way!" Tim replied. I hang up the phone as I heard a faint explosion from down the hall. People are starting to take up positions behind anything they can get cover from. "BOOM, BOOM BOOM!" The sounds are getting much louder now. What the fuck are they doing? My hand starts to shake as I feel that I might not be seeing home tonight. "BOOOOOOM!" Fuck that was a big explosion; they must be throwing hand grenades into the buildings. I'm not going out like that, I need to escape outside. I start running upstairs and open the men's room and look for a window that wasn't welded shut. No luck, so I make my own exit by shooting out the bathroom window and climb down onto the kitchen roof. If I just hug the walls and crouch down, no will see me. I can hear automatic gun fire from the house next door. What's going on!! Come on Michael, fucking get here now and sort this out. Where the fuck is Tim?? I feel myself start to lose all sense of reality. The British are coming to finish us off I thought. No, no, that's impossible. They wouldn't have the balls to do this.

"RATATATATATA!" Automatic gun fire sounds like it's coming from next door. BWOOOM!.....BWOOOM! I hear muffled voices and screams of agony coming from next door which chills me to the bone. There is no running away from this so I take position below the window of the second floor where I heard the gun fire. I keep my weapon ready and my eyes fixated on that window ready to take out our uninvited guests. I see something, a fucking video probe? I reached up and snatched it from the hole in the window and fire my weapon at the person using it. "BRAAAAAAPPPPPPP!" The window is blown apart and hopefully with it the enemy.

"Chaka, chaka, chaka, chaka, chaka!" Someone was returning fire from the window. I hug the wall so they can't see me as they will not want to poke their head out in case I fucking put a hole in it. I can't risk it here anymore, I am too exposed and it's too high to jump down. I make the decision to climb back into our building. I slowly walk over the glass trying to be as quiet as I could, when "CRUNCH!" I walked on a noisy bit of glass. The walls started to open up in gigantic holes as the intruders were firing their weapons in all directions towards me. There was dust and smoke everywhere which suited me as it would give me a little cover to escape. I clamber up the piping and into the toilets. Once I was in the men's room, I threw my gun out of the window. We have no hope of winning this I thought to myself, might as well surrender. I make my way downstairs and I could see everyone was hiding behind the bar.

"Hurry up you stupid fucker and get behind the bar. Michael is going to hit next door with a mortar!" One of the men shouted at me as I entered the bar area. I was too late for that as the blast sent me hurtling across the room. It was like slow motion and I didn't feel a thing. Our men got up from behind the bar and ran past me with their weapons drawn. Opening fire into the next building via a small hole in the wall now created by Michael. I can't focus as I am seeing in double vision which is making me incredibly dizzy. I hear another loud explosion which rocks the entire building and brings down a portion of the roof. I didn't care; I just lay on the floor, watching it happen before me. I wasn't afraid either as I was drunk with a concussion. Nothing made sense to me now. There were people I knew running about the bar and flashes of light exploding all around the room. It was like being on a bad trip of acid, but my brain kept telling me it was real even though I didn't want to believe it. I can see small bursts of flames coming from holes in the roof and from the hallway. I can see many of my friends are now lying still on the ground or hiding in corners. I close my eyes and try to wish myself away.

"ENEMIES SITUATED FRONT ROOM!" Someone shouted, and I looked up to finally lay eyes on who it was that beat us. Two large men kept their weapons pointed at us, waiting for someone to make a wrong move. They don't see me behind this rubble yet. I take advantage and crawl slowly around the corner and up the fire escape exit to the second floor. My wits were coming back to me and I felt in full control again. I need to get out of here quick! I open the door at the top of the stairs and make my way into one of the bedrooms. There is fuck all places to hide. I hear footsteps coming! I quickly hide in the closet and hope for the best.

I can hear the door open. "MAKE YOURSELF KNOWN OR DEADLY FORCE WILL BE USED!" a man shouted loudly. I believed him, with all my heart I knew if I didn't step out he would riddle the room. I hold my breath and open the closet door. I see a man before me I recognise but couldn't put a name to. He told his men to leave him and continue the search of the building. Now he is putting his weapons down against the wall all the while staring at me like I killed his mother? He wants to fight me? He looks like a British soldier, he can't do that! I have fucking rights! I thought to myself. "You have to arrest me!" I said. He continued to take his bullet proof vest off and ignored me. "What your doing is illegal and against the Geneva Convention of warfare!" I added. I put my hands up as I know I can't beat this guy. "I surrender; I have a wife and kids! I FUCKING GIVE UP YOU CUNT! YOU FUCKING HUN BASTARD, THIS IS MURDER!" I desperately shouted as I am now scared. He throws me a small sword and backs up away from me. "I'm not picking it up. FUCK YOU!" I shout. He just stares at me, he's fucking psychotic! Shit, he is now punching me. I fight with all I have... fuck I'm caught with a ...wire. ARGHHHHHHHHHH, gasp, nnnnnn, aahhh.

Chapter 11 - Loose ends

Jason has survived what most men wouldn't have. He finds himself alone, with no one to call on for help, as he is now wanted dead by his government and is the number one target for the RVA. The odds are greatly stacked against him and any normal person would try to run from the trouble he is heading towards. The truth is that Jason doesn't have anyone left to finish the job. Either he completes REVERT or accepts that the operation is a failure which will mean all he has achieved thus far won't eliminate the RVA, only just slow them down.

I am nervous as I don't have all the weapons I need to do a solo mission. 10% left on the hit list, equates to 23 Terrorists to put down which means the odds are vastly against me, so I need to approach this with guerrilla tactics. I have no explosives or high power tactical rifles. The solution to my problem would be finding RVA targets that do have the equipment I need and use their gear to finish this operation.

Driving around in Andersonstown 1:30 pm, I go to my old stomping grounds. I know the majority of these scumbags better than my own relatives. It doesn't take long for me to see a potential lead. Nora was a young girl in her early twenties who never experienced the troubles but somehow has the biggest chip on her shoulder about any British citizens being allowed to live in this country, calling them Colonists. She applauds the evil work of the RVA and defends the use of the bombs they use that not only try to kill the police and army but also in the majority of the cases civilians. She can be regularly seen spouting her warped views at the illegal memorials of these dead assholes. I would fucking shoot her, but she doesn't fit our code for termination, YET. I have been keeping her constantly monitored to see when I can take her out as I rather it be her, than an innocent regardless of their race or religion.

I don't think I have to worry about the code as I am now a fugitive, so I don't have that red tape attached to myself anymore. Most likely after yesterday's events I would more likely be killed than arrested by my turn coat peers. That fucker Trevor will pay and anyone else who has turned operation REVERT into a witch hunt. I am that flustered with my own thoughts about it that I nearly miss Nora going into a house. I know that house... That's Nora's sister's place. That will be a good place to watch for stragglers on my hit list. I don't have long to wait until I see more and more people enter her house. Right! I don't have any sophisticated equipment with me, so I do this the old school way. I need to get much closer to the house to see if I can get a positive ID on someone that's on my list.

A few hours go by and no one leaves the house.

I need to take a slash but can't afford to take my eyes off that house. I look up and down the street to see if it's clear of people who could walk past the car in the time it would take for me to have a pee. Clear! I open the door and carefully aim beside the car whilst keeping my back turned so no one can see me being uncouth. I always have my eyes on the door. I'm about to finish when I see a police car come down the road. I quickly stop what I am doing and pretend to open my boot to look for something. The police car slows to a stop beside me and rolls its window down which produces a typical electric window whine. I try not to look at them. "Excuse me, sir? I was wondering if you could help me with some information about an incident that took place close by here yesterday afternoon," the police officer asked. "I am just back from Portrush today, sorry I can't help" I replied. "What about giving me your name for a start?" The officer further enquired. "Bernie Andrews," I replied and looked at him with my head tilted under the boot, so it would distort my face.

I could see a mark on my list exiting the house but couldn't pursue them as this fuckwit was holding me back. "Thank you, Mr Andrews, for your time," the officer said before the patrol car slowly pulled away. Dam! I have lost sight of him. I get into my car and take the road behind the house as that would be the fastest way to escape my view. I was correct. I have a positive id on Colin Timmons, I just get to him on time to see him climb onto his dirt bike and put on his helmet which strangely doesn't seem to have a strap. That will do me nicely as I can make his death look like an accident. I need to spook him so he speeds right up and then he will kill himself as the area we are in is dense with traffic and obstacles. If he doesn't die or I see him moving I will just run him over. I might just run him over anyway to be 100% sure he's dead.

I slowly pull up beside him as he was messing with the gears on the dirt bike. I roll down my window and point my gun at him, then thought fuck it! "Braap! Braap!" I shot him several times in the head and chest with my pistol on automatic before driving off. I thought it would be more work the other way and what if he didn't die? Then all that blood over the car I would have to clean.

Yeah, I made the right choice I assured myself. I speed off but circle back and wait at the side of the road for the others to come out and inspect Colin's body. This is a classic baiting trap used in guerrilla warfare. Minutes later they come pouring out and over to Colin who is laying on the footpath with the dirt bike still on top of him. I lock and load with an extended magazine.

Everyone in that house is guilty by association as I spy two more targets that I can positively identify so I commit to killing them all in a worst-case scenario. Best case would be to only kill my marks and hope my aim is as good as it used to be when I trained in the military's kill rooms. I drive over to them at the speed limit and spray the crowd around Colin. I shoot low on purpose, to make them immobile but need to get out and finish off my two RVA targets. I pulled over and jump out of the car, keeping the door open. I then on closer inspection positively id another two on my list. "Fucking A! I've got more of you bastards!" I shouted.

I don't prolong it and quickly shoot each one in turn in the head. Boom! Boom! Boom! Boom! I took the automatic off to conserve bullets. I pat down the deceased and found only two shitty hand guns. The others didn't have any weapons on them. FUCK! I need more munitions fast. I see Nora, she is shot in the leg and is flopping around in agony when I approached her. I kneel down and whisper in her ear. "Hurts, doesn't it?" I asked her. She then spat at me. "What you don't realise Nora is " before I could finish my sentence she screamed "How the fuck do you know me, who the fuck are YOU!" I pointed my gun against her face and she stopped talking. "Like I was saying Nora, this is called Karma. I want you to think long and hard about that and consider this chat a final warning." She looked frightened as she erratically nodded her head in agreement. Almost as if she knew the road she was on, was going to lead to an early grave. I get up all the while aiming my gun at her. I then holster it quickly as I hear screams and yells from the public around me.

I get back in my car and drive off towards my safe house avoiding the usual shitty ANPR cameras along the way. Five more terrorist scumbags to strike off the list and in one day I might add. Nineteen left which includes Michael. Michael, Michael, Michael... I kept repeating his name in my head. I'm going to kill you slowly and disintegrate your body in acid, so you can't become a fucking martyr. I want to make it look like the prick has gone into hiding like the coward he is. It was pushing 3 pm when I parked the car at the Crispy Chickens car park near my place. I started to gingerly walk towards home looking forward to a long sleep when I notice the road down to my place was cordoned off with yellow tape and a big land rover blocking the entrance. I don't even want to know what's happening I thought to myself as I begrudgingly head back to the car. I'm so tired now that I might just sleep in the car but I don't. I take out my gear from the boot and make my way towards the docks. I know of another wee hidey hole I can take a doze in. It takes me a little while to get there but I am soon at the harbour. I walk along one of the many boats perched high on the dry docks. Which one...hmm...needs to be high enough so no one can see in very easily I thought to myself. Wow, she's a beauty, I see a gorgeous boat with a double decker cabin that also has its own wooden deck. I could never afford one of these, but it won't stop me from experiencing how the other half live.

I look around the boat and try to pick the best route up onto the deck as it was quite high off the ground. I use part of the scaffolding to climb up and reach the anchor as this will be my starting point to lift myself up and over the railings on the front of the boat. As I climb up I make sure I am not spotted as I have to lay low here for a few hours. The huge cabin covers me from view as I approach the locked door on the main deck. FUCK, it's one of those new anti-snap locks, this will be difficult to pick. Ahh, just remembered how to get around one of these. You need to unscrew and remove the handle cover first, then remove the bolt connecting the two sides of the handle before sticking your screw driver in and pulling the snib back. I'm in. I need to screw the handle back on and then lock the door behind me. It takes about 12 minutes in total. Way too long for someone of my calibre. I quickly suss out where the main bedroom is to have my long overdue snooze. I need to be fully alert with my wits about me to complete my mission. I turn on my tablet and connect to my neighbour's WIFI to see if I have any correspondence from my team. Sure enough, before my head hits the pillow I get an email from someone. It was from Ryan.

His email starts off *"How's things working out with your new wheels ?? ??"* then he goes on to say *"Our brothers have seen your latest moves on the news and are most impressed. The man on the inside wanted me to send you this Intel update as a gift and pass on his appreciation for the good work you have done thus far. Speak soon."* I download and open the attachment. I was excited as I knew everything we use to get in the day was top notch information that made what we had to do very easy.

As I read the Intel which has been forwarded to me by Ryan, it explains in quite some detail on an RVA gathering in Galway at a hotel called The Fox and Whippet with the added bonus of a certain political party also in attendance. You can almost guarantee some of the people on my hit list will be there. I have a date, time and address of the hotel with a cheeky little note on the bottom to me. "Tell them we send our best!" which was a double meaning that some of these poor unfortunates at this party would soon understand. Eight hours pass and the docks are now flood lit. It's now 9:40pm. I get up and use the boat's bog. It's a chemical toilet so no DNA can be used unless you do a number two. That's a different story altogether. I check the fridge and cupboards in a futile look for food and drinks. Nothing! I then gather my things and leave the place the way I found it. I walk onto the deck and check to see if anyone is close by in case I get spotted.

It all looks to be clear. I throw my ruck sack over my shoulder and begin the climb down. Fucking wind is colder than a witch's titty today. I try to pull my coat tighter around me as I make my way back up to the car.

It's a good twenty-minute walk but as good fortune would have it, the car was still there and the road to my place is unblocked. I don't need anything I don't already have, I thought to myself. No! Wait, I could use some body armour and ammunition. I all of a sudden remember a stash I put into the floor safe and get excited. "Shit I almost forgot about that!" I said aloud. I quicken my steps as I make my way towards my place. I then remember the old dear who got robbed the night before and start to count through my wad of notes in my pockets. I take 2k and roll it up tight and push it through the letter box of her house. I then quickly run around to the back of my place and unlock the door and make my way in. I don't want her to know it was me.

I pick up my full body combat armour which can be hidden under my clothes, more ammunition and what guns I could use from my floor vault. I also bring some low-tech gear to scope the place out. I am now locked and loaded and ready to crash a party. I get to my car and make the journey along the gorgeous coastline to Galway. I love travelling by the sea as the scenery never gets old and it always looks as pretty as a picture no matter what the weather. The gathering is tomorrow night which is a Thursday so that gives me a solid 24 hours to set up. I make my usual stops and decide to change the car again as I have had it more than three days.

I see a beautiful looking black Mercedes parked in front of a news agent. It's just the colour I was looking for I thought to myself. I pull over down the road a bit and make my way up leaving my kit in the car. I get the Mercedes and hit it a kick with no one noticing. Sure enough, the car started squealing and before long the owner was made known to me. I see this quite fit looking bird come quickly walking down and as she fumbles through her purse to find the car key fob to disarm the alarm. I find myself not moving towards her, I could quite easy stun her and take the keys but I'm not that person anymore who would involve an innocent bystander to fix my problem. She has a quick look around the vehicle and arms the alarm once more while walking back to where she came from. "Wok Palace Gardens," I said under my breath. I decide against this direction I was heading towards. I choose to keep the car I already had and hope for the best, it lifted my heart in a way and I felt better for not doing it. I walk back to my car and drive off towards the border where I am hoping my ducks in a barrel will be waiting. It is late evening when I arrive near the hotel in Galway. I pull up into a car park near the hotel, so the car would be close if I needed it.

I then open the boot and kit up for a possible assault if Intel is confirmed to be correct. I walk over to the beach and make my way down it until I am about 400 feet away from the premises of the hotel; now I need to find some cover.

I see a public toilet I can use. I get into a cubical and unload my micro drone from the open window behind me. I have my VR glasses on that allow me to see what the drone does which is not exactly new tech but it works. My drone is a twin blade micro helicopter which has great range and superior HD cam quality which is precisely what I need to see what I am up against. I can see the entire perimeter of the hotel now which shows me a car park about one-third filled. They must have booked the whole place out as this is prime tourist season and it would most likely have a car park full of patrons. I now check around the sides of the building. Two floors... several entrances...no visible guards on the outside of the building.... WAIT...scratch that...Three men patrolling the hotel's communal gardens...no visible weapons.... possible RVA as none of them are engaging in conversation as each man is visibly occupied with checking the surroundings.... interesting... they are no more than ever 6ft away from each other at any time. The car park has a barrier up to stop anyone coming in. There is a sign on it, moving the drone closer to read it. "Private function tonight, no admittance! Kind regards The Fox and Whippet."

146

I bring the drone back and land it just outside the pay toilets. I get my gear and head out. "OH FUCK!" I blurted loudly as I was about to get my drone when those three RVA men who were on patrol are making their way over to where I landed the drone.

This might be a good time to engage the enemy. I run over and pick up my drone and run back into the toilets. I park myself against the side wall of the door entrance and ready my two silenced ballers. I remember the way they stayed only 6ft apart and knew I was going to rush the other two after I take the first one out. Like clockwork, I see the tip of the gun first coming around the corner so I go low and drop in front of him. "PAP,PAP,PAP!!!" One in the bollocks, one in the gut and one in the head. He didn't even get a chance to look down. As he fell on top of me, I use him as cover instead of going for the rush, I waited for the other two dopes. BOOM! "FUCK!" I shouted as a round nearly hit me in the head. The fucking window was opened and those two twats were firing through it. I quickly roll to the side and make my way to the exit, quick glance left and right and I come out pointing a gun to the front of me and one behind, hugging the wall closely. I side shuffle along quietly and see no one, then I shuffle back the way I came and there they were, busy looking down the entrance to the crappers. I whistle, they both look and at the same instance, I shot both to the head. I grab their coms and listen in... yeah, they know I am here. I take my gear and pick up my drone and run across the road to the hotel, taking the garden entrance as it has more cover. I load up, my sheathed swords, two Ballers holstered, my body armour secured and my tactical rifle with extended magazines loaded.

I bet someone already reported that shot that fuck nearly got me with to the police; hopefully the public were not spooked by those RVA pricks. I don't need any more noise alerting them as it would severely fuck with my mission. I fasten a silencer to my rifle and proceed further into the hotel grounds. I see Michael, Fuck yes!! I think to myself but then panic sinks in....Trevor?! I quickly get the drone camera and point it in their direction and hit record. Trevor has his gun out and is pushing Michael out of the hotel and towards a car on the road. They seem to be in some kind of argument about leaving the hotel. Trevor hugs Michael and holds the driver door open and guides him in. Michael seems reluctant to leave.

As Michael shuts the door and Trevor waves his gun in the direction he wants him to drive, anger starts to well up in me. What the fuck? I'm flustered and greatly confused, as Trevor was at the docks a few days ago with the firm intention of nutting me which I would have expected but now he is with the RVA here? Is he a double agent? It slowly makes sense now when you start to look at it from this perspective; Trevor ...is... working with the RVA!

I grit my teeth and lock and load my rifle with my hands gripping tightly around the weapon. I fire a volley of shots at the car and Trevor, emptying my entire clip before taking cover again. I think I have hit both of them but not good enough as the car speeds off and Trevor ducks for cover. I have made a positive id for both of them and have it videoed as evidence; I send the file quickly to Headquarters and to my cloud server for back up. It took me less than a minute to fucking ruin that turncoat bastard. Now I start to make my way towards Trevor. I am covering the ground between us at a dangerous pace. I had tunnel vision as everything that has happened now makes perfect sense in my mind. I'm twenty feet away from him, using a large tree as cover. I lock and load another clip. "Jason, is that you?" Trevor shouted. I ignore him and concentrate on my surroundings as I could have enemies on all sides of my position. I see a row of houses to my left that I will use to flank him as he focuses on where I'm not. "Really sorry about your wife Jason... I am even sorrier that we didn't kill that fucking rat kid of yours!

30 seconds of Silence

Jason, you still there...ERRRAGH..ERahhgh!" I managed to circle back on Trevor and stick my sword through his fucking scrawny neck. Trevor is jiggling around like a fish out of water, I can't help but laugh. As I keep guard of my surroundings I whisper to Trevor that I was going to cut his face off and bankrupt his family.

His pension and insurance would be void after I get through with him and he knew I could do it. Trevor tried in vain to speak, his eyes were bulging in anger. He was paralysed from the neck down and could only shake. I take out a picture of my wife and son and hold it close to his face. The dirty cunt wants to look away, but I won't let him as I keep their picture right in front of his face. I turn my blade to open him up and increase the flow of blood leaving his traitorous body. I made sure that my wife and my boy would be the last thing he sees before he departs this earth, straight to hell. It only takes seconds to bleed him out after I turned the blade.

I was about to cut his face off but I held back and didn't as there was nothing to gain from mutilating his body. I took a deep breath and had a quick look around before I hacked his nose off and stuck it in my pocket, you know, for DNA confirmation. I then cut an "R" and a "V" then an "A" onto his forehead, whilst keeping watch for his comrades, just to let his family and friends know he was a scumbag. I finish and slowly get off him and look down to admire my handy work. "Yes, that look does suit you, YOU RAT FUCK!" I said aloud.

Now back to work. I knew that fucking coward Michael would not be back here as he is well known for his guerrilla warfare tactics but even better known for running away from a fair fight. It seems oddly quiet for an RVA party. I bet they are hoping if they are quiet enough I will go away. I laugh to myself, as if. This is going to be fun, I thought to myself as I stealthily make my way to the car park of the hotel. I am nearly there when the hotel suddenly explodes into a billion pieces. The splintered wood and roof tiles litter the sky like a huge flock of starlings in synchronised flight. My ears are bleeding again and the dust and gravel hit me like pellets from a shot gun. I'm in a lot of pain but I can't stop laughing as I know what probably happened when Michael left. The stupid dick left his gear with the dopey RVA fucks who blew themselves up. Probably by moving one of their primed bombs! "Ha ha ha ha!" I'm laughing out loud as I make my way back to my stashed gear. I'm not surprised, to be honest as the RVA have had loads of volunteers blow themselves up by accident. I then pause and think about the collateral damage that bomb would have done to the staff and other innocents that had nothing to do with those terrorist assholes. I put my rifle down with my gear bag and take only a pistol with me back to the hotel.

I quickly conceal my weapon and check for any innocent survivors that might have been caught in the explosion. I see a waiter lying in the hallway and go to him first. He is knocked out cold and had his left arm missing. I carry him carefully out to the car park and go in again. This time I make my way through the rubble to where it looks like the explosion happened.

It's heavy in flames but I hear groans near me. I look around and see a man in a collapsed door way, covered in blood and debris. I clear enough of the rubble away to pull him out of it and carry him to safety which again was the car park. As I am about to put him down the police and fire rescue services were pulling up. The man I just saved comes back into life and starts to stare at me, then feebly tries to get on his feet but he can't. He just slowly crawls away from me like he is scared of me.

149

I don't recognise him as an RVA member, but his face does look familiar, nevertheless, I leave him as he tries to make his way towards the police. That was indeed my queue to exit this situation. That's gratitude for Ya, I thought as I go back into the burning building. I navigate through the thick smoke and try to find a room I could use to access the gardens at the back of the hotel. I find the dining room which is adjacent to the garden and quickly use a chair from an over turned table to smash a window to escape through. Running through the garden of the hotel I could hear more sirens approaching my location.

I gather my gear and make my way back across the road and walk down the beach, back to my car. I open the door and throw my shit into the back seat as I make a hasty departure back along the coast and up to Northern Ireland. I drove for about an hour and pulled off the road to check my Intel on my team and where that fuck Michael is. I have an email from the agency which I open first. It reads "Well done Jason! You and your team along with the Intel you have sent shows the serious damage this agency and government has caused the U.K, under these now identified rogue agents. We are in a great deal of debt to you and your team for uncovering this on-going espionage. All charges against you and your team have now been quashed. You are hereby reinstated to your former rank immediately upon receiving this email. You are also advised to come in and get debriefed on the current status of operations and of the updated amendments to the UK's security. Regards, Fredrick Norman - Chief of the Secret Intelligence Service." I breathe out in relief as now I am no longer a fugitive. My heart is beating fast, I never expected to make it this far.

I also see that I have a message from Ryan. I wonder what he wants as all he has done was send me a number to call. I ring the number through a social media app under a code name that would be recognised by Ryan. It rang only once before it was answered by the man himself. "Hello?" I said. "Hello Jason, we just wanted to clear the air about what happened today," Ryan said. "Yeah, go on!" I replied sharply as if I was not going to like what I was about to hear. "We were watching you and you fucked up. You let Michael escape." Ryan stated. "So, it was you fuckwits that nearly blew me up!

You fucking bastard, I had that under control. What about the innocent workers in that hotel? Did you even stop to think about what you have done? You're no better than them!" I shouted. "Listen, you know the score. We had an opportunity to end this once and for all and that's what we mostly did. Yes, unfortunately, some bystanders got caught up in this, but we have saved how many lives by taking this group out all at once. They never meet up like this. I wish it could have been different but at the end of the day, you know we had to, no matter how much you don't want to hear it!" Ryan calmly said back. "Even if you were in the building, we would have done it anyway. You understand that don't you Jason?" Ryan continued.

As much as it turned me, I knew Ryan was right. If this war was to stop, we had to kill all of the terrorists before they have a chance to regroup. "Yes, I understand. War is never fair or pretty but it's war at the end of the day. I object to what you did as I could have cleaned that place out myself, but I understand why you did it." I replied to Ryan. "You have mortally crippled their struggle and the next generation of RVA have seen now with their own eyes, how you have beaten them, in a matter of days. You have also embarrassed the government as this went against their code of ethics when dealing with terrorists, as it now shows what they were pushing down the public throats all these years of bringing these murderers into politics was utterly ludicrous. The British government had now set a dangerous precedent, which other terrorist groups around the world could mimic this madness as it was proof positive that you could kill and maim for your beliefs and be rewarded for it. Politics could be now be influenced by the bomb and gun instead of the ballots. We could not let this happen and that is why the shadow government introduced Operation REVERT. To restore our once noble and lawful democracy of this country." Ryan said in a triumphant voice.

I agreed with him whole heartedly and was very impressed with what he knew about us and his vision for the country as I just knew him for being a loud drunk Loyalist with no inkling of what to do next in his life. I was taken back as this was not the Ryan I knew but it was the Ryan I now prefer. I was speechless. "Jason, you still there?" Ryan asked. "Yes, yes mate, I am" I replied. "We wanted to also update you on Michael. He has boarded a plane to Toronto just a few minutes ago from the Galway Airport. The man on the inside believes he will use your son to flush you out of hiding as you are now considered a high-value target for what's left of the RVA. To restore their army's so-called honour, you and what's left of your family have to die by their hands." Ryan said in a sombre voice. Reality hit me hard when he had said that! I immediately end the call as I don't have a moment to lose to get my ass on a plane to Canada and protect Daniel and Gerard.

I ring HQ and order them to set me up transport from the Galway Airport and safe passage into Canada, landing at Thunder Bay airport. Everything I asked for was approved without question. It only takes twenty minutes to arrive at the airport and sure enough, my trusted pilot Captain Rodgers was there waiting for me. "Major Wright!" Captain Rogers shouted as he saluted me. "Captain Rodgers my old friend, I need you to perform the fastest trans-Atlantic flight you have ever done in your career." I requested. "5 hours 30mins would be the fastest I could do, we need to go a little higher than normal for it to happen though" Captain Rodgers replied. "Fantastic!" I shouted as I got into the Gulfstream. The Captain follows me into the plane and sits behind the controls. Flicking the switches on that bring the jet to life. I noticed there doesn't seem to be a co-pilot with the Captain today. Not that he needed one as he was the best pilot I knew.

"Flight checks are already done. The agency has diverted all air traffic from this airport so you can leave right away. We have new clothes and gear for you in the back along with a fully stocked fridge, help yourself." Captain Rogers stated. The jet trundles from its parking bay and starts to taxi down a deserted runway. I immediately call Gerard and get a busy signal on his cell phone "Fucksake Gerard!!" I shouted. "You, all right?" Captain Rodgers shouted back to me. "Yes, mate! Trying to get through to the family at the moment." I shouted back.

Five hours pass and still Jason cannot get through to Gerard. Jason still does not trust that all RVA members within the security service are identified. He reluctantly holds off informing the RCMP of the situation as he does not want to tip the RVA off to his son's location.

I phone again and again until I finally get through to Gerard. "Hello?" Gerard said. "Michael is coming to you now and has probably regrouped with what's left of the RVA. Where are you?" I desperately asked hoping he would say at home.

"I have just arrived home, took the kid fishing on Trout Lake. We weren't expecting a call from you as the little man got bored cooped up in the house. Apologies if you were trying to ring, no cell reception up there. Anyway, how would he know where I live?" Gerard said. It was a good question as I have never mentioned anything about him to anyone outside of the family. Then I remember the phone call those assholes made using Olivia's mobile. They have her phone and the only Canadian land line number on her mobile was Gerard's. "They are going to find you through the landline number on Olivia's mobile. They could have already been checking out the place for weeks!" I replied. Gerard fell silent as it was all too possible for the RVA to be capable of such a task.

"We have fucked up Jason, we didn't plan for this, but we are prepared for it!" Gerard answered. "I will get help to you now, secure the house and prepare to defend yourselves! Don't you let anything happen to Daniel, you hear me?" I told him in a firm voice. "I'm going to send these Irish bog bastards, straight to hell. They won't get Daniel, I promise you." Gerard replied. "I have agents on the way to your location. Do not let anyone in until I confirm it's them!" I instructed. "Fuck! Powers out!" Gerard said. "That's them, they're on you already! Get Daniel to the safe room now!" I replied, "Done, get here fucking quick!" Gerard said before he hung up.

I immediately ring the RCMP in Thunder Bay and ask for assistance. "This is MI6 Agent, Major, Jason Wright 45035XXA, we have a terrorist situation (Code 10-35) Need assistance (Code 10-78) 2 miles north from Crystal Lake on the Trans-Canada Hwy, Jamison residence, number 81. Shots fired, Shots fired! Recommend land and air intervention. Confirm?" I ask the operator. Within a few seconds, the operator replies. "This is RCMP, acknowledged and authorised ETA 20 mins."

I lied about the shots fired as they would have done a risk assessment that would have took longer so I helped them with the category this situation fits into by placing the action into a code red. I can't risk anything when it comes to my son's safety. "Thank you for your assistance!" I then hang up and get prepared for my arrival in Thunder Bay. I'm thinking about my promise to Olivia and how I have put my boy in danger again. I won't hold anything back, this time, they all die!

Chapter 12 - The new king of nothing

Michael is planning a coup within the RVA as he finds himself backed into a corner by Brendan and Trevor. If Brendan is out of the picture, then Trevor becomes Michael's obedient bitch. Michael understands he can't risk doing it himself as all the RVA would turn on him. Time is against him as it won't be long before Brendan will find out that Jason and his kid are still breathing. Michael knows he has at the most a few days or in the worst-case scenario, a few hours.

I will invite Brendan to the party we are having and get him shot by the Loyalists when he attends the gathering. Getting him to attend is the easy bit, getting him shot will be hard as he has been playing dodge the bullet with the Brits practically his whole life, so I can't expect him to go down easy. I can't do it... I just can't fucking do it. He's my mentor, a father figure who almost raised me like one of his own boys. Plus, what if the Loyalists fuck up, I can't risk it!

Michael sits down on his steps outside his home and puts his head in his hands.

I know Brendan will kill me as it's the code we all govern ourselves by. The code declared to us on entry to the RVA brotherhood, which every volunteer vowed to live by. I had used this very same code to execute traitors and defectors who were among us and yet I can't justify that the same code should apply to me. If I die by Brendan's hands will I still be honoured amongst the ranks or will they turn my memory into something that would dishonour my achievements? I want to rip my hair out as there is no one I can turn to in my hour of need. I'm on my own and that's that.

Fuck the code. Brendan's a dead man. "I've got it!" Michael says aloud to himself. The two new boys wee Paul brought over to me won't have any notion of who Brendan is! I will go pay their granny a wee visit to find out where they are.

Michael looks across the road and sees the light is still on in the old girl's house. Time to introduce myself to the old doll. Michael looks about and makes sure that no one sees him going over to the house as the fewer people know what's going on the better. "Knock, Knock, Knock" Michael wrapped the door gentle as to not scare the old woman as its late evening. The door slowly opens and the old woman peeks her head around the door to find out who was there. "Awk, hello Michael, come in, come in!" she said with delight. "How are we doing missus? You're looking well so you are!" Michael said trying to complement her. "Hello Michael, Hi Michael!" said the boys who were eating a take away on the couch whilst watching the telly.

"Gran, do you mind if I talk business with the lads for a wee minute?" Michael asked the old woman. "No problem Michael, I've smoothing to be done in the kitchen. You work away here and I will close the door." She replied. "You're a wee doll, so you are!" Michael said to the old woman with a smile on his face. The old woman shuffled out of the room and closed the door gently. "Right you two! I got a job that I need both of you on with me. You pull it off, you're in!" Michael said to the boys. "Fantastic Michael!" The older boy said as they both kept eating and looking at him a little dumbfounded. Michael went over to them both and asked them their names. "So, what do they call you?" he said to the younger boy. "Aodhan!" he said. "What about you?" He asked the other. "Ruari!" said the older brother. "Well, boys, where are your parents?" Michael asked. The boys looked ashamed and were hesitant to answer. Michael just waited patiently for an answer. Aodhan spoke first. "Our parents were drunks and didn't look after us too well so our gran stepped in," Aodhan said. "We don't miss them, they don't give a shit about us!" Ruari added.

Michael thought that this situation was perfect for what he needed to use them for. "You boys fancy a pint?" Michael said. They both said yes and left the house and shouted to their gran they would see her later. The old dear, shouted back at them not to be too late coming home.

"Which pub are we going to Michael?" Ruari asked. "One across the border. The pub I am taking you to has the best pie and chips on the island. Trust me you will love it!" Michael replied in an excited voice as he guided the boys over to his old grey beat up truck. "Get in, I won't be a moment!" He said to the boys before disappearing into his house.

Michael went to the kitchen and opened up the cupboards under the sink and began to shove everything out onto the floor. He then began lifting an edge of the bottom floor in the cupboard to reveal a stash of weapons and munitions. Michael put on some leather gloves before picking up the guns and ammo and throwing them roughly behind him on the floor in a hurried mess. Michael then began to put the flooring of the cupboard back down again and started to throw all the cleaning products and pots he had just taken out, back in again and closed

155

the cupboard doors. Michael needed a big ruck sack to carry all of the weapons in and was struggling to find one down stairs. He rushed up to his room and pulled his duvet off the bed and brought it down stairs. He laid it out across the kitchen floor and started to pile the weapons and ammo into the middle of his duvet. He then folded the corners over and gave it a spin to pack the stash together and make it easier to carry.

Michael then ripped off his gloves and brought the stash of weapons outside and placed them into the back cabin of the truck as the boys looked on. "What you doing Michael?" asked Ruari. Michael ignored him and made sure the stash was secure behind their seats. "Right, let's get going!" Michael said as he turned on the stereo loud enough, so they couldn't ask him questions. They travelled for over an hour till they got to the pub Michael had told them about. The pub is close to Brendan's village and it should be just starting to get busy. "Right lads, out you get! We ARE here!" said Michael as he rubbed his hands together excitedly. "What if they don't serve us, Michael? We're under age?" Aodhan asked. "Shut up Aodhan! Who is going to say no to us with Michael King of the RVA here.

Let's fucking wreck this place!" Ruari said with a smile on his face. "That's the spirit lad!" Michael said. "Tell your little bro to put his big boy pants on and fucking relax!" Michael said into Ruari's ear. The boys and Michael enter the pub and drink for hours on end. They danced with the women and share stories with each other about what they have done for the RVA in the past. The boys began to relax and trust Michael more and more after each round. The trouble was Michael was not drinking the same quantities as the young boys and this was all part of his plan.

"Right, let's go boys. We have a wee job to do. You still up for it?" Michael asked excitedly. "YEAH!!! Chucky Your Ma!" Ruari said drunkenly. Both boys burst out laughing and even Michael started to chuckle as they made their way back to the truck. "Are you tough guys?" Michael asked the boys as they clambered into his truck. "What do you mean? Like can we fight?" Aodhan replied. "Yeah, I suppose. I was actually thinking more along the lines of whether you guys have ever fired guns at Loyalists?" Michael replied.

"Not many around here, sure there's not Michael" Ruari laughed to himself. "No, we haven't done anything like that before. We've thrown petrol bombs at the police and proddy band parades if that counts?" Ruari continued. "Yes, I suppose that does. Well, I got a treat for you two. Look behind the seat, in the duvet." Michael said. "Wow! Look at all these rifles and guns! We could take out anyone we want with this lot!" Ruari said as he pulled out a rifle and was admiring it in his hands. Not to be out done by his older brother Aodhan pulls a hand gun out of the stash and struggles to cock the weapon. "FUCK!" Aodhan shouted as he dropped the gun and clasped his hand. "What's the matter boy!" Michael asked slightly smirking to himself. Michael knew what Aodhan did as he watched him try to cock the weapon, only for the loading chamber to spring back and cut his hand on the bit of skin between the thumb and index finger. Michael put on his leather gloves again.

"Let me show you how it's done. You hold firmly the top part of the gun and slide it back, pointing the weapon away from you. You then check if the chamber is loaded. Then release the top half which cocks the gun. You will know it's cocked as you can see the hammer is down, ready for you to pull the trigger." Michael explained as he handed the gun back to Aodhan. Aodhan tried to pull the trigger of the gun but nothing happened. Michael, waited gleefully as he knew the safety was on but wanted to see if the young boy could figure it out for himself. "Ya stupid fucker! You have the safety on." Shouted Ruari. Michael wanted to be the one that showed him where he was going wrong before Ruari butted in. Aodhan pushed the safety off and began to click away at the trigger. Ruari, on the other hand, looked a bit too confident with his rifle as he was able to check it and load a clip. "Don't be firing that fucking thing here Ruari! Push over and let me get behind the wheel!" Michael shouted.

As their truck pulled out of the pub car park, Michael started to explain to the boys about the job he wanted them to do. "Right, you both listening! There is a tout just outside this village called Brendan and we are going to nut him. He is in his late fifties, dark hair and has a bit of a belly on him. There is no one in his house except for his wife. You guys will go in and shoot the bastard dead and leave the wife alone." Michael instructed. "Do you got any masks or gloves, Michael?" Ruari asked. "Nah, you don't need that shit for this job. It's going to be over quick before you know it you will be out and back in the truck with me as fully-fledged members of the RVA," Michael said.

The boys were getting excited and were ready to do what Michael had asked of them. They had no idea that Michael knew that they didn't stand a chance against Brendan. All he was using the boys for was a distraction, so he could locate and stealthily kill Brendan. As they got closer to the house Michaels' nerves were kicking in as his hands started to shake as he was steering the truck. He pulled over and got the boys out by the side of the road. "Right lads...um...I need Ya to..." Michael started to mumble as he grabbed each of their weapons and loaded them. "What Michael?" Aodhan asked with a confused look on his face. "Just gathering my thoughts about how best to approach this as we can't let the fucker escape. Give me a minute!" Michael snarled.

Michael handed the older boy the 9mm hand gun. "Ruari, you go to the front of the house and knock on the door. Wait for someone to answer and ask if they could phone a tow truck for you as you left your mobile at home." Michael ordered. He then turned to the younger brother and gave him the automatic rifle. "Aodhan, you go around the back of the house and watch through the window to see who answers the door.

If it's a man, shoot through the glass and riddle him. If it's the wife just meet me back here. That goes for you too Ruari." Michael instructed. The boys nodded and Michael led them to Brendan's house through a cabbage field. Michael froze as he could hear the dogs barking in the distance. "Shit, forgot about them!" Michael said aloud. Michael then started to let out a low pitch whistle which attracted the dogs, The dogs started to run towards them across the field. "Give me that hand gun Ruari!" Ping, Ping "Yelp", Ping, Ping "Whimper".

Michael kills the two dogs with the silenced pistol.

"Right boys, there is the house, now off you go and remember what I told you!" Michael said whilst giving Ruari his gun back. The boys split up and did exactly what they were told as Michael took up position behind the parked car at the back of the house and readied his rifle. Michael could no longer see Ruari as he went around to the front. He could see Aodhan looking through the window of the kitchen waiting on his brother to knock on the door. "Knock Knock." That was Ruari signal given, now all we had to do was wait to see who answered the door. All of a sudden, the entire property went dark, including the exterior property lights. "Lads, run back here now!" Michael shouted. The boys started to run back into the field they came from as the back door of the house flew open and gun fire erupted. Ruari was hit in the leg and fell face first into the ground. Aodhan went back to his brother when he saw he had dropped. The boys got their weapons ready and scanned the field for movement. Michael stayed where he was and watched Brendan slip out and around the back of the garage, out of his sight. There is no going back now, Michael thought. It was almost like he was waiting on us.

I see Brendan again, slowly approaching the boys, using the overgrown hedge to walk in front of so he blends into the background. Michael started to keep a fix on Brendan's position as he lined up his scope on him. He had seconds to get a clean shot in before Brendan got to the boys. Michael loaded the chamber and tried to slow his breathing down as anxiety was creeping in. "Boom!" Brendan went down hard as the bullet struck him in the chest. Michael breathed a sigh of relief as he got back up on to his feet and began to walk over to the boys. "Fucksake lads, that was too close! Ruari, give us that gun you have." Michael said. "Aye, here you go!" Ruari replied. "Thanks!" Michael said before quickly shooting each brother in the head. Michael then threw the pistol beside their bodies. Michael had always planned to kill the brothers once the job was done as he couldn't risk any trials that would lead back to him. He calmly walked over to Brendan and stood over his body. He was clearly dead. Michael took Brendan's gun and slowly walked back to the house.

He had one more witness to take care of. After finding Brendan's wife and killing her, Michael made himself a cup of tea. He sat outside and started to relax as he no longer had a death threat over his head. He was now in charge. I need to get back home quickly and pretend to be surprised at the news of our leader's death. As I make my way back across the field I can see the outline shadows of the recently deceased. They stay where they lay I thought to myself as I focused on climbing up and over a gate.

Climbing into the van, I carefully place my rifle under the duvet cover behind the seats. It will take me over an hour to get back to my place but it's a pleasant enough drive home. I turn on the radio and go into auto pilot as I sail down the road back to Belfast. Dawn was breaking as Michael pulled up to his house. He got out of his truck and grabbed the duvet from behind the seats. He locked the doors and went up the steps and into his house. He was very tired after that long drive and just wanted to go to bed but he knew he had to stow the guns he didn't use, away again. The guns that were left scattered around Brendan's property will, however, paint a most confusing story for the authorities. As long as they didn't have his prints on them he didn't care who found them.

The guns were now stowed away and the duvet ready once again to be used on Michaels bed. He needed to get some sleep as tonight was going to be the gathering. It was 8 am when he finally got off to sleep. Michael's phone rang and rang later that afternoon but he ignored it. When he finally got up around 3 pm, he had seen that he had a missed call from Nula, his older sister.

Michael phoned Nula to check on the progress of the provisions for his party. "Well, how's it going down there? Is everything set up?" Michael asked the person who picked up the phone. "Yes, it's going good.... who is this please?" A little voice replied. "Is that Bernadette? My wee friend? It's your uncle Michael. Is any of the adults nearby?" Michael said with a smile of his face as he hasn't spoken to his niece in months. "Yes, Uncle Mike, hold on and I will get mummy," Bernadette replied. "MUUUM, can you come here, please? IT'S UNCLE MIKE!" Bernadette yelled. "Hold on, she's coming." Bernadette put the phone down and went away. Seconds later Bernadette's mum picks up the line. "Hello, Mike. What's wrong, why you not answering your phone?" said Nula as she starts to look around the room she is in and shouts out instructions to the decorators as she is impatiently waiting for Michael to speak. "Listen Nula can I phone back later, things going alright though?" Michael asked. "Yes, everything is looking great, speak later," Nula said as she hung up the phone.

That is all Michael wanted to hear. Getting tired again Michael switches his phone to silent and tries to grab another sleep as he wanted to stay up late with the lads and restore their faith in him after the death of wee Paul. He threw his phone onto his side cabinet and found a sweet spot in his bed which made him fall asleep quite quickly. "DZZZ, DZZZZ, DZZZZ!" Michael's phone was vibrating a few hours later which only made him stir him as he did not get up. "DZZZ, DZZZZ, DZZZZ!" His mobile went again before a groggy Michael answered. A man from the social club where his gathering was taking place had screamed down the phone they were under heavy attack. Without hesitation, Michael threw on a top and buttoned his jeans up before running down stairs. He ran into the kitchen and grabbed the weapons he needed and ran outside to his truck. He then took out his pistol and fired four rounds into the air to get the attention of his troops. Only a few were left on the estate as the majority had already gone ahead to the gathering. To be more accurate, there were only three of them and they were nothing more than foot soldiers guarding the estate. "Right Hughes, get that fucking mortar tube from your garage and make sure it's welded to the big foot plate as its going into the back of my pick-up truck!" Michael shouted. "Now you two, go to the weapons stash and get me all the rockets we have. HURRY!" Michael ordered.

All of the men did what was asked of them and rapidly get the truck ready with the weapons they were going to use. They all got into the truck, well except for one who had to ride in the truck bed to stop the mortar cannon from jumping about while on transit. "Michael, who the fuck is attacking the club?" Hughes asked. "We don't know, the only things we know for sure, is that they are coming in heavy!" Michael replied. I have to get there fast; Michael thought to himself as he climbed curbs and ran traffic lights in order to gain time. You could start to see smoke coming out of the area where the club was located. Michael knew they were counting on him to save them and he wasn't about to let them down. As he swerved around the last corner he could see gun fire coming from all directions. Before he could even stop the truck, his windscreen disintegrated as bullets came roaring into the cab.

Hughes was hit multiple times along with the other foot soldier who was next to him. They were both screaming out in agony asking for help but there was nothing Michael was prepared to do. They were no use to him now. He drove nearer to the club and screeched the truck to a halt before jumping out firing his weapon at his attackers but couldn't get a bearing on any individual targets. "FUCK THIS!" Michael shouted as he pushed the body of his RVA comrade off the back of his truck and positioned the mortar to where he could see military men dressed in black.

He loaded the mortar with a missile which hit the bottom of the tube and thumped out the top with such ferocity it shook the entire vehicle. The missile gave a whistle before it hit the building where he had seen the military men. It was a good hit as some of the walls caved in on top of them. Michael was about to load another missile when gun fire and ricocheting bullets started to hit all around him. He was made, and he could see where the enemy was firing from. "BOOM!" A chunk of the road near his back vanished in an explosive hit, debris flying through the air killing his third comrade. That was a high calibre round, fucking great; sniper has eyes on me, he thought to himself. The sound of approaching helicopters could be heard getting ever closer.

Michael was hoping the police would arrive soon as they could take the heat off him, so he could move from behind his truck. "Boom!" A bullet tears through the truck rear panelling and bursts the tire near Michael's head which blows him off balance and into plain sight. "Mother Fuckers!" Michael yelled as he scrambled to get on his feet to run for cover. His head was dizzy from the impact of the exploding truck tyre; he had just made it behind a concrete flower bed. It was run and fight another day or die right here, right now he thought to himself. "Fuck it!" Michael said as he ran for cover around the back of the building. I've done my part, those fucks will have to hold their own, I'm out of here. All I need to do is leave in this direction away from the fight and I will be home free. The fighting was overwhelming for Michael as he walked with a blank look on his face almost like he saw the beginning of the end for the RVA.

He did not care about the comrades he just lost, as empathy just wasn't in his nature. All he could think about was revenge on whomever it was that was behind the attack. The police sirens could be heard now, and they were coming fast. I need to pick up the pace a bit to get out of here, Michael thought as he knew he couldn't get the revenge he wanted behind bars if he was caught with a weapon. It was a long walk home and his estate seemed deserted. Michael looked around the houses to find them mostly empty. He could see the old doll across the road looking at him through the curtains of her bedroom. She looked angry like she knew I had something to do with the disappearance of her grand kids. Well if she is smart she will stay away from me as I would be just as easy for me to kill her as it would to tell her to fuck off! Michael wanted his phone to ring or someone to come over to his house and tell him what the fuck happened tonight. He sat for hours looking out the window and checking his phone every five minutes. "Ring! Hello, hello!" Michael said. "Thank god you're still alive! I have been really worried over today's events." Trevor said.

"You should have known about this shit ahead of time! My people are lying dead all over the fucking streets, slaughtered like pigs whilst you're tucked up safe and sound in your fucking office! You better fucking have an air tight explanation of how this happened or you're a dead man!" Michael screamed down the phone at Trevor. "Listen MICHAEL! I know who was behind the attacks and unfortunately it's really bad news for you," said Trevor. "How is it bad news for me just tell me who it is so I can kill the bastard?" replied Michael. "It was Jason and the operations team behind REVERT," Trevor said in a sombre voice. Michael said nothing as he realised he had vastly underestimated this man and what he was truly capable of. "It also means that you yourself are on borrowed time as I have to inform Brendan you failed in killing Jason and his son.

I am truly sorry about this but if this organisation is to complete its goals we can't have fuck ups like you running the show. Good bye Michael." Trevor said. "Brendan's dead," Michael replied. There was silence on the line again as it was now Trevor who was quickly recalculating the situation he now finds himself in. "When did Brendan die?" Trevor said hoping to find out more about what happened if anything at all. If this is indeed true, Trevor knows the balance of power has now gone indisputably to Michael. Thus, making his unceremonious threats to him seconds ago, utterly worthless, and quite possibly, detrimental to his own life.

"I will deal with you later!" Michael said as he disconnected the call. Michael knows he still needs Trevor but wants him to stew for a while, thinking his life was under threat. This way Michael can be assured that Trevor will finally give him the respect and fear he now deserves. I will phone that fucker back in a few days to assert my authority over him and let him know where he stands with me. In the meantime, I need to gather my troops and what senior members we have left for a war meeting. I won't know the damage to our numbers until we have all areas checking in with us.

Michael phones the RVA political wing and asks them to contact everyone of importance to meet across the border in Galway at a well-known hotel called The Fox and Whippet. Trevor will need to be there as well to advise our next steps to counter these attacks and how to rebuild what we have lost so far. What if this attack was one of many happening around the country, for all I know, I could be the last man standing. Michaels phone rings and as he pulls it from his pocket a smile comes across his face as he looks at the caller ID, "Colin Murphy".

Chapter 13 - Last man standing

Jason's son and uncle are on their own. The power has been cut to the property but nothing else has happened yet. Gerard has Daniel secured in his safe room as a precaution as he does not know what exactly awaits him outside. Jason has alerted the authorities which are en route to Gerard's homestead.

I fucking hate this. I can't be there when my son needs me the most. Gerard has this, don't worry! I kept thinking to myself as I often was forgetting the fact that he was a decorated war hero. He knew how to handle a weapon and could out think most people by at least ten moves. Why can't this fucking plane go any faster!

Meanwhile

Gerard was waiting on assistance coming as he knew Jason would have sent the police his way for assistance. What was more worrying to Gerard was the utter silence, there was no noise coming from anywhere. No one was trying to break in or could be seen lurking about the property. Gerard was no fool and knew most of the obvious tactics of terrorist groups like the RVA. They mostly stuck to guerrilla tactics or masquerading as public officials to get the jump on their target. "Knock, Knock, Knock" went Gerard's front door which slightly startled him as he had seen no one come down his driveway. Gerard readied his rifle and stood behind the support wall in the living room, which was hidden from any of the windows. "WHO IS IT?" Gerard yelled. "IT'S THE RCMP; WE ARE INVESTIGATING A POSSIBLE HOME INTRUSION," The voice said behind the door. "WHO TOLD YOU THIS?" Gerard asked as he was not yet convinced who they said they were. "WE NEED ACCESS TO YOUR HOUSE NOW IN ORDER TO VALIDATE IF THERE IS A PROBLEM AT YOUR RESIDENCE. GERARD, OPEN THE DOOR OR WE WILL FORCE ENTRY!" The voice said.

Gerard quickly phoned the RCMP to ask whether they had sent officers to his house. "Sir they are on their way now, I'm looking at the GPS of the officer's cars in real time and can see they are 10 minutes away from your location." Before Gerard could reply to the young lady on the phone. His front door was blasted into pieces in what seemed to be military plastic explosives due to the smell it gave off. Gerard knows who was most likely behind the explosion. "Gerard, is it?" said an unfamiliar Irish voice. It's him, fucking Michael on my own door step, Gerard thought to himself. Gerard took a deep breath and took aim around the corner carefully, waiting for the voice to speak again. "Geo..."

"RA TA TA TA TA TA TA" focusing his aim on the door and windows Gerard let out a volley of shots to let them know he is armed. "THAT WASN'T TOO FRIENDLY GERARD, BUT YOU HAVE MADE MY MIND UP ABOUT HOW BEST TO DEAL WITH THIS SITUATION! GOODBYE GERARD!" Michael yelled into the house before throwing a large satchel charge through the front door. "FUCK!" Gerard said as he ran to the back of the house. "BOOOOOM!" The explosion ripped through the house with a shock wave that destroyed nearly everything in its path. The roof of the house caved in along with some of the walls. "Well if I didn't just kill everyone in that fucking shed he calls a house, I will eat me fucking hat!" Michael said out loud to his three Canadian comrades. Michael could hear sirens in the distance. "Right, let's go. My pal will follow me now, where I want him to go!" Michael shouted to his men as they ran back into the woods.

The RCMP cruisers sped down Gerard's drive way and strategically parked their cars, so they could use them as cover. They were met with a smouldering wreck of a house that looked like it belonged in a war zone. The officers called for further assistance immediately. Gerard was starting to come around, after being knocked unconscious. "DANIEL!!" he shouted as he made his way from under the debris and wreckage that was once his home.

"DANIEL!! UNCLE GERARD IS COMING, DON'T WORRY!" he shouted again as he made his way to the kitchen and pulled open the floor latch which was hidden under a rug in the middle of his kitchen. Gerard pulled the doorway open to reveal the safe room entrance he had built under the house. Gerard carefully typed the key code into the hatch entrance and opened the heavy metal door. Daniel was sitting on a chair with a blanket around him, too scared to even look at Gerard. "You alright Daniel?" Gerard said as he put his arm around him to comfort him. Suddenly a loud mega phone can be heard "THIS IS THE RCMP, GERARD JAMESON. PLEASE MAKE CONTACT WITH US TO LET US KNOW YOU'RE IN THERE." The officer said. Gerard took out his mobile and contacted the RCMP which patched him through to the officers at his house.

He had informed them the house was clear but structurally damaged and advised the officers to be vigilant as the terrorists could be anywhere on his homestead. Gerard's property was swarming with emergency services and they were now treating Gerard and Daniel for any injuries they may have received. "We found a back-dirt road which was most likely used to escape the area. We are following the road now to see if we can get an idea of where these fugitives are going." The officer said to Gerard.

Gerard looked back at the officer and told them "I have a good idea where Michael and his goons are going." Gerard said whilst looking at a Toronto Blue Jays hat blowing around his front porch. "How do you know where they going?" asked the officer inquisitively. "I'm not a baseball fan!" Gerard replied as they both looked at the baseball cap. The officer leaves Gerard at the ambulance and goes back to his cruiser immediately to call in check points for a 200-mile radius of his location. Gerard continues to stay right beside Daniel as he is being checked over. You could tell he was reliving the nightmare he had lived through once before on the night his mother died. Daniel looked pale and lost in his thoughts. Gerard knew the one person who could bring him around and that was his father Jason.

"Hello, Jason...Now hold on a minute till I explain the current situation. Yes, he is 100% fine.... Are you going to let me get a word in edgewise? Thank you. Daniel was in the safe room as agreed while the house came under attack. It was that Irish fuck Michael that paid us a visit and nearly levelled the house. Listen, he left a Blue Jays baseball cap here which is a message obviously for you. The dumb fuck thinks we are dead or he wasn't bothered about finishing us off. I doubt he knew I had a secure safe room. Regardless, he did what he came to do and left you that message on the porch of where you can find him. Toronto is a big place Jason, where do you even start?" Gerard said. "Listen, more importantly, you have a wee man here who needs to speak to his daddy." Gerard continued as he handed his mobile to Daniel. "Son, it's daddy. You Ok?" Jason asked.

Daniel nods his head without saying a word and hands the phone back to Gerard. "Why are you not talking to your daddy?" Gerard asked. "I don't have a daddy anymore. He left me again with bad people. He doesn't like me!" Daniel said as tears started to come down his face. Jason heard every word and it broke his heart. He was on a plane and his boy yet again was put through what no child should ever have to face time and time again. He felt ashamed that he didn't keep his promise of being there for him. Jason wished with all his might he could hug his only child and tell him again it would be alright but how could Daniel ever believe him again. "Gerard...Gerard, are you there?" Jason asked. "Yes, Jason," Gerard replied as he took the phone off Daniel.

"I have let my son down badly. I should have got those fuckers before they got anywhere near him. I'm diverting the plane to Toronto and finishing this tonight. Please keep him safe." Jason said in a sombre voice. "You know I will! We are staying under police protection at a military base near the state line.

Don't you worry about Daniel, if he knew what you have done so far for everyone, he would be very proud. Just make sure you get that prick and any of his goons. God speed Jason!" Gerard said as he disconnected the call. Jason sat back in his chair in the cabin and started to take off his tactical gear. This was now a man hunt and he needed to blend in with the crowd. He put on a smart black suit and tie, white shirt but kept his bullet proof vest on as he could conceal it under his shirt. He then started to sort out his weapons he would use and came upon his razor wire Garrotte. He gently stretched it into a straight line then back again to make a snare like loop. Jason fantasized about putting it around Michael's neck, but he thought that was too good for him and placed it to the side of the table. He then got his swords out and knew he could dice him from the feet up, which the thought of, put a smile on his face. "You're going to beg for me to kill you, Michael!" Jason said quietly, gripping his swords ever tighter.

"Sir, 20 mins ETA!" Captain Rogers shouted back to Jason. "Ok mate, thanks for the heads up," Jason shouted back. Jason then got the rest of his gear ready and waited for the plane to land. As the plane came drifting down lower Jason could see the twinkling skyline of Toronto once more. He felt energised and refreshed after such a daunting time whilst on operations in Northern Ireland. Jason quickly fixed his hair, ready to leave the plane. Jason held onto the door frame looking into the cockpit as the Captain landed the plane. As Captain Rogers taxied the plane, Jason stood by the door impatiently waiting for the plane to stop.

As the captain pulled into their parking spot away from the main terminal at Pearsons, Jason pulled the latch on the door and opened it. "LET ME KNOW WHEN YOU'RE FINISHED JASON!" Captain Rodgers shouted as Jason jumped down onto the tarmac. Jason ran to the hangers and looked around for any vehicle he could boost. He stopped and shook his head. No! I'm not going to cheapen this manhunt by breaking the laws I have sworn to serve he thought to himself. Jason made his way to the back fence and threw his duffle bag over it before he quickly scaled the fence and made his way over to the other side. He then made his way to the front of the airport and waited in line for a taxi.

It takes a few minutes at the taxi rank for Jason to finally get a cab. "Hello sir, where do you want to go?" asked the taxi driver. "Take me to the corner of Adelaide and York street please," Jason replied. As the taxi moved onto the slip road and into the city Jason started to lock and load his weapons inside the duffle bag on his lap. He made sure the man in front couldn't see what he was up to. The taxi man strained every so often to get a glimpse of what Jason was up to but to no avail. Jason paid the taxi man and even gave him a generous tip before parting ways.

Jason knew Michael wouldn't be at where the Blue Jays play but knowing he was a twisted cunt, it would be a safe bet he was in the area. Jason tried to narrow his chances by seeing if Michael would be so blatant to show his face at the Irish bars. Jason checked his mobile map search and found there were a few in the area to investigate. However, he also knew Michael most likely would not be alone and would be looking for him also. The good news is that Jason had got to Toronto a few hours ahead of Michael and play it smart if he was going to kill him today. Jason roamed the streets and when he found a bin got rid of the duffle bag. The first Irish bar Jason approached was small and didn't have windows you could see through due to the frosted stencilled glass. Jason carefully walked through the doors and into the dimly lit pub.

The music was blaring, and it was packed. Jason was relieved to see the pub was full of punters as he now had cover to scan the place over. He went to the back of the pub and stood at the gambling machines whilst keeping an eye on the front entrance, hoping the next people in would be his targets. Jason gave it a few hours before moving to the next pub on his planned route. As he walked outside he got a glimmer of a face he thought he recognised. He couldn't place the face and continued to walk to the next pub. As he was walking Jason felt like he was being watched but could not place eyes on anyone that would be a threat to him.

Jason thought about the best way to find a tail is to go in a circle and that is what he did. This time he concentrated his focus of colours and outfits making sure that if he saw them again he would know he was being followed. He also remembers from his time in the Loyalist paramilitaries they used at least three people at a time to track a person's movements. There it was again, that face and grey coat. Now it was time to flush them out. Jason went into the hotel that was adjacent to him and used the stairs to get to the second floor. As he got to the second floor, he looked down over the balcony and focused on the hotel entrance. Sure enough, the same man in the grey coat came in shortly after him. Now to lure him in for questioning Jason smirked to himself. Jason stood by the elevators on the second floor until he was sure the man had seen him. The man in the grey coat was looking in the wrong areas and was at risk of leaving the building. Jason took out his phone and pretended to talk to someone as he laughed out loud. This did the trick as the man in the grey coat was slowly making his way towards him from the ground floor.

Jason hit the elevator button and took it to the ninth floor. As soon as the elevator stopped, Jason got out and waited in the hall by the vending machines. "Ding!" the elevator opened and the man with the grey coat stepped out.

Jason could see him approaching as he was watching him carefully using the glass on the vending machine to see his stalkers reflexion. Suddenly the man in the grey coat pulled a gun on Jason as he came closer. Jason fired his silenced gun through the side of his coat and hit the man in both legs. The man involuntarily threw his weapon out of his hand after being shot which quickly put him on the ground. Without hesitation, Jason grabbed the man's gun and quickly holstered his own as he lifted the man onto his shoulders and brought him down the hall. The man was in dire pain and didn't even talk; he just kept gritting his teeth and grunting whilst trying to hold his wounded legs. Jason threw the man roughly off his shoulders and onto the floor at the end of the hall before he started to knock on the door beside him. Jason needed a room to help encourage his new friend to talk to him.

Jason knocked the door once more and still, no one came to the door. Fair game, he thought to himself before stepping back and booting the door open with one mighty kick. The room was unoccupied which was a bonus as Jason didn't want an audience for what he was about to do. His interrogation was going to have to be short as the area was not a secure location.

Jason went back to the man in the hall and grabbed a fist full of his hair before dragging him into the room and then continued into the bathroom. He then grabbed the man by his coat and picked him up and placed him in the bath. The man was crying out in pain and asked Jason to stop, to which he made no reaction. Jason searched the man and took all the contents he had on him and placed them on the floor to inspect. He then flipped the man roughly over and hand cuffed his wrists behind his back before turning him around again on his back. The man looked terrified as he was watching Jason prep the bathroom for what looked like his execution. As Jason yanked the shower curtain off the railing and threw it on the ground he turned on the taps at the sink. He then took one of the hotel towels and ran it under the tap to make it thoroughly wet before slapping it over the man's face.

The man jolted right away as the weight of the towel and the amount of water being held in it made it impossible to breathe. Jason looked at his watch and gave it fifteen seconds before removing the towel. "I will tell you everything! Please don't kill me!" the man pleaded with Jason. Jason didn't even look at him as he ran the towel again under the tap and for a second time slapped it onto the man's face. This time Jason gave it twenty seconds which for anyone breathing heavy already would put them on the cusp of unconsciousness. As the man flopped about in the bath struggling to breathe Jason started to feel bad for his assailant.

Jason whipped off the towel and made sure the man understood to be quiet until he was finished speaking. "I am a member of the secret service for her majesties government and have a licence to eliminate targets when deemed a viable threat to our national security. You need to understand that I know a great many things and will be cross examining you to see if the Intel you are about to give me is indeed correct and up-to-date. The repercussions of not cooperating or giving me no viable information will result in me leaving this towel on your face until you die. Are you ready for my questions?" Jason asked the man. The man quickly nodded his head and waited for Jason to ask his first question. "Why were you following me?" asked Jason. "I was paid to as there is a bounty on your head of $60000." The man replied. "Who set this bounty and whom do you work for?" Jason asked. "I work for myself as a bounty hunter for anyone that pays well. I found out about your bounty through an Irish man at a pub nearby this hotel.

The guy didn't give a fuck who heard him as he stood up on a pool table and offered anyone sixty thousand dollars to bring you to him alive. He had loads of your pictures and said you would be in the area now" The man said. "HOW LONG AGO WAS THIS?" Jason shouted. "Less than an hour ago, I was thinking how lucky I was to have seen you first." The man said. I need to get to that pub and track Michael from there but first I have to find out if I am talking to a killer. "How long have you been doing this job?" Jason inquired. "All my life, I do it as a side-line to support my family as my main job doesn't pay so good." The man said.

"Do you realise that you have dragged your bounties all those years, most likely to their deaths?" Jason said. "No, No, I wouldn't take a bounty if I knew they were going to be killed at the end of it. No way!" the man replied. Jason knew the man was full of shit and the world would be a better place without him, but he didn't want to execute him. He would give the man a choice. "Ok, I think we are done here," Jason said as he turned the man on his side and un-cuffed him. Jason purposely left his holstered gun exposed and in easy reach of the man. He pretended to fumble around in his pockets to see what the man would do.

To Jason's surprise, the man did nothing but start to shiver a little as his gunshot wound seemed to be giving his body notice that he needed fixed and soon. Jason got his gear together and asked one final question to the man. "Which pub did you see this Irish man in?" The man who was now starting to slur his words said: "The pubsh is called th Irish Gent." Jason went over to the telephone beside the bed and rang room service. "Yes, can we help you?" a polite voice said down the line. "Yes, there is a man in my bathtub who is bleeding all over it. Could I get a room change?" Jason replied and then threw the still connected receiver onto the bed.

Jason then left the room and made his way out of the building. As Jason makes his way to the Irish Gent pub he was thinking how close he was to finally ending this operation once and for all. The mistakes he had made throughout this mission and how he would do it differently. Jason was in and out of his thoughts whilst keeping an eye on his mobile phone GPS map to make sure he was going the right way. Nearly twenty minutes later and Jason is practically at the pub deciding which way he would enter it or where he could watch it from so he could clap eyes on Michael.

Jason noticed another Irish bar across the road from the Irish Gent and decided he would go there instead to see what exactly he was up against across the road. As Jason entered the pub he was scanning everyone as he was taught

171

to do by the firm. Watching their body language and counting exits as he made his way deeper into the venue.

The bar wasn't too busy for 5 pm and had a right mix of people in it of all ages. Jason walks into the bar and orders a drink. "Double port please," Jason said to the barman. As the barman was getting his drink, Jason noticed a fairly good vantage point on the second floor of the bar that overlooked the Irish Gents pub. "There you go sir, that will be fifteen dollars." The barman said to Jason. FUCK, Jason thought to himself as the drink was way overpriced to what he would pay back home. Jason gave him a twenty. "Keep the change," Jason told the barman.

Jason noticed some black and white photos of some deceased RVA men on the wall, each of them dressed in a suit. "Who are the snooker players on the wall?" Jason sarcastically asks the barman. "Yeah, very funny mate. You wouldn't be saying that aloud after 7 pm here if you knew what was good for Ya!" The man snarled. Jason laughed as he made his way up the steps to the second floor of the bar and said under his breath, "I only think it's funny, because I put most of them there!" Jason began to fumble around in his pockets for his micro telescopic lens. He found a seat by the window and sat down. He then attached the device over his camera lens on his mobile and switched the camera on. As Jason was drinking his port he was using his phone to zoom in and scan the Irish Gent pub. He searched the roof tops, the front of the building and finally started to fixate around the door. If there was one golden rule Jason knew about surveillance, it was that of patience. It was now 9:45 pm at night and the bar he was in started to get busy and to make matters worse the indoor lighting was affecting the glare on the windows and making it difficult to see anything with his equipment. Jason made his way quickly to the men's room as he noticed a fire escape earlier whilst using the gents. This was his access point to the roof.

As Jason made his way out the door and onto the metal staircase outside he felt anxious that he was going to miss Michael leaving the pub, that's if he was there in the first place. "EXCUSE ME!" a loud voice said behind Jason. Jason turned around quickly and had his weapon pointed at the man who shouted at him. "YES?" Jason asked. The man looked like he was sucking a lemon. His face was contorted in fear and Jason didn't know what he was going to do now as this person has now fucked up his surveillance. "Get over here!" Jason ordered the man as he was looking around where to cuff the bar staffer. "Listen, sir, I am sorry if I made you angry. I..I ..just wanted to inform you that no one is allowed up onto the roof. Company policy." The man said in a weak voice. "SHUT THE FUCK UP!" Jason snarled as he grabbed him by the scruff of his neck and directed him to some piping near the water tank.

"Hands!" Jason ordered. The man cooperated with Jason as he was handcuffed around the piping. "You make a sound and you won't like what I do next!" Jason told the man whilst eye balling him. Jason made his way to the ledge and brought out his surveillance equipment again. Jason didn't have to wait too long on the roof. "BINGO!" Jason said as he made a positive id on Michael and Colin leaving the Irish Gent premises. Jason was able to work out that they had about eight other men with them which was good as it was now much easier to track them. As he ran down stairs the man he had cuffed earlier shouted over to him. "Hey what about me?" Jason stopped and got the handcuff key out and threw it over to the man at his feet. Jason gave him a smile before he darted off down the fire escape stairs. "How am I supposed to reach that you fucking prick!" the man shouted after him. Jason knew he would be released soon as someone would notice him missing. Jason caught up with the crew and followed them for a short distance to this enormous sky scraper. Michael and his men went into the building and then waited by the elevators. Jason read the neon sign "Skye Club."

He then looked all the way up to the top of the very tall building where he could see flashing lights and hear the music faintly playing. It was easy to see where Michael and his men were going. "Hope they are playing house music!" Jason said to himself as he crossed the road and made his way into the building. Whilst walking across the floor Jason tried to tidy himself up so he wouldn't get any hassle from the bouncers at the door of this club. Once inside the empty elevator, Jason checks his weapons over. I only have two clips, so I will need to be careful and try to take them out one at a time. I can always take any guns or ammo I find on my first kill, so I will be alright. As the elevator slowed down near the top floor, Jason was amazed at the scenic night view of Toronto and all her dazzling lights. "Ding!" The lift door opened, and Jason was face to face with one of the men on Michael's crew.

Before the man could even get into the elevator Jason had him pulled in and knocked out cold on the elevator floor. The doors started to close, and Jason hit the button for the next floor down. As the elevator started to move Jason took the unconscious man's weapons which was a Glock 17 and several full clips.

The door opened again, and Jason threw the man out of the lift so hard he hit the wall across from the elevator. As the door closed again Jason pressed the button three or four times impatiently for the top floor. Hopefully this time he could exit the lift without any issues. "Ding!" The doors opened, and Jason casually walked out of the lift and over to the entrance of the club. The music was hypnotic and loud but more importantly, it was good. "Welcome to Skye Club Sir!" the woman at the entrance said. "Thank you," Jason replied. The bouncers on the door were too busy yapping to even look at Jason as he strolled in. The club was packed, and everyone was dancing and enjoying themselves.

There! Back middle table! Jason spots Michael and his men smoking and drinking. Jason circles around and prepares to attack the men as they are very close together but would risk killing civilians on the dance floor. Jason waits patiently by the bar which is behind their table, waiting for the men to make a move when he suddenly notices Colin Murphy making his way into the gents. Jason spots the opportunity and follows right after him making sure no one else from Michaels crew follows. Colin makes his way to the urinals at the back. There are two men in the rest room, one using the sink and the other the hand dryer as Jason comes in. The end cubical is open by Colin, Jason swiftly walks up to him and pulls out his garrotte and quickly puts it around his neck before jolting him back into the cubical he had just opened. The two men in the gents were totally oblivious to what just happened. Jason struggled to keep the razor wire tight around Colin's neck as he was over six feet tall, so he climbed onto the toilet seat and raised the tension which did the trick as Colin's neck succumbed to the death grip and killed him quickly. As Colin's lifeless body was being held up by Jason, his actual head was starting to detach from his body as the razor wire was digging into Colin's neck. Jason had to quickly sit Colin's body down on the toilet seat before that happened. As Jason placed the corpse on the bog, he started to search Colin's pockets. He pulled out a mobile... It was Olivia's.

It instantly brought back those terrible memories of that night Olivia died and before Jason knew it he fired three rounds into Colin's face using the silenced gun. Jason knew it didn't matter what he did to this piece of shit, he couldn't change what he did. What he forever took away from him and his son. Jason then began to take Colin's weapons and ammo. I left the cubical and closed the door behind me.

I had a job to finish and there was nothing going to stand in my way of doing that! The music was thumping, and it was the type I loved, electric house! As I was leaving the gents and making my way round to Michael's table, gunfire erupts throughout the club. I was fucking made! I fired a round through the window to gain access to the outside balcony. As I threw myself through it, it smashed into countless shards all around me. My face was cut and bleeding from the glass and I had taken at least two hits to the midsection which hurt but didn't penetrate my armoured vest. As I was getting my breath back and looking for cover one of Michael's men comes running at me. I was about to shoot him but he had grabbed a hold of my wrist and was pointing the gun away whilst trying to move his own gun near my head which I wasn't about to let happen. We were wrestling on the ground as the other men from Michael's crew were coming up fast behind us.

I spun around and held the man's neck between my legs and used him as a shield as the bullets started to bounce off the ground near us. I wrestled my gun away and shot three of the men coming towards me before shooting the guy I had gripped in the head. I rolled behind the outside bar and changed my weapon for the Glock 17.

The bar was not putting up any kind of resistance to the bullets flying through it, so I had to move fast to alternative cover. I crawl behind the bar and make my way to a wall which leaves me nowhere to go but a vertical drop down. I have killed five of the crew plus Colin so looks like it's only Michael and two militia men left. Which is plenty enough to handle as Michael is good with a gun! It was quiet due to most of the crowd running away from the gun fight. The music was blaring and the disco lights were still in motion. There is only one place I can safely move to next and it's beside the wall behind me. Sure, as shit Michael will be waiting for me to pop my head over for a peek. "JASON!" Michael shouts. "Do yourself a favour and jump over the edge and I promise I won't kill anyone else in your family!" Michael continued. Jason ignored him.

"Hold on Jason, I can't keep that promise, can I? I already killed what's left of your family!" Michael sarcastically said. Michael was unaware that his hit on his son and uncle was not successful. Jason takes out one of his swords and uses the blade to look around the corner. He can see the last of Michael's thugs trying to sneak up on him whilst Michael was busy distracting him with insults. As the Men got closer, Jason was ready and waiting. The man rushed the corner but failed to look down at his feet, it was his last mistake. Jason fired a volley of shots upwards as he lay on his back at the man's feet. The man's skull cap took off like a bloodied Frisbee.

To say the man died instantly would be an understatement. Suddenly the second thug jumped over the wall and had hold of Jason's two hands. The man was able to knock the gun out of Jason's hand and was working on loosening Jason's grip on his Wakizashi sword. Jason then brought his legs up and started to pry the man's grip he had away by pushing against his chest with his foot. It was working as the man shouted for help from Michael. "Michael, get over here before this fuck breaks free. I have hold of both his arms!" Michael approaches cautiously but not fast enough as Jason's wins the tug of war with the sword and puts it through the thug's chest. "Just you and me now Michael!" Jason shouted. Jason uses the bloodied blade again to look around to spot where Michael was hiding.

The sounds of many sirens could be heard coming closer to the building. "Fuck this!" Jason said as he dived behind the bar once more to get a better look around him. Jason holstered his swords and took out his other guns so he had a weapon in each hand to cover more area as he made his way slowly back into the building. "MOTHER FUCKER!" Jason shouted. Michael had slipped away in the carnage. "Not this fucking time, NO WAY!" Jason continued to rant as he ran down to the fire exit. Jason quickly looked down the centre of the stairwell to see Michael scrambling down the steps.

Jason fired a volley of shots at Michael which ricocheted off the railings and hit Michael in the leg. "AARRGH, Bastard!" Michael shouted as he fell against the railing of the stairs. Jason took no time in getting caught up to Michael; they both had their weapons fixed on each other. "Well, well, well. The fucking Hun bastard finally graces me with his presence!" Michael said whilst trying to keep on his feet. "If you only knew what was coming next, you would put that gun to your own head you fucking terrorist, child killing cunt!" Jason shouted back to Michael as he gripped the handle of his pistols tighter. Jason wanted to kill Michael so bad he was shaking but he had better plans for him. Michael pulled the trigger first and to his astonishment, nothing came out. Jason smiled and pointed his gun at Michaels gun arm and shot two rounds into it. "AAAAAAAAGHHHH! YOU FUCKING CUUUNT!" Michael screamed in pain as Jason wrapped his fingers into Michael's long hair and began dragging him by it, up the fire exit stairs to the roof again. Jason was taking utter delight in knowing that he had complete power over Michael and that he was seconds away from killing him. Once they made it to the top floor, Jason continued to drag Michael along the hall and across the dance floor by his hair. Michael was writhing in pain and Jason could care less. "WHAT THE FUCK ARE YOU DOING YOU HUN BASTARD!?" Michael screamed.

"I want you to know something before you die, my son and uncle are still alive!" Jason said as he ran Michael to the edge of the building still holding his hair and threw him up and over the side. Jason watched Michaels screaming descent onto the street below. His body exploded into three raggedly torn parts as he smashed into the pavement. He was quickly surrounded by police and bystanders. "That's the end of you, so it is," Jason said as he stood back from the ledge. My work is done; the operation for all purposes was successfully completed. All Jason could think about was meeting his son again, knowing that he was now safe. That Ulster was once again safer than it was before the RVA. The police officers started to make their way through the club and onto the balcony. They screamed at Jason to raise his hands. Jason didn't put up a fight and followed every instruction given to him as he was placed under arrest.

I can't believe I fucking made it through that! Jason thought to himself as he walked into the lift with the officers. "Look what this sick fuck had on him!" an officer said whilst showing the other officers my swords and bloodied garrotte. "Fucksake, you will be locked away for a long-time buddy!" another officer said to Jason. Jason just ignored them and enjoyed the view of the city on his way down to the lobby. "Ding" The ground floor. The lift doors opened, and the officers escorted Jason through the crowded lobby and outside to the waiting patrol cars. "STOP!" a familiar voice shouted. "We will take it from here!" the man said. It was Mark and a few of the operations team from REVERT. The leading police officer radioed into HQ and walked over to a quieter spot in the road to validate the handover. A few minutes later he came back to the group with a disappointed look on his face and revealed to the rest of the officers to let Jason go. One of the officers began to un-cuff Jason with a very confused look on his face. "Dickhead, my stuff?" Jason shouted over to the mouthy officer who had his tactical gear. The officer slowly handed over Jason's weapons and made his way quickly back to the hotel. "I can't believe you guys are here! Better late than never I suppose!" Jason said to his crew. "The Commander gave us orders to bring you back safe and sound once we found out where you were. Your boy and that uncle of yours are making their way down as we speak to meet up with you at the Kings Hotel. You ready to go?" Mark asked Jason. "Yes mate, take me to where I am staying. I need to clean up before I see Daniel."

Jason replied. With that, the team all got into a large black van and departed from the scene. Jason finally met up with Daniel a few hours later in the lobby and gave him the longest hug he ever had. He knew he had a lot to make up to his son as no child should ever have to go through or witness what he had. He also hugged his uncle for keeping his boy safe. Jason could finally relax and celebrated the reunion of his family and friends in peace.

Chapter 14 - History repeats itself

Life has been moving fast for Jason as a few weeks later he finds himself settling into his old routines again but this time in a new home by the sea near Portavogie. Ian raved about the area so much to Jason that he took it upon himself to check it out and immediately fell in love with it. Jason was doing the same job with the same team but in a different Northern Ireland. Since weeding out the collaborators, the firm seems more productive and well-resourced than it did before. Jason was happy with the progress that is being made all around, but he had to deal with a big headache that would be arriving on his doorstep any day now. He understood that Michael and Colin's bodies would be repatriated to Ulster in a few days, so their families can bury them. This in itself, was a major problem to Jason as some die-hard Republicans will use this event as a stage to recruit more idiots and this simply could not be allowed to happen.

It is a Thursday morning and Jason is at work.

"Ian, what do we know about the funeral arrangements for the RVA leader?" Jason said. "We have heard increased chatter throughout the RVA network which is all pointing to a show of strength which we have connected to a mass protest in several key areas of Ulster. The ceremony most likely will try to push a show of bravado with masks and guns." Said Ian. "I want two eyes in the sky and CCTV vans along with all officers to wear body cams. We need to build up a proper database of who these sympathisers are and if they are a credible threat. Where is the burial taking place or do I even need to ask?" Jason said. "You already know where it is sir!" replied Ian. "St Ava near the motor way! Well, he will fit in well there with the rest of the terrorists!" Jason replied. Jason was pleased he was now basically doing Trevor's job and was able to protect Northern Ireland unhinged. Michaels funeral will be heavily policed, and the area surrounded to thwart any chance of weapons being used over Michaels coffin. Jason finished his day at the office and made his way home along the scenic coastline. Daniel would be at home waiting with Granny and Granda as they were staying at his house for a while till they got settled in.

It's unusual pulling up to a strange house and one as nice as this. Olivia would have loved this place Jason thought to himself as he got out of the car. Jason could hear a commotion of children's laughter coming from the backyard of his house.

Daniel had made some new friends and was kicking a ball about with them whilst granny and granda were outside sunning themselves on the deck lovingly watching over them. "DADDY!" yelled Daniel as he ran over and gave his dad a big hug. "Well, who's this?" Jason asked. "This is Robbie from next door," Daniel said. "Hello!" Robbie said whilst squinting to keep the sun out of his eyes. "Nice to meet you, Robbie!" Jason replied. " You boys have fun while I talk to the old people!" Jason said to the boys. "Ok, Dad!" Replied Daniel. Jason walks over to Olivia's parents and sits down with them. "It's lovely to see Daniel smiling again!" said Amanda. "It is! Thank you, guys, for coming down here and helping us settle in." Jason replied. "Right, time for the BBQ!" Thomas said as he stood up and made his way over to the BBQ at the back door. Jason got up as well and went inside to the kitchen and put his work bag on the table before going into the fridge for a cold Pear cider. "Knock, Knock, Knock!" went the front door.

Jason casually went to the front of the house and peered out the side window. It was an old man with a card and flowers. Must be a neighbour with welcome gifts. Jason then made his way to the front door and opened it. "Hello?" Jason said. "Hello!" said the man. "This is a fine house you have here!" said the man whilst looking at Jason. "Yeah, it's alright. Who are you mate?" Jason inquired. "Oh, yes, I do apologise. My name is Michael Mordha." The old man said. Jason was taken back at the name as it was the same name as the man he just killed a few weeks ago in Canada. "Where are you from Mr Mordha?" Jason asked. The old man laughed and said, "Guess!" Jason was starting to lose his patience but was curious to see if there was indeed a connection to the RVA leader Michael Mordha.

"Andersonstown!" Jason said firmly. "Correct! That didn't take you long Jason!" the old man said. Jason quickly opened the card he was given which turned out to be a condolence card with nothing written on it and the flowers were white lilies. Now, this is making more sense Jason thought to himself. "I suppose you think I will be threatened with the card, flowers and the fact you know where I live. Don't you Mr Mordha?" Jason said. Mr Mordha said nothing and just glared at Jason. "That's my son you killed! I will never forgive or forget what you did to my child! You took him from me and now I will repay you in kind!" Mr Mordha snarled. Mr Mordha then turned around and walked down the long path to Jason's front gate. Jason threw the flowers down on the ground and ripped up the card as he walked towards his car. Jason got down and looked underneath his vehicle and quickly spotted a smart phone duck taped to the underside of his fuel tank. Fucking armature night for a car tracking device but 100% effective. They could have tracked him anywhere in the UK or Europe until the battery ran out. Jason ripped the phone out and placed it carefully in his pocket as to not smudge any prints.

Jason then went into the backyard and shouted over to Thomas and Amanda that he would be out on a message for about an hour. With that done, Jason got into his car and drove back to HQ in Bangor. After a short drive back to work, Jason headed down to the labs to push the forensics through on the phone as a priority. "Jason, we have the results of the phone. Purchased two days ago at this store for £45. The phone signal triangulation shows it travelled from the shop to this area of Andersonstown, then to our HQ. Then from our HQ to your house. The only prints on our file we have out of the set of three we found was Mr Michael Mordha's." Said Taylor who was head of forensics.

"Thank you, Taylor, that's all the information I need," Jason replied before leaving in a rush. Jason knew that it was just the old man who was on his case and needed to find more about Michaels father. Jason went into his office and pulled Michael Mordha's file and looked for any links to his father. "Yes, here we go," Jason said with glee. Michael Mordha senior was a Republican hood in his youth but nothing significant in his file. Jason felt relieved as he had visions of all sorts of problems this guy was going to cause but at the end of the day, he was a nobody that was going to be burying his murderous son in a few days. Jason took down Mr Mordha's address and contact just in case he would need them for later. The old man has a grudge against me for killing his shitbag terrorist son. If he thinks he can intimidate me, let him have that. I got bigger fish to fry. Jason shuts down his computer and went home.

The media buzz was going crazy as the dead bodies of the RVA were finally arriving at Belfast airport. The news of Michael's death and the extermination of the RVA were making headlines all over the world. The media were in a frenzy to know more about what happened but as you and I know, that's classified. That sparked a question in my head, how did Michael's father know it was me that took his son out? Intel probably leaked from Canada law enforcement would be my guess as our agency is now tight, water tight. It didn't matter as the old man has no priors and was of little threat.

As I was coming up to my house I see an unfamiliar car in the driveway and a young man leaning against it. I pull up near him and step out of my vehicle. "Hello, Sir! My name is Harry. I've just graduated from the sweat box and was sent to your jurisdiction for my formal training. I have been told you're expecting me." Harry said. Jason smiled. "Did a man called Mark send you this way?" Jason asked. "Black hair, 5ft 6", Tattoo of a wolf on the left arm?" Inquired Harry. "Yes, that's him. He has sent you out on a fool's errand." Jason sniggered. Harry looked embarrassed and unsure of what to do next. "Sorry sir, I will be on my way," Harry said as he opened his car door.

"No! You, my friend, are going to come with me." Jason said as he closed Harry's car door and guided him towards the backyard. "The agents are just having a bit of fun with you and trying to wind me up at the same time. Grab a seat and I will bring you a beer. Hungry?" Jason asked. "Yes sir, I could eat," Harry replied. Thomas was dishing up the BBQ and the kids were tucking into their burgers. Jason comes out of the kitchen with the beers and throws two of them Harry's way which he caught both and then began to fill two plates with the BBQ feast. "Here you go, mate!" Jason said as he gave Harry a plate full of food. "Just hold on one moment. Take a drink of the beer whilst flipping the bird to the camera." Jason instructed as he got his mobile out for a pic. "What's the photo for?" Harry asked. "The pics for your work buddies down at HQ to show their little joke backfired!" Laughed Jason, as he sent the picture message to Mark. Harry laughed and started to tuck into the food he was given.

When the meal was finished Jason took Daniel for a walk along the beach and Harry joined them. "Listen, Harry, I have a bit of a situation which I think you would be perfect for as a first assignment. You might think I am throwing you into the deep end with this one but I am really not. You remember that RVA Michael Mordha that was killed?" Jason said. "Yes, it's all over the news. It was you, wasn't it that killed him?" Harry replied. "Yes it was me and now I have his old man making veiled threats against me. He has found out rather quickly where I live and I am concerned about it. He has no priors but that means nothing as he could have easily been smart enough to stay out of the limelight with the Republican movement." Jason replied.

"Understood Sir, I will keep a tail on him and his associates," Harry said. "No. Just him. His name is also Michael Mordha like his son. I need you to stick to him like glue as there has been chatter on wires that there will be a show of strength at the funeral of his son. What that show of strength will be, could be anything. We first must remember what Michael was known for." Jason said. "Bombs!" Harry replied. "Exactly Harry!" Jason said. "I have a feeling that his father could have been the one to teach young Michael how to make the tools for terror. I need you to find something so I can stick him in jail where he will hurt no one. If you find nothing, then all's good and we know he is all mouth. Can you do this for me?" Jason continued. "Of course, sir," Harry said. "Good, you're on active duty as of this very moment. Go to HQ to make a file on Michael Mordha and you will be on him 24hrs a day until I personally say otherwise. Ask Mark for a suitable experienced partner so you can get a shift pattern going. I need video, audio, wiretap, car tracking and GPS location grid and movement mapping as data evidence. Give this note to Ian; he will get you geared up with weapons and surveillance. Good luck agent!" Jason said as he saluted Harry.

Daniel saluted Harry as well. With the new orders, he has received Harry went immediately back to his car and made his way back to Bangor HQ to carry out his orders. Upon arriving at HQ, Harry noticed Mark leaving the building and quickly made his way over to him. "Mark! Jason wants you to set me up with an experienced partner for an active assignment on Michael Mordha's father," said, Harry. Mark sighed. "I was so close to going home on time! Come on and I will get you sorted." Mark replied. They both went into the building and went upstairs to the top floor for operations. Mark was pondering who to use as an experienced partner for young Harry. "How old are you Harry, around 25?" Mark asked. "Yes, that's right. I am 25, good guess." Harry replied. Need to pick someone who can show this young guy the ropes that won't put him astray like Ian. "I've got it! I'm your new partner!" Mark said out loud. Mark knew he had some damage to repair to his reputation and this would be the perfect opportunity for him to do just that. Harry smiled "Well then, let's get over to Ian and down to work." Harry replied.

Mark and Harry went to find Ian who had now been promoted and no longer a temp at the agency after his outstanding work in operation REVERT. Ian was now a full-time agent that will have to conform to the firm's policy's and give up his freelance killing.

Ian was only too happy to set the new partnership out with the weapons and surveillance gear they needed. "Now my friend, we need to draw up a file and a plan of action to carry out our new orders. For time-saving I will do that, and you will take notes on what I do and how it's done correctly." Mark said to Harry.

The new team spent four hours putting together a file on Michaels father and a plan of action to shadow his movements. They agreed that they will take two vehicles from the police recovery compound and use two different vantage points to keep an eye on the old man. They quickly fit their vehicles with the surveillance equipment and make their way to Andersonstown to stake out Michaels fathers house. Unsurprisingly the estate where Michael's dad lived was busy with activity. Michael's body had arrived at their house already. The streets were lined with people making their way in and out of Michaels fathers house. "Keep frosty Harry, this is not a place where you want to get cornered. Have that automatic rifle locked and loaded. Keep the safety on until you feel threatened." Mark said over the coms. "Understood sir!" Harry replied.

Mark took the first watch for four hours whilst Harry slept in the car. Mark noted that no clergy or priests had visited the house and made note of that. He found that over 200 people came to Michael's father's house to pay their respects. That was somewhat worrying because if the dead Michael had this many fans after the atrocities he committed it would be only reasonable to assume that more recruits could come from his death if he is portrayed as a martyr at the funeral.

Mark was nearing the end of his shift and buzzed Harry to wake up and continue the watch. "Good morning dickhead!" Mark blurted down the coms. "Mmm, morning sir!" Harry sheepishly replied. "Your watch, wake me in 4 hours. Remember what you are watching for and if you feel something's wrong, no matter what it is, wake me." Mark replied. "Yes, sir!" Harry replied. Harry was starting to pull himself together. He forgot to keep his window open a crack and had all his car windows fogged up. As he was cleaning them he could hear voices behind the car. Harry couldn't make out what they were saying but to it as a signal to move positions. "Mark! Position may be compromised moving to location B." Harry said. "Roger that!" Mark replied. Before Harry could start the car, a knock on the roof of the car was heard and a man appeared beside him on the driver's side. The man motioned him to roll down his window which Harry did but just an inch. "Yes, what is it?" Harry said to the man.

"You mind telling me what you are doing here? You lost?" The man asked. Harry noticed the other men starting to make their way in front of the car. "I had a bit too much to drink and I couldn't drive home," Harry said whilst he started to move the car forward and the men slowly got out of the way to let him pass. Right, that's this car marked. "Harry, any issues?" Mark shouted down the coms. "No, but I am sure you heard all that. Need new wheels." Harry replied. "Yes, heard everything. Good job keeping your cool. Park up at location B and make your way down to me." Mark said. "On route sir." Harry replied.

Harry parked the car well away from where he originally was seen and proceeded to empty the car of its contents into a back pack. He then made his way carefully to where Mark was situated. "Fucking typical, no sleep for me," Mark grunted as Harry threw his gear into the back seat and got into Marks car. "Pass me that flask!" Mark asked Harry. Harry handed it over to Mark who began to unscrew the top and took a long drink from it. "It's black coffee. You want some." Mark asked. Harry declined the offer.

"Oi, look! Action time my friend!" Mark said excitedly. Michaels father was leading his coffin out into the street where people put a tri colour and gloves onto the coffin. The coffin was set on a pair of wooden stands. "Wait till you see how fast the rats come out in military gear to fire a volley of shots over the coffin then run away to hide," Mark said whilst adjusting the video surveillance. But nobody came to do that. Instead, the old man saluted his son and the other four men did the same. A few minutes later a funeral hearse came into view and made its way beside the coffin. The men picked up the coffin and put it into the back of the hearse carefully and proceeded to get into their cars to follow the coffin down to the burial site.

"Wasn't expecting that!" Mark said surprised. Mark got onto the phone with Jason and said the funeral processions were starting. Jason acknowledged the update from Mark and set the ball rolling for a high police presence. The army bomb squad was sent in first to do a quick sweep of the area where the officers were to be positioned to see if there was any IEDs in the area. Once they got the all clear the police armoured division could move in and take up their positions. Armoured units then were sent into line the streets in case any riots broke out. The final unit to be sent out was the police helicopters so they could video the event and spot any trouble from the air.

The whole thing took 30 minutes to roll out. Everyone was in position as the streets started to fill with RVA supporters. News cameras and journalists were trying to get as much in as the time would allow before the burial took place.

Jason got on his tactical vest and made his way down to the proceedings. To his surprise, there was nowhere near the crowd he thought would be present for the funeral. If there was a hundred people in attendance that would be it. Not to make the police presence look like over kill, Jason ordered half of the squad back to their stations, to wait on standby. Jason watched as the coffin went into the chapel, followed by the mourners. Michaels dad stood outside the Chapel staring at Jason. His eyes were filled with hate and Jason knew if the old man could, would want him dead. After the last mourner went in, so did the old man. Jason knew he couldn't use surveillance inside the chapel and had to just wait outside until the proceedings where over.

Meanwhile in the chapel

Michael's father had sat in his seat waiting for the priest to begin the eulogy of his son. As the priest was giving his sermon, Michael's father took out a small cigar box which was wrapped neatly in brown paper. Michael's father had written on the top of it "For you son. Love always Dad." Michaels father began to get teary eyed and opened the box carefully, using the front pew to hide what he was doing. Inside was two bars of semtex and a mobile. Michael armed the bomb and closed the lid of the box and began to wrap the paper carefully around it again. He then tied a string around both ends so it could not be opened easily. Michael leaned over and asked his nephew if he would take this box outside and place it in the bushes near the navy BMW that was in front of the church. This was the car that was nearest to the police and close to where Jason was positioned. Michael's nephew knew what was in the box as he watched his uncle the night before putting it together. Nervously he took the box and placed it inside his coat which he kept a hold of through his pocket. Making his way outside he did exactly what his uncle had asked.

He made it look like he was just having a cigarette whilst leaning against the navy BMW but with his other hand, he placed the box on top of the front wheel. After he finished his smoke, the man walked casually back into the chapel which was a good distance from the car. Harry had been watching the man but didn't see what he had left. Being nosey he got out of Marks car and made his way down to where he saw the man standing. He carefully scanned the area and seen nothing until he got a little further away from the car and noticed the brown package on top of the tyre. Harry picked the box up and read what was written on the top. "Shit, the old man lost this package for Michael. I will bring it in and place it in his coffin. He will be none the wiser." Harry thought to himself. As Harry started to walk towards the Chapel, Jason went on coms.

"What the fuck are you doing Harry? Get back here now!" Jason ordered. "Michaels dad had left a keepsake for the coffin outside. I am just going to give it to him." Harry replied. "Proceed, then immediately get out of there!" Jason replied. Jason thought it would look like a good will gesture from the police if they gave something they had which belonged to his dead son, back to him for burial. Jason assured himself that this could be a positive move to bring closure to his son's death.

Harry came into the chapel as people were lining up to past the coffin saying their last goodbyes. Harry made sure he was at the end and leaned over Michaels body and stealthy slid the box down the side of Michaels' arm. As he leaned up straight again he met with Michael's father and shook his hand. The old man couldn't place his face but shook his hand anyway. As Harry was leaving the men put the lid of Michaels coffin back on and began to tighten the coffin screws down.

The whole congregation made their way out of the chapel and to where the burial place of Michael was prepared. As the crowd made their way out of the church and through the courtyard and over to the cemetery. Michaels coffin came out being flanked by masked men. "Hold, keep eyes on the mask men for pick up after!" Jason ordered over comms. Michaels father kept looking back to see where Jason was. Jason and a number of officers were moving forward with the crowd. Ever keeping the same distance between them so the police presence didn't intrude on the burial. Once Jason got to the front of the church near the blue BMW, Michael's father broke rank and got his phone out. Michaels father gave Jason long and deathly stare. Jason started to realise something wasn't right. "GET TO COVER!" Jason screamed as Michael's father pushes the call button on his mobile. BOOOOM, Michaels coffin exploded into thousands of tiny splinters which creates a bloody mist.

Everyone carrying Michaels coffin was blown to bits which included his father. The noise of shattering glass and car alarms erupted, filling the air with a deathly tension. News reporters at the scene were blown down and had varying degrees of injuries. Crying and screams could be heard all around. Jason was on his back looking from one place to another and was very disorientated. As he came around and looked at all the carnage that was left and started to figure out very quickly, that Harrys found package with Michaels name on it was meant for them.

Jason rolled slowly onto his side and tried to clap eyes on Harry and Mark. Harry was already looking at him from behind a car with a worried look on his face. Jason spotted Harry and shook his head. "FUCK!" Jason said.

THE END